Clouds and Earth

Clouds and Earth

The Peace Outside: I/III

Sayde Scarlett

Copyright © 2018 by Sayde Scarlett.

ISBN:	Softcover	978-1-5434-9323-8
	eBook	978-1-5434-9322-1

All rights reserved. No part of this book may be reproduced or transmitted in any form or by any means, electronic or mechanical, including photocopying, recording, or by any information storage and retrieval system, without permission in writing from the copyright owner.

This is a work of fiction. Names, characters, places and incidents either are the product of the author's imagination or are used fictitiously, and any resemblance to any actual persons, living or dead, events, or locales is entirely coincidental.

Any people depicted in stock imagery provided by Getty Images are models, and such images are being used for illustrative purposes only.
Certain stock imagery © Getty Images.

Print information available on the last page.

Rev. date: 01/08/2019

To order additional copies of this book, contact:
Xlibris
800-056-3182
www.Xlibrispublishing.co.uk
Orders@Xlibrispublishing.co.uk
787576

"He who fights with monsters might take care lest he thereby become a monster. And when you gaze long into an abyss the abyss also gazes into you."

— Friedrich Nietzsche
From *Beyond Good and Evil, Aphorism 146* (1886)

"The great object of life is sensation—to feel that we exist, even though in pain. It is this 'craving void' which drives us to gaming—to battle—to travel—to intemperate but keenly felt pursuits of every description, whose principal attraction is the agitation inseparable from their accomplishment."

— Lord Byron
From *The Letter of Lord Byron to Annabella Milbanke, September 6, 1813*

"If men want to oppose war, it is statism that they must oppose. So long as they hold the tribal notion that the individual is sacrificial fodder for the collective, that some men have the right to rule others by force, and that some (any) alleged 'good' can justify it—there can be no peace within a nation and no peace among nations."

— Ayn Rand
From *Capitalism: The Unknown Ideal* (1966)

"We must love one another or die."

— W. H. Auden
From the poem *September 1, 1939*

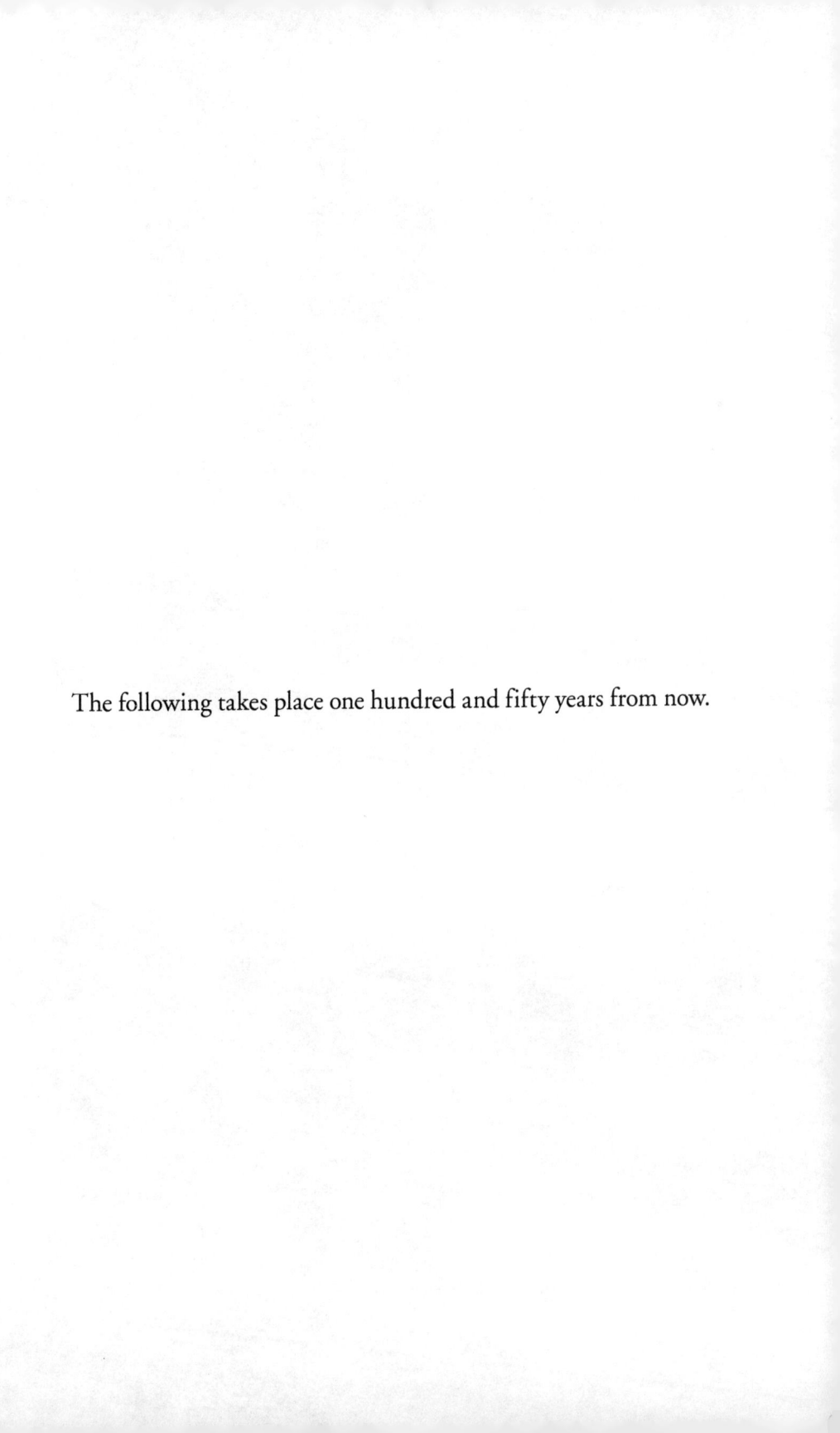

The following takes place one hundred and fifty years from now.

CHAPTER ONE

A mixture of tears and blood dripped sporadically from the woman's chin. The pink fluid stained her otherwise pristine white lab coat. She was seated, shivering and weeping, in a cold office. When she tried to move her arms, the cuffs that bound her to the chair made soft clinking sounds that echoed throughout the room. The imposing space had high ceilings and beige walls without much decoration. The woman's dark hair was strewn across her face, some sticking to the sweat on her forehead. Her left eye was a throbbing purple mass, and her nose was broken and bloody. It was the last day of her life.

Although what little vision remained in her right eye was blurry, she could still make out the desk in front of her. The piece of furniture itself was old-fashioned: made of carved, varnished wood and expensive-looking. There was nothing extraordinary about it other than it seemed out of place in such a modern room. Her mind temporarily drifted from the pain of her injuries as she was struck by the peculiarity of the objects on the desk. She had been in this office many times before but had never noticed them until now. They were precisely aligned and symmetrical. Items on each side of the desk – a pair of paperweights, two matching lamps, and two pen holders – mirrored one another in a state of perfection that seemed forced and uncomfortable.

Lyndon Hamilton, a tall, slim man in his early fifties with impeccably groomed brown hair, entered the room, interrupting the woman's thoughts. Instead of taking his place in the large leather chair on the other side of the desk, he stood in front of her and removed a handkerchief from his suit pocket. He took her chin in his right hand and, with his left, softly dabbed the blood from her face.

"I'm very sorry for the actions of my subordinate, Doctor. I fear Mr. Farlow overreacted somewhat when he saw you tampering with our project. His behaviour was <u>rude</u>."

She looked at him, her dark eyes large and vulnerable.

"That being said," he continued, "power is the ability to mobilise your resources, and I am deeply disappointed that, at this stage, I lack the resources I need."

"The model is as complete as I can get it," she spluttered through spit and blood, "and you must know that the nature of the projection means the underlying database must constantly adapt and change."

"That's quite all right."

"To take it any further requires action that I am not capable of." Her face hardened. "Action that I'm not comfortable with."

"I understand," he nodded, "and you must know that this means our association has to come to an end."

"Just let me go, Lyndon. Please."

He sat on the front edge of his desk. His face was relaxed and emotionless.

"Lyndon, please. I have a child. She'll be asking where Mummy is now."

"Your daughter will be fine, Maria. She'll be taken care of."

"Lyndon, you know that I'm discreet."

"You've already compromised the project, Maria."

"Lyndon—Lyndon, please."

"Don't beg," Hamilton hissed. "It's beneath you. It's dirty. It's what dogs do."

At that moment, Farlow, a man in his late thirties, appeared at the door, his muscular build taking up all the space within the frame. "Sir, the room is ready." He spoke without acknowledging the woman in the chair.

"Thank you, Farlow," said Hamilton, as he proceeded to uncuff her. "It's time to go."

The two men guided her down the hallway, away from Hamilton's office. She was hustled into a lift, which descended to the basement. From there, she was led to a sterile-looking room that contained nothing but an empty bathtub. She stood at the end of the tub, a porcelain coffin.

Farlow handed Hamilton a syringe. Hamilton took hold of Maria's left arm and stabbed the needle into her.

"I'm sorry I disappointed you, Lyndon," she said, making peace with her fate.

"There are no hard feelings," he responded.

"I still believe…I still believe," she blurted out whilst looking into his eyes. They were the truest words she had ever uttered.

"I don't doubt it," he said, pressing down on the syringe.

The scientist fell backwards as the poison entered her brain. Her lifeless body collapsed neatly into the tub. Hamilton motioned to his subordinate; in return, Farlow offered him a cloth in which to drop the spent syringe.

The two men made their way back upstairs. Once in his office, Hamilton moved to the seat behind his desk.

"I am at a loss, Farlow. I thought I'd made the nature and complexity of my little project clear from the very beginning." He rocked back in his chair.

"Sir, I think you need someone who would be willing to do a little more reconnaissance work," said Farlow.

"I think you may be right."

###

Three small catboats raced across the deep, sparkling waters of the Potomac River. It was warm for early spring. The sun was shining, and the sky was a cloudless powder blue. A strong breeze rustled though the verdant trees and made the water choppy beneath the boats. Sandy Attiyeh's lips curved into a slight smile. She preferred it when the water was rougher; it made things so much more interesting.

It was hard to tell Sandy's age or background just by looking at her. She was physically fit and ethnically vague. Her hair was a bit too unruly to belong to someone with a nine-to-five, and her brow was furrowed so that, even at rest, her face was serious and lined, making her look older than she was. If not for that, she would have been good-looking—with her long, dark, wavy hair and tanned skin. She was often chatted up in bars and clubs on the few occasions she visited them, but those would-be suitors soon came to realise that her outwardly feminine appearance was deceptive. There was also something steely and unnerving about her: a confusing defensiveness.

Her two competitors were worthy adversaries and, despite being older than she was—both of them were approaching middle age and out of shape—they had been ahead of her for most of the race. After negotiating the last bend, Sandy pulled ahead, almost at the expense of Phillip Manning, who had avoided taking a dip in the deep, cool blue. Peter Hackett was a tougher opponent but was outrun in the end due to a lack of stamina on his part.

Sandy smiled and laughed as she pulled ahead of her competition.

Once they were back on the northern Virginia side of the river, the two men rehydrated and caught their breath while Sandy dried herself off with a towel.

"I was certain I had you at the last bend this time," said Manning.

"And yet, you lost again," said Sandy, boasting playfully. "That must suck. Or at least I think it must suck. I wouldn't know."

"Another race?" Manning asked, smiling.

"I can't. I'm giving a talk at the Academy this afternoon. Tomorrow?"

"Tomorrow's Monday—we'll be at work," said Hackett.

"Ah! How are things in the old ivory tower?" asked Sandy.

"If you showed up for work, you'd know," Manning teased.

"I don't have a desk at HQ anymore."

"Muro got rid of you? Finally?" Hackett feigned surprise.

"No," said Sandy, shrugging. "I'm a soldier; I never needed a desk."

"You're an intelligence officer. We all have desks," said Hackett. "What are you doing tomorrow if you're not coming in to work?"

"I don't have plans yet," said Sandy, backing down.

"I see," said Hackett.

Sandy left the boats and walked back up the beach. Her motorbike was waiting for her by the side of the marina. How strange it was to have spent the entire day with other people and still feel alone. Manning and Hackett were not her friends; they were colleagues, and they were keeping an eye on her. Sighing, she zipped up her uniform, which consisted of a white body suit, black ankle boots, and a WristWatt, a high-tech cuff on her left forearm, which used the unique information stored in a chip under her skin. Although wrist devices were common, this particular one was the most advanced of its kind and was only issued to the officers of Intelligence Command.

The bike's tires screeched beneath her as she sped away.

Massi and Natalia huddled together, clutching their guns tightly. They surveyed the dimly lit terrain, their faces squinting to see in the dark. In any other walk of life, these two youths would have had nothing in common and no reason to ever associate with one other. Yet they were both dressed in grey camouflage combat uniforms. War made unlikely allies. Matthew 'Massi' Moretti was a muscular adolescent with dark hair, pale skin and blue eyes. He would not have looked out of place in a boy band. Natalia was a righteous young woman of mixed ancestry, who possessed a striking long, straight black braid trailing down her back. Lithe and catlike, it was Natalia who crept out of the darkness first, immobilising an enemy soldier so Massi could get a clear run to their next position. They moved stealthily, shooting several more enemy soldiers, who fell to the ground. One of their assailants crawled on the ground in an attempt to retrieve his gun, but Massi slammed his boot down, crushing the man's hand. The enemy soldier squealed in pain.

Massi's eyes flickered left and right, scanning the landscape as he crouched without making a sound. Then he lurched forward. As soon as Massi grabbed the flag, a bell rang, and the lights came up on the training ground. The loudspeaker announced that it was all over.

"Paratag exercise completed. Cadet Moretti, Matthew, 373 points. Cadet Sanghera, Natalia, 184 points."

Massi smiled and swung his gun around, enjoying his winner's high. The cadet he had injured got up, clutching his hand in pain as a medic ran over. "You take paratag way too seriously," he yelled at Massi.

Massi snorted derisively. "If you're going to do something, do it right."

A female cadet shot Massi a contemptuous look as she comforted the injured cadet. "He's an ass," she whispered, deliberately within earshot.

"Hey, I'm a soldier, not a ballerina. You'd be thanking me if this was actually war," said Massi.

"That's enough, cadet." Colonel Mathers stepped in, sensing that the argument was about to escalate. Mathers was a spry but stern-looking man in his sixties, with a bald head and a neatly groomed, greying moustache. "Return your paraguns and immobilisation vests to the equipment locker. Put on your dress uniforms for this afternoon's lecture. Post-haste."

The cadets hurried out of the mock war zone, taking their vests off as they left.

Sandy moved through the Academy's barriers. The small army of security guards instantly recognised her, even with her helmet on, and waved her through. She parked in front of the state-of-the-art building, being sure to take in the sight of the place. She had to make a real effort to control her recollections. She wanted to experience the real thing; she did not want to be surprised when reality did not match her memories. There it was—festooned with the best security and surveillance technology money could buy. Her feelings about this place were sometimes overwhelming. Had she hated it, really? No, there had been times when she had been happy here. She appreciated that this school had challenged her. She may not have looked back fondly on all her time at the Academy, but she was grateful for it. This place had kept her alive. She looked up and was shaken from her thoughts. Cadets had gathered at the upstairs windows, fighting to get a glimpse of her. These were different times.

Massi rushed into the lecture hall and ploughed through the accumulating mass of grey uniforms. He could not quite make it to the front row. Colonel Mathers took to the stage and saluted. The cadets saluted back in near-perfect unison.

"Attention, cadets. It's not every day you get to hear from a genuine war hero. All of you know the name of our guest, and there are many reasons for that. For Lieutenant First Class Alisande Attiyeh—ATTENTION!"

The cadets saluted again. This time, their salute was longer; it lingered as a solemn sign of respect. Sandy found herself smiling and was surprised to feel a warm connection with the cadets as she returned the salute.

"Thank you, Colonel." She moved towards the podium, shuffled her papers and began. "At ease."

The cadets relaxed.

"All of you know my name because of my supposedly heroic deeds during the Long War. But I can't tell you anything about the past that you haven't already been told in history class. Not just because I don't want to, but also because even if I did want to, I couldn't. I am bound by the Military Information and Secrets Act, and one day, when you graduate, all of you will be too. So the buck stops there.

"Let us, instead, talk about the future. If we look at human history, the future is promising to be ever brighter. I am proud of the peaceful, prosperous society we have created. I am envious that your youth is not filled with the fear, dread and <u>hatred</u> that was ever present in mine." She paused for a moment. She had not meant to emphasise the word.

"The way we capture, handle and process information is crucial. Information is a precious commodity, and information serves you better when it is treated as such."

For the first fifteen minutes of Sandy's speech, Massi was enthralled by her words. It was not until someone nudged his elbow that he became aware of what was happening in the room. He looked around and realised that some of his fellow cadets were struggling to suppress their giggles. Someone jostled him again from behind, and a small piece of paper was shoved into his hand. Briefly redirecting his gaze from Sandy, he eyed it and then glanced around to see if anyone else had seen what he was looking at.

He took a longer look at the piece of paper and felt his heart skip a beat as he read the words written on it:

WANTED: ATTIYEH
FOR WAR CRIMES & MURDER

It pictured Sandy with a crosshair hovering over her right eye and a pile of dead bodies behind her. The blood rose to Massi's face. The hair on the back of his neck stood up sharp and cold, like hundreds of tiny steel needles. He crumpled up the flier and threw it on the floor. He looked around, terrified that someone had seen him. Thankfully, no one had. He breathed in and felt a pang of shame just for having viewed the piece of paper. Possessing it was an offence worthy of suspension. Creating it, or anything like it, would mean certain expulsion.

###

After the lecture, Sandy walked towards the exit. A couple of female cadets pushed notebooks in front of her, and she graciously signed her autograph on each of them. Massi ran up to her, bulldozing the other cadets out of the way.

"You're my hero!"

"Am I now?" she asked. It was not the response he was expecting.

"If there's ever another war, I'll be the first to sign up for a black-ops mission," he continued.

Sandy grabbed him by both his arms and aggressively pulled him close to her face. She looked him in the eyes. Massi felt the full force of her gaze. He was too shocked to move. The other cadets nearby looked on the scene with quizzical expressions. Sandy suddenly remembered herself and let go of the youth, her face reddening with embarrassment.

"If that ever happens, give me a call." She took out a business card. It was white and had nothing on it except a single phone number. "Not a lot of people have this number. Think about what I said in the lecture before you share it."

Massi nodded and clasped the card close to his chest, not wanting the other cadets to see it.

Sandy left the Academy through the large glass doors and disappeared into the evening's light.

CHAPTER TWO

Theme music played as Jason Casillas, host of the *Goodnight Show*, said good-bye to his latest guest. He had just finished interviewing a young blonde underwear model in a short, strappy red dress. While the blonde teetered offstage, Sandy waited in the wings. To Sandy, the model seemed like a different species, though their differences were hardly noticeable at that moment. Sandy's hair had been blow-dried straight and was thick and shiny with product. Her face had been meticulously made up, and she was wearing a simple, white knee-length dress with elbow-length sleeves. She was also wearing heels. She decided there and then that she liked wearing heels, having previously had no strong opinions on them and not owning a pair herself. *These are okay,* she thought, *as long as I don't have to wear them for very long, or very often.* They felt unfamiliar and thrilling. It also crossed her mind that maybe she should also wear more makeup now. Throughout her service during the Long War, it was neither allowed nor a priority. The war had swallowed up her adolescence and her early twenties. Things that other women had spent their time learning, such as how to put on makeup and walk in heels, still felt foreign to her. She resolved to buy some red lipstick tomorrow. She liked the way she looked tonight, like a different—a better—version of herself.

Her heart was beating excitedly. She felt embarrassed—not by the attention but by the fact that she was enjoying it.

"My next guest tonight is a genuine war hero. Her military career is the stuff of legend. That's right, a living legend. She's also a philanthropist. A true humanitarian. It was just announced that she'll become the seventh recipient of the Medal of Outstanding Service. Please give it up for Sandy Attiyeh!"

The audience applauded and whooped, some of them even rose to their feet. Sandy walked in front of the camera and waved to the audience, indistinguishable from any other starlet who had graced the stage. Sandy kissed Jason Casillas on both cheeks and sat down opposite him, grinning and trying to be as ladylike as she could.

"Welcome back, Sandy," he said.

"Thank you for having me," she said. Her body language was relaxed and open.

"You look fantastic, by the way. What's your secret?"

"Well," she said, giggling nervously, "there is a painting of me in my attic, just rotting."

The audience laughed.

"Ha-ha!" His laugh was loud and genuine. "You're such a wit."

"I still have to stay combat ready. That's the truth."

"You're still technically a soldier, am I right? You could be called up again at any minute?"

"Oh yes, absolutely," Sandy said, nodding.

"You served in what we now know were probably the most decisive campaigns of the Long War—and now another medal. Where on earth are you going to put this one?"

The audience laughed.

"Oh, you know, I'll just add it to my collection."

"Am I right in thinking that you're the youngest recipient of this award?"

"Yes, you're right."

"How old are you now? May I ask?"

"I've just turned thirty-one," she said, blushing.

"Now I feel old. Over the past couple of years, you've become somewhat of a media darling. Most recently I saw you in a cream soda ad."

"What can I say—my new kitchen won't pay for itself."

More laughter.

"You're such a great guest, Sandy. Such a wit. This is why people like you . . ."

His voice trailed off as a smattering of discontent erupted in the audience. Sandy was the first on her feet. Casillas stumbled from his chair. An angry voice pierced the jovial atmosphere. A group of security guards ran towards the stage, but it was too late.

"WAR CRIMINAL! MURDERER!"

The first protestor stood with her anti-war poster right in front of the camera, her back to Sandy. Another woman directed her fury at Sandy herself.

"YOU KILLED WOMEN AND CHILDREN! WAR CRIMES!"

Horror enveloped Sandy. She felt a type of panic that the Academy had not prepared her for. It was then that Casillas made a slicing gesture across his throat, and the transmission was cut. Just as Sandy felt a short moment of relief, the egg hit her chest. With honed reflexes, Sandy evaded the second and third egg, garnering small cheers from the audience. The fourth egg smashed straight into her face and neck. She did not even try to move as the fifth egg hit her thigh. The security team dragged the protestors out. There were three in total: two women and a man. Several members of the crew rushed onto the stage to help a shaken Sandy.

"I'm so sorry." Casillas picked a piece of brown shell off her. "We can get you cleaned up."

"Thanks."

"We don't have to continue filming," he said, concerned.

"It's okay. I'm fine." She felt her throat tighten but she had learnt how to stop herself from crying many, many years ago.

"Give a round of applause for a courageous war hero, ladies and gentlemen!" Jason started to clap.

The audience cheered.

Jason leaned in close to Sandy and whispered, "Only a few crazies think what they think. We all think you're a hero."

Sandy swallowed and held back her tears.

Sandy returned home alone to her spotless penthouse apartment. She flopped down on the sofa and picked the last vestiges of eggshell out of her hair. Despite taking a brief shower at the studio, she had not been thorough, as she had been keen to leave New York. She removed her WristWatt and placed it on her glass coffee table, methodically checking it for any remaining sign of egg. She had changed out of the white dress at the studio and was now wearing a pair of dark blue jeans with a brown belt and a pink vest top. Civilian clothes. She took two phones out of her pockets. One was black and the other white. She adjusted them until they were perfectly parallel to each other on the coffee table. Her head was buzzing, and she was distracted by her thoughts even though she was sitting still and in silence. One of the protestors, the second woman, had looked familiar, but Sandy could not recall her name or where she had first seen her. She picked up the remote and switched on the TV. Perhaps if she concentrated on something else, the name would come back to her. A dark haze of sadness had crept over her.

After she had flicked through a few channels, she switched the TV off. Two large ceiling-to-floor bookcases framed the TV on each side, and both were crammed tight with books. She had a well-worn tablet for reading, but tonight only a real book would do. She picked a book of poems and made her way to bed, keen on losing herself in the past.

The cadets' barracks were Spartan and brightly lit, with rows of beds and lockers on each wall. The beds were dressed with stiff white sheets and an itchy, grey fleece blanket during the winter. Each bed had one pillow—two was considered decadent.

"What did she give you? Come on. Tell us!" one of the male cadets teased.

"That's a secret, I'm afraid. A good intelligence officer is careful with his secrets," said Massi, grinning.

"Perhaps it was a list of all the people she murdered," a second cadet offered.

"It's not murder when it's war." Massi sat up in bed, offended by the other cadet's words.

"Did she give you her number? There are hardly any men her age in IC now. Going to take her on a date?" the first cadet continued.

"Don't be ridiculous," said Massi.

Colonel Mathers appeared in the doorway. "Enough of this. Why are your beds unkempt? Inspection in ten." Massi wondered if the colonel had been listening from out of sight.

"Sir, thank you, sir." Massi straightened his bed area.

"Keep your head down, cadet. You've made too much of yourself lately. You're part of a unit. Forget that at your peril." The colonel enunciated every word as he approached Massi.

"Sir, yes, sir."

"At ease. Let's speak freely."

Massi cringed at the words.

"You're a lot like her, you know," said Mathers.

"She's the best," said Massi. "I want to be the best one day too. Better."

"You have the same arrogance—that's for sure."

As the colonel looked down to read something on his tablet, Massi continued, "I call it confidence. And honesty. False modesty is just another lie."

"That sounds very much like something she'd say. I've just got your latest psych profile back. Your patterns are very similar to hers. Some differences, though."

"What are those?"

"Those are classified." He looked up and shouted, "Inspection in five!"

The next day, Sandy had the porter bring her breakfast from a deli down the street. The only food she had in her home was a box of eggs. She ate on her balcony and then dressed in civilian clothes. Discomforted by the events of the previous day, she felt the urge to do something active. That morning she pushed her furniture to the walls, strapped on a pressure vest and ran a gunfire simulation on a basic console in her living room. Trying to prove to herself that she was as sharp as ever, she hit almost every target until another avatar came up from behind and stabbed her in the back. Before she had a chance to see who had fatally wounded her, the vest tightened around her waist, leaving her spluttering and gasping for breath on her living room floor.

She went to the gym and lifted heavy weights. Back home, she showered, and for the first time in a long time, she was acutely aware of the scars on her body. Her skin felt tight where they marked it. Turning around, she caught a glimpse of the regimental tattoo on her left shoulder blade in the mirror, but she could not look at it for too long. How many others owned one like it? One. That was all. He was the only one still alive. Only one other individual out of the twenty-four who had gotten matching tattoos that day, and he did not speak to her—to anyone—anymore. She missed him, and she missed the others. The holes they had left in her life were like the scars on her body. She ignored them most of the time, but every now and again they crept into her mind.

Back on her balcony, she sat in a white dressing gown and summoned the courage to make the call. Both her black phone and her white phone were before her on the table. She picked up the black phone and dialled.

Claudette Muro was slender and remarkably physically fit for a woman in her early sixties. Her shoulder-length, chestnut-brown hair was always immaculate and had a smattering of expensive, tasteful highlights. Muro's fox-like features had never seemed warm to Sandy, but to the other soldiers in Sandy's regiment, Muro had been regarded as a motherly figure. To Sandy, she was more like a high-class madam, maternal but exploitative. Only seventy-five per cent of Intelligence Command was funded through taxation. Outside Intelligence Command's official operations, Muro would often ask her officers to carry out corporate espionage on foreign companies and other entities. These missions were meant to be voluntary, but officers who refused would find themselves last in line for promotion. Sandy had resented being sent to gather intelligence for the army's corporate sponsors while Muro took a cut and worried about the influence IC's sponsors had over Muro's decision-making process. Those were thoughts and feelings she kept to herself.

When the phone on Muro's desk flashed with Sandy's name and picture, she rolled her eyes and answered. "Good morning, Sandy."

"Good morning, Commander."

"What can I do for you?"

"What can I do for _you_, Commander?"

"If there was a mission that required your unique skill set, you'd be contacted without delay."

"There's really nothing?"

"Please appreciate that I'm very busy," said Muro as she hung up on Sandy.

The next day, Sandy sat in Muro's office fidgeting in the chair in front of her. The only decoration in the office was a single picture frame on the desk. Sandy had never seen whose picture occupied it. Sandy had served in the war with Muro's son, Martin. Perhaps it was a picture of him? She did not ask. There was a line between her and Muro, a line that was better not crossed.

"Why are you here, Sandy?" Muro waved her hand in annoyance. "Nothing has changed since our phone call yesterday."

"I can't believe there's nothing for me," said Sandy. "There's no such thing as one hundred percent security. Even in peacetime."

"We're doing just fine, but thank you for your concern."

"Don't you think you could be doing better with me?" she asked, almost pleading.

Muro exhaled. "Your style of operating is not what we hope to aspire to in peacetime. High Command considers you emotional and reckless."

"That's news to me. They never said anything before." Sandy was indignant.

"Sandy, I find you to be emotional and reckless," said Muro.

At last. The truth.

"Whatever I've done—it's worked, hasn't it? I'm the best there ever was."

"And you have been remunerated handsomely for your work during the war. It's time to enjoy your wealth. Find hobbies. Spend time with your friends."

Sandy's eyes began to tear. Muro was taken aback by this rare and uncharacteristic show of vulnerability but remained unmoved.

"I do enjoy my wealth. I have plenty of hobbies. But the reason I know that I'm the best there ever was without any uncertainty—without a shadow of a doubt—isn't because that's what everyone is saying. It's because I'm the only one in my regiment who came back alive and able-bodied. I'm compos mentis, and I have all my limbs. There are only a handful of soldiers my age who can say that. All my friends are dead. You sent us to die." Sandy spat the words out through her teeth.

The two sat together in silence until Muro finally stirred. "That doesn't mean I owe you anything now." She ran her fingers through her silky hair. "And winning by default has never been my preferred way of winning."

Sandy stood up and left Muro's office, moving like a wounded wild animal.

Massi was lying on his bunk in the barracks with his hands behind his head, enjoying a rare spare moment alone. That moment, however, was interrupted by Natalia, who startled him by entering the men's barracks. His heart leapt into his throat. She was wearing her uniform zipped down to the waist, and the arms of her suit were tied around her hips, revealing her tank top underneath.

"Hey, you can't be in here." Massi sat up, smiling.

She climbed onto his bed and whispered, "I thought you wouldn't mind."

"It's a lovely surprise for me, but I'm not the one you should worry about."

She kissed him hard on the lips and pushed him back on the bed. He ran his hands down her back and then unzipped her suit down lower. She helped him take his shirt off and moved her hands across his lean shoulders. The skin on her back was so soft. He loved it when her hair was loose. He hardly ever saw it that way. What a beautiful creature she was. It was not just the way she looked but the way she moved, too.

The barracks' doors snapped open. Massi sat up in bed, his daydream rudely interrupted. Three male cadets, each of them wearing the Academy's grey suits, complete with the balaclava masks usually reserved for combat, seized Massi before he could get off the bed. They bound his hands behind him and put another balaclava on him backwards so that he could not see. They dragged him to the main courtyard and began moving towards the flagpole that stood at its centre. Massi resisted his assailants as they dragged him, but they ducked and blocked his blind swipes and kicks. The three masked cadets hoisted Massi onto the pole with rope and tied him to it, his feet dangling a few metres off the ground. Throughout the whole ordeal, none of them said a word, and Massi could not tell who they were.

Hearing the commotion, a few other cadets entered the courtyard, as did Colonel Mathers. Satisfied with their work, the three rogue cadets secured Massi with the tight, intricate knots they had learnt in outdoor survival class. The colonel did not stop them. Massi was left squirming on the flagpole like an insect trapped in a spider's web. Before the cadets left, they wrote something on a piece of cardboard and placed it at the base of the pole.

CHAPTER THREE

After her meeting with Commander Muro had failed to go her way, Sandy had exited the building, but not without exacting a small measure of petty revenge. Before she left, she typed a series of numbers into a keypad mounted on a wall in the lobby. Once she finished typing, sirens sounded, and Intelligence Command HQ began its lockdown protocol. Sandy slid beneath the giant concrete blast shields as they lowered to the ground, pulling her motorbike helmet through with her in spectacular style. With a hollow THUD, the blast doors closed, locking those in the building inside.

Sandy now sat in a fast-food joint, eating in full view of ICHQ and watching in silent delight at the unfolding chaos that she had created. She was also sitting with her back towards a giant billboard. It was yet another soft-drink advertisement with her face front and centre, her lips stretched into an unnaturally wide grin. At twenty-metres high, it was a vulgarity she could not stand to look at right now. She was usually smug and satisfied with her endorsements—until she saw them. But no matter how phoney they seemed or how gaudy the products were, she liked seeing the numbers in her bank account rise. A cheque was a cheque.

Commander Muro sat with her officers, Hackett and Manning. Manning was thumbing through a messy, overfilled folder. Hackett had several more files on his lap.

"According to her last medicals, she's not suffering from post-traumatic stress disorder." Manning pulled out a sheet from the file and slid it onto Muro's desk.

"Frankly, it's been an enduring mystery how she ever passed the psych test at first entry," said Hackett.

"She passed the psych test like she passes all others—with flying colours," Manning said while gesturing to another sheet of paper.

"Are we wise not to rule out other possibilities?" asked Muro.

"Like what? Cheating?" asked Hackett.

"How do you cheat a psych test?" Manning protested.

"There must be something," said Muro.

"Maybe she's just depressed," Manning offered sympathetically. "We all know what happened to Lucian Scott."

"I heard she spends all her endorsement money on his treatment," said Hackett. "All of it."

"She's not that selfless." Muro sat back in her chair.

"It's not like she doesn't work hard. In the Academy, she had near-perfect scores. She is unfailingly loyal. She speaks three languages, and apart from recent, mild insubordination, she has been a model officer." Manning's words sounded more defensive than he had intended.

Muro smiled to herself.

"What?" asked Manning.

"There's something else," Muro mused, sounding as though she were talking to herself. "I sent that girl on operations I was certain she wouldn't come back from." Muro would never throw away a soldier's life intentionally, but sometimes the missions just seemed so insurmountable, she doubted if the corresponding exit plans were worth the time it took to draft them. "For now, she's just going to have to adjust to a world that is no longer in chaos."

Sandy finished her meal and started playing with her black phone. She flicked through her calendar, then saw a missed call from her aunt; she set an alarm as a reminder to return it later in the afternoon. There were several invitations: more talk shows, more endorsements, more events for troops and veterans. She was only included on those lists as a courtesy. In truth, she wanted to forget the period known as the 'Soft

Terror,' which led up to the Long War, and most of all, she wanted to forget the war itself. If she had her way, she would never go to another memorial event again. Her childhood had been marred by the ever-present threat of terrorism. Attack came after attack, increasing in ferocity and frequency until every shopping mall had metal detectors at their entrances and every school had armed guards. Living a safe, civilian life had become a luxury. Many chose to move out of big cities, taking their families and hefty pay cuts, preferring to live in poverty than in constant crippling fear. The war that had once been confined to foreign lands seemed to become an ever-present part of life on home soil. A new army was formed to take on a new threat, and Sandy had been determined to be a part of that army since she was a child. Whatever she had done in the war, and she had done many things, she had done them all for freedom from fear.

A child playing nearby dropped something, and the sound it made as it hit the floor shook Sandy out of her thoughts. It was a little silver robot. The head, arms and torso of the toy had slid across the floor and stopped beside Sandy's right foot. The little girl walked up to Sandy to retrieve its missing pieces, and Sandy helped her put the two halves back together again, twisting a shiny metal bolt back into place at the robot's waist. The little girl thanked her and ran back to her own table. Sandy watched discreetly as the girl and her parents gathered up their things and left the restaurant.

Sandy felt his eyes on her before she saw him. A stranger was staring at her from the other side of the restaurant. She looked away, but she still felt the strange man's intense stare boring into her. He was clean-shaven, but his clothes looked unkempt, and he was holding something in his hands. Sandy felt the urge to reach for the miniature pistol she kept strapped to her right ankle at all times. She knelt down as though she were going to tie her shoelaces, but when she got to the floor she realised she was not wearing shoes with laces. She straightened herself up abruptly, readying herself to run, but before she could, the man was right beside her.

"Hi," he said, startling her. She jumped backwards, almost losing her balance. "You okay there?"

His smile, concern and passive demeanour calmed her.

"Yes, I'm fine," she replied.

"Great! Can I have your autograph?" he said, thrusting a notepad and pen towards her.

"Ah, yes, of course." She returned his smile and took the pad and pen.

"Thanks. I've been waiting a long time to get you," he said, looking delighted. I thought it was you, but I wasn't sure. Sorry if I was staring."

"That's quite all right. I get that a lot." She winked at him and handed the pad back.

"Thanks. This is just great." He clasped the notepad as though it were made of gold.

"Who else do you have?" Sandy asked, though she was not really interested.

"Oh, I've got them all now. Peter Mac. Charlie-Ray Hanney. Arianne Vanner." The colour drained from Sandy's face as her 'fan' read the names of the country's best-known living serial killers. "You usually have to write to them in prison, though," the man said. He chuckled to himself and added, "You're just walking about."

Sandy sucked in the air around her and turned on her heels. She grabbed her motorbike helmet and darted out of the eatery without looking back, sending several trays of food flying in her haste.

Sandy had run back to her bike as fast as she could, then made her way to the hospital. She walked into the one of the rooms, still catching her breath and feeling shaken. She sat beside the bed and let her head fall onto the soft, clean blankets that covered the comatose patient. Fumbling beneath the sheets, she found his hand.

"Luca? Luca? Lucian? Are you there?" she whispered. He did not stir. "I don't know why you're not here. Why did I wake up, when you didn't? There's no place for me in this world without you. I need to save you. I will find a way to save you."

The familiar pang in her chest never really went away. It dimmed, and it sharpened. It waxed; it waned. But her heart was always sick. She rolled his hand in her own and renewed the covenant she had made a long time ago. She swore to him that she would love him deeply, passionately, fervently until the day she died.

A young female doctor brandishing a tablet walked briskly into the room. It took her a while to notice the hunched figure at the side of the bed.

"Oh, sorry. I can come back."

"No, it's okay." Sandy wiped away her tears and then turned to face the doctor. Sandy did not recognise her; she must be new. "How is he?"

Straightening herself up, the young doctor said, "Lieutenant Scott is still in a coma, as you can see. Our most advanced conventional techniques have stabilised him, as you know, but I would be uncomfortable saying there's been any improvement. Not for a while now. He's the same."

"Can I speak to the consultant, please?"

"Of course."

The young woman seemed irritated, as though Sandy had suggested her own competence was not enough. She left the room with the same professional, brisk stride that she had entered with. She re-entered a few minutes later with Dr Leroy Ennis, Lucian's long-term physician.

"Hello again, Sandy." He sounded cheerful but reluctant. "I'm not sure if my colleague informed you, but I'll be transferring soon. Dr Reuben will be taking over Lieutenant Scott's care." He gestured at the female doctor who forced a smile across the bottom half of her plump, appealing face.

"You're leaving? Where to?" Sandy's body twitched in agitation.

"Back to Florida. I've been here a while, working on the same type of cases, and I just . . . I just needed a change. I want to be closer to my parents. My wife loves the weather down there, and she's not keen on another winter here. You know I got married recently."

"Oh, oh okay. I didn't know, but I get that." Sandy felt the sting of betrayal envelop her body. Dr Ennis had looked after Luca from the beginning, and even though she knew his decision was not personal, it still felt that way. She paused for a moment, suppressing her raw and irrational feelings.

"Good, good. I'm glad," he said to fill the awkward silence.

"Before you go, what's left? There must be something that we haven't tried."

"Now that he's stable again, we could try nano-surgery to repair the damage to the nervous system. We would have to make a single-camera drone and have it look around to pinpoint exactly where the damage is.

If there's anything we can do, we manufacture more nano drones and set them to fixing all that we can."

"Whatever it takes," Sandy responded.

"I'll do everything I can, Sandy, but this is also the part where I have to manage expectations."

"Tomorrow. Let's have that talk tomorrow," said Sandy, looking back at Lucian.

As evening descended on the Academy, Massi continued to hang helplessly from the flagpole in the deserted courtyard. Eventually, a female cadet dressed in a grey uniform, complete with balaclava and visor, walked up to the pole and loosened the cord. She undid the knots and lowered Massi to the ground.

Massi stumbled, trying to get back on his feet. "Nat, is that you?"

She did not answer and instead turned to walk back inside.

"You didn't have to miss the ceremony for me," Massi said. "Nat!"

He called after her, but she did not acknowledge him. Massi rubbed his wrists. They were sore and scorched with red rings where the rope had gripped his flesh. His eyes stung, but he did not remember if he had been crying or not. It was then that he noticed what had been written on the sign:

ICARUS LIKES THE HEAT UP HIGH!

He took it and ripped it up. He threw the torn cardboard to the ground and stomped on it repeatedly. Collapsing at the base of the flagpole, he let his head drop into his hands.

That evening the night was cloudy but beautiful. Sandy stepped out of a taxi in front of the opera house, unsteady in brand-new gold strappy heels. Her knee-length little black dress made her hobble, but she managed to compose herself. Before the taxi sped away, she checked her neat chignon and make-up in its window. She was especially pleased with the effort she had made with her appearance. She had even bought some of the same products that the makeup artist on the set of the *Goodnight*

Show had used. Her only other accessories were a little gold clutch and her medals.

"Good evening, Sandy." Commander Muro was resplendent in a shimmering black ball gown.

"Evening, ma'am," said Sandy standing as straight as she could.

"You do still have a dress uniform, do you not?"

"Yes, ma'am. It's not black, though." Sandy had wanted to be someone other than a soldier tonight. Annoying Muro was icing on the cake.

"Of course. Because of the occasion, I will give you a free pass for mufti, but dress uniform for ceremonies and formal events from now on."

"Yes, ma'am."

"At least your dress has enough material for you to attach all your medals to it this time. Well done."

"Thank you, ma'am." Truth be told, Sandy's many medals made an awkward spectacle on the front of her frock. Their weight caused the fabric to sag in a rather unflattering fashion and ruined the dress's attempt at simplicity.

A limousine pulled up beside them. A man got out and opened one of its doors for Lyndon Hamilton.

"Claudette, you're a vision." He greeted Muro with open arms.

"Lyndon, you polish up rather nicely yourself," said Muro. "Not just a sharp mind and a generous heart."

He kissed her hand to return the compliment.

Sandy cringed and discreetly entered the building to avoid the spectacle.

The inside of the opera house looked glorious. Cadets and officers parted as Sandy was ushered to her seat at a long table on an elevated platform overlooking the main stage. The cadets were clad in their grey dress uniforms and stood in the stalls like polished tin soldiers. Some of them were looking up at Sandy, and, feeling uncomfortable and out of place, she slid downwards into her chair to avoid their gaze.

Muro, still deep in conversation with Hamilton, was ushered to the same table as Sandy. Thankfully, the two were seated next to one another. Sandy would not have to feign interest or make small talk with either of them. Sandy had already sensed that Hamilton wanted to engage her in conversation, but she distanced herself from him every time he made eye contact with her.

Sandy had never met Hamilton properly; she resented him for being a typical corporate sponsor of Intelligence Command. He was not as bad as an arms dealer, but he still provided technology, security infrastructure and other tools of war. He was also a sponsor of many of the Academy's cadets. Sandy had always avoided him at similar events, and she had no intention of breaking that winning streak tonight.

"Thank you again for coming, Lyndon," said Muro. "We appreciate that you prefer not to make public appearances."

"Claudette, it's times like these that humble me and remind me that my sacrifices are nothing."

Sandy took a deep gulp of the drink she had picked up in the opera house lobby before she was seated. It was going to be one of those nights. The politicians and other facilitators of war who came to these events would fawn and pat each other on the back, never knowing the full extent of their actions. If only they really knew what men and women like Sandy had done to fulfil their orders, perhaps they might have shown more respect. Their missions had sent young men and women to their deaths or home to their families incomplete and irreparably broken. It did not seem like a waste to them now that there was peace, but Sandy could only see what was missing—missing faces, missing limbs, missing friends and missing family. Whole clusters of humanity and resources wasted. Sandy found herself working hard to suppress the rage boiling inside her. The sight of a medal on the lapel of a politician who had never seen active service made her face feel hot. She clenched her fist to fight the urge to walk up to him and rip the medal right off his chest.

The lights darkened, and the ceremony began.

"Ladies and gentleman, will you please stand?" a civilian, the master of ceremonies, said. "Officers and cadets of Intelligence Command, stand to attention."

The cadets stood and saluted in sharp unison. Sandy wobbled up onto her heels and saluted as well.

"High Commander Drummond will now give his address."

Christopher Drummond was an arresting man—tall, solid, clean-shaven except for a neat black moustache, and dark-skinned. His uniform was a deep sanguine red, and today it sported so many gold embellishments and medals, it was almost comical. Sandy had to stifle a laugh as she looked at it.

"At ease," he said. "Ladies, gentlemen, officers and cadets of Intelligence Command and distinguished guests, we are here this evening to remember and honour the dead of the Long War. Our dead.

"I take great pride in seeing mankind once again enjoy lasting peace. To know that my daughter will never know fear such as the Soft Terror is a prevailing comfort. We have created a more perfect world, and it was forged with fortitude and bravery. Security and progress have come at a price, and the souls of the valiant and glorious men and women who came before you were the levy paid.

"I now call upon Lyndon Hamilton—a generous donor to the Veterans of the Long War Memorial Project—to present High Command's Medal of Outstanding Service."

Sandy was no longer paying attention. She was working on concocting a drink stronger than the one she already had from the various bottles on the table in front of her. When Hamilton stood up, she spilt it. Muro shot her a dirty look that stopped her in her tracks.

Hamilton walked onstage, his strides swift, long and confident.

"Thank you, High Commander Drummond," Hamilton said, his voice loud, articulate and calming. Drummond shook Hamilton's hand and retired from the podium. "No doubt you have all heard the heroic deeds of Lieutenant First Class Alisande Attiyeh. She served in Russia, Indashin and the Middle East. Most notably on Operations Locket Vault, Surabaya and Jazan. A first-class intelligence officer, a humanitarian and a true patriot. We owe so much to the service of individuals like Lieutenant First Class Attiyeh that a mere medal seems a paltry way of expressing gratitude, but I don't make up these traditions."

A polite wave of laughter rippled through the crowd of cadets and junior officers.

"For outstanding service in the face of danger unfathomable to a civilian such as myself, Lieutenant First Class Alisande Attiyeh, I honour you."

Sandy had clambered down to the stage just in time. She saluted Drummond and then the cadets. Hamilton handed the medal to Drummond, who attempted to pin the medal on Sandy, but could not seem to figure out how to do that without touching her inappropriately. Sandy discreetly stuck her thumb under her dress at the armpit and pulled the fabric away from her body. Drummond pinned the medal to the dress, causing the neckline to sag a little further and expose her bra. Her lingerie was a conspicuous shade of metallic aquamarine. Sandy noticed but made no attempt to rearrange her clothes. Drummond shot her a look of irritated embarrassment as they saluted each other again. Sandy then exited the stage as quickly as she could without running.

"It's now time to remember all those who did not come back from the Long War," said Drummond.

The orchestra began to play as Sandy retook her seat. A female opera singer began to sing 'Dido's Lament' from Dido and Aeneas.

Sandy's eyes fixated on a violin bow sawing at its strings. She felt moved by the music and regretted the extra alcohol; she was not able to control her mind.

Her body was wet and intensely cold, and she was back on the outskirts of the Ural Mountains. She was hacking away at a piece of rope with a blunt knife. When she finally cut the rope, the body of a dead female officer slumped into her arms. Sandy wailed in despair.

She slapped a hand over her mouth before she could make a sound. Muro flashed her another dirty look. Sandy shook her head and instead stared at a flickering light.

The scent of spiced meat filled her nose. The man beneath her, another officer, convulsed as she electrocuted him again and again with a small device she held in her hand.

Sandy had to blink rapidly to clear her mind.

Before her was a wall of flames that lapped at a city of tents. Screams of pain echoed in the distance.

Sandy writhed on her chair in discomfort as a percussionist beat a drum.

A copper pot was in her hand. She was beating a faceless man with it again and again and again.

Sandy reached for a glass of water but knocked it instead and then fumbled at it while it spilt. Embarrassed, she excused herself to the ladies' washroom.

###

Sandy splashed water across her face and neck, removing some of her makeup in the process. She wiped her eyes and closed a toilet cubical door behind her. The lock was broken, so she jammed a pen into it to prevent it from opening and took a seat.

She lay on a beach, her black-ops combat suit soaked. It was night, and a male officer lay face down in the sand next to her. Seawater washed over them as the rising tide threatened to drown them both, and she struggled to lift him farther onto the beach.

She opened her clutch and pulled out what looked like a lipstick case. The cap took some effort to unscrew, but when it did, a mechanism pushed up to reveal a concealed tube. The tube dispensed a tiny tab, which Sandy pressed her little finger onto. She rubbed the tab on the inside of her bottom lip, closed her eyes and rested her head against the side of the cubicle.

She was back on the beach. Bullets were flying in her direction, but just before they reached her they dissolved inches in front of her face. The sun rose, and Sandy was alone on a sunny tropical island. Three birds chirped in the fronds of a nearby palm tree, and she watched them for what seemed like a very long time.

###

Natalia was alone in the computer lab. She had finished up her homework a while ago, and it appeared to Massi, who had just entered the room, that she was now working on an unfamiliar project of her own. Natalia did not look at him as he approached. Massi sat facing away from her, still feeling ashamed. He opened his workbook and looked over his shoulder, marvelling at how much more advanced Natalia's work was compared to his own.

"They did it on purpose," he said, "so I'd miss the ceremony. They knew how much I wanted to go."

Natalia ignored his remarks.

After a few more minutes, he swallowed his pride. "Thank you," he said softly.

"You're welcome," she replied.

Massi wanted to hold her, touch her, put his lips on her smooth skin, but above all, he wanted to actually know her. Most of the time, he felt as if they were speaking different languages. His attempts at deepening the relationship had thus far not yielded any progress. Natalia was now engrossed in what looked like a Web chat.

"Who are you emailing?" Massi enquired.

"Someone whose username is 'Corio'."

"Is he another cadet?"

"No, I think he's my soulmate, though."

A shiver went up Massi's spine. He sat bolt upright in his seat and turned to face her even though she was not looking his way.

"Do you see him regularly?" he asked.

"No, we've never met," she said.

He relaxed. "How do you know him then?"

"Found him on a forum. It's nothing. We just like the same things." She continued typing.

"What do you two chat about?" he asked.

"We don't chat in real time. He just leaves puzzles for me. I solve them. This is the first time I've encountered anyone better at this than me."

"You shouldn't go meeting people from online."

"I've no intention of meeting him. We share a dark corner of the Net, so that would definitely not be wise. We just both play these online games that no one else plays."

"Okay. Good. Just looking out for you." Massi turned back around and smiled to himself. Though his jealousy had not receded entirely, he was still in the game.

###

Sandy was awakened by the sound of her own drool hitting the bathroom floor with a loud splutter. She was slumped in the toilet cubicle, her head still resting on one of the walls. Her expensive clutch lay open on the bathroom floor in front of her. As she picked it up, she realised that she could still hear birdsong. She un-jammed the lock and stumbled to the mirror. Her vision was blurred, and her pupils were dilated. She undid her hair from its chignon and let it cascade over her shoulders.

She looked at her reflection in the mirror. Her eyes twitched at her appearance. All the years she had wished for the war to end. How she had longed for the days when she would no longer have to wear a uniform. Those days had shone in her mind like the light at the end of a tunnel. Now those days had come, and she felt naked without her white suit. The war had defined her. Even her full name, Alisande. Alisande. Alisande. She repeated it in her mind. A floral, feminine name that was so ill-fitting that almost no one ever referred to her by it. Her parents had named her for a different life. She would have been another person had the war not happened. But it _had_ happened. Every violent act she committed had stripped away the person she would have been, and now she was left with the malformed creature looking back at her.

What could she do with this creature? Go to college? And study what? Get a job? Where? Doing what? And who would employ her when she could not come to work because the nightmares that haunted her kept her up for as many as thirty-six consecutive hours? Or when she did not leave her apartment because subduing the ghoulish, accusing faces of her fallen friends and comrades required a small pharmacy's worth of psychotropic drugs that incapacitated her for days?

She walked into the room where the cadets and officers were now socialising. Looking around, she began walking down the corridor where the birdsong seemed to come from. It became louder, and she made her way through several rooms until finally she found a small aviary full of songbirds. Without hesitating, she opened the aviary door, and the songbirds flew straight out through an open French window, over the balcony and into the night sky. She followed the birds onto the balcony and slipped off her high heels. She unpinned the medals from her chest, let them fall through her fingers to the floor, and dropped her clutch beside them. Sandy moved a chair and, stepping onto it tentatively, climbed onto the stone balustrades. A midnight breeze moved the hair away from her face as she looked down at the street below.

The tabs could remove the visions from her mind, but they could not take the sorrow from her heart. There were wounds beneath her skin that were just not healing—that would never heal. Now they were festering and churning her guts. Every day she would wake up, and the pain would still be there, ever-present on her chest, making it hard to move, to eat and to live. She may have once been a hero to some, but she was not anymore, and she never would be again.

"Careful!" Lyndon Hamilton strode onto the balcony. "You might fall."

His voice jolted Sandy from her trancelike state.

"I'll fall only if I want to," she said without turning around.

"Okay, but why don't you come down from there anyway?"

Sandy did not respond.

He looked around and said with some trepidation, "Please come down... you're making me anxious"

"I'm fine," said Sandy. To prove that she was in perfect control, she performed a round-off on the balustrade and hopped down, giving a little curtsey after she landed soundly.

"Wow," he said, gesticulating as if though he were applauding, a coy smile on his face. "I never believed you were as impressive as everyone says you are. Not until this very moment."

"You still shouldn't believe what they say," she said wryly. "The truth is much worse."

"I've been wanting to make your acquaintance for some time now, Sandy. I'm a fellow epistemophiliac." He picked up her medals and clutch and offered them back to her. She slid them off his hands and held them close to her body.

"You must be." She sounded impressed. "Very few people know that."

"I know you collect books. You outbid me at an auction. Have you ever considered working in the private sector?"

"All I've ever been is a soldier." Sandy looked uninterested.

"But you're much more than that. In the private sector, you'd be called a hacker, a detective, a thief, a murderer...a mass murderer."

"If you're not upholding the monopoly on the legitimate use of force, you're constrained by it. You're gaming the system, or you're a victim of it," Sandy said, trying to stem the conversation.

"Oh, my goodness. That's rather contrarian for a soldier. Don't worry, I won't tell Commander Muro." Hamilton gave Sandy a little wink.

"It wouldn't matter. She's giving me the silent treatment."

"How so?" asked Hamilton.

"I'm being...decommissioned," said Sandy, forlorn.

"Are you seeking work?" he asked.

"I'm seeking adventure."

"In that case, I need someone to act as a consultant on a project that is semi-complete. It's a hobby. Would you indulge me?"

###

Sandy stood in the most sophisticated computer lab she had ever seen. The logo of Hamilton InfoSec, Hamilton's company, was plastered across everything. Hamilton was an outstanding entrepreneur in his field, and his company provided information storage, but they were most well-known for supplying the best encryption software, firewalls, anti-phishing programs and other security infrastructure in the world. Data protected from would-be hackers by Hamilton InfoSec's software was thirty-five percent less likely to be stolen than had it been guarded by the next best information security company.

In front of her was a large digital sphere representing the earth, surrounded by what looked like a green net. The image was projected from a high-tech machine housed in a waist-height round table in the centre of the room.

"I see; it's a map," Sandy said.

"That's right. It's a map of the other information storage companies and their links to the significant individuals who work for them. It's not complete; it's missing the clients of my competitors, and I would like to know who they are, and why they chose them instead of me."

"Of course, you would," said Sandy.

"On top of this, I want to know where those clients get their original research from, specifically in relation to those companies in the technology, IT, manufacturing and medical sectors. Who creates the information that they need locked away by my competitors? In the end, this projection should be a complete network of the relevant relationships all around the world. I should be able to touch this model and have all the information appear at my fingertips."

"You're thinking about this wrong. These companies may say they're multinational, but they're anchored in real locations on earth for a reason. They're also anchored in human relationships," Sandy spoke as if she were thinking out loud.

"Interesting. If I asked, would you be willing to put the other pieces into this puzzle and map these relationships entirely?" he queried. "I'm an entrepreneur, not an engineer."

"It's a long-term, time-intensive project."

"I have deep pockets," he said, and smiled. Everything about Hamilton reeked of a quiet, tasteful opulence.

More money means better treatment for Luca, Sandy's mind reasoned.

"Interesting hobby. Should I ask why?" asked Sandy.

"Curiosity," Hamilton answered quickly. Too quickly.

"As simple as that? It looks like corporate espionage to me."

"I've made my money by making data more secure. This is my domain. My life's work. After thirty years, I feel as though I've barely scratched the surface. If my competitors know something that I don't, then I want to know what that is. I doubt you could ever understand this, but it's about completeness. Fulfilling one's potential. All I wish is to know my domain in its entirety."

An elegant speech, thought Sandy. "I do understand. But the legality of this project is tenuous. And you know that." Her words were spoken cautiously.

"Legality wasn't an issue for you on Operation Jazan. Have I at least piqued your curiosity?"

"Pay me in advance, and never mention Jazan again," she said abruptly.

"You're not hired yet. I've only heard anecdotal evidence of your hacking skills. They're not the type of skills an IC field agent usually has. How can I know you're up to the job?"

Sandy stepped further into Hamilton's lab and approached a laptop. She started to type. After a little while, she closed the laptop and turned back to Hamilton.

"How do you get to the roof of this place?" she asked with a sly grin on her face.

###

Massi struggled with his computer science homework as Natalia continued to work on the puzzle left for her by the mysterious Corio.

Natalia screamed.

"What's wrong?" Massi cried out to her.

"I didn't save!" Natalia's computer screen was blank. Massi turned back and saw that his screen was also blank. Then the lights in the computer lab shut off.

Across the city, the lights went out—mostly one by one, sometimes in rows. Electric cars shut down on the roads. Big screens blinked off. Streetlights dimmed to blackness until the entire East Coast of the United States was plunged into darkness.

###

Sandy stood on the roof of Hamilton's building, and Hamilton watched in disbelief as the city went dark before them. Sandy's long hair was whipped around by the turbulent night air. For the first time in a long time, she felt powerful. For a fleeting moment, Hamilton considered the possibility that he found her intensely attractive. But as quickly as the notion had come upon him, he stopped himself from indulging in that type of thought. Undisputed queen of the dark city in front of her, she raised her arms triumphantly to the heavens.

CHAPTER FOUR

Sandy entered her apartment and kicked off her high heels. She poured herself a small glass of red wine and sat on the balcony of her penthouse to watch the sun rise. The sunlight sparkled on the river and began to spread a soft radiance over the monuments. The lights she had extinguished were slowly coming back to life too. Her despair had been vanquished in the dark. Muro could not give her work, so she had found new purpose for herself. In the early glow of the new day, she could finally see a life beyond the white suit of her youth. Her little power cut would be dismissed as a glitch, and she would make a career working as a spy for hire. Not just for companies; she knew of several nations that could use her skills and would pay for them. She would never do anything that harmed IC, of course; she would be ethical.

When she went inside to sleep, she found that even her usual nightmares had abated. The terrifying ambushes and automated fire that more often than not shook her awake had been replaced by two scared little boys who stood weeping in front of her. They were dressed in rags, and their feet were bare. They were standing in red sand and crying because it was too hot: every step they took burnt their feet, so they just stood still and cried.

This image was still unpleasant but not loud or scary enough to rouse her, and without the use of any pills, she slept for several unbroken hours.

Sandy was awakened by a loud knock at her door. She turned to her alarm clock— an out-dated digital she kept for sentimental reasons—it flashed 00:00. The power cut! Still in her dressing gown, she opened the door and was greeted by Hackett and Manning.

"Good afternoon, Sandy." Manning looked serious.

"Hey," was all she could muster.

"Long night?" Hackett enquired.

"Err…tiresome. What time is it?" Sandy played with the belt on her robe.

"It's fourteen thirty. Sandy, we were sent here by Muro." Hackett tried to ease through the doorway, but Sandy blocked him.

"Why?" asked Sandy, irritated.

"Just let us in," Manning insisted.

Manning and Hackett stayed in Sandy's living room while she made coffee and breakfast for herself. She sensed that this conversation would not be confined to her apartment for long. When she returned, the TV was on.

"There was an incident last night, and we don't know what caused it," Manning offered.

On the screen, a newsreader said, "We are now going to a press conference Commander Claudette Muro held earlier today."

The news show cut to an ashen-faced Muro.

"Last night, at approximately twenty-three forty, we began hearing reports of electrical failure. This electrical failure affected power substations citywide. It took three hours to restore the grid to full capacity. As of yet, we are still trying to ascertain what exactly caused this, but engineers have been able to confirm that this was a software infrastructure failure. This was not a terrorist attack." She looked up from her notes and stared directly into the camera. "I repeat. This was not a terrorist attack."

Back to the newsreader. "High Command are urging calm, but questions are arising about the soundness and security of our nation's infrastructure—"

Hackett snatched up the remote and turned off the TV.

"What does this have to do with me?" said Sandy with a petulant shrug.

"We're not sure this was as cut and dried as a simple electrical fault. It's still possible it was caused deliberately. The truth is…we don't know." Manning's voice was hushed.

"This may still turn out to be a terrorist attack and you, being a high-profile officer of Intelligence Command, may be a target." Hackett turned to face her square on.

"I can handle myself, thanks," she said.

"We'd still like you to come to HQ with us." Manning was trying hard to be the good cop.

"Your uniform. Find it. Get dressed," said Hackett with authority.

In the Academy's uniform locker, Massi and Natalia were polishing their boots. Natalia's usual cool, impregnable façade had slipped. She was agitated and struggling to keep the polish off her skin. She never smudged even a slither of polish anywhere other than where it was intended. For some reason, Massi liked seeing her like this. She seemed vulnerable, messier. It was as if her seams had been unpicked. *Although,* he thought, *I like her when she is playing her steely ice-queen act, too. I just like her.*

"What's up?" he ventured.

"Nothing," she answered sullenly.

"Lie."

"What do you want?" she asked.

"For you not to be upset. Did I say something?" he asked.

"It's not you."

"Okay then." Massi looked away.

"Yes, actually, it is you," she snapped.

"What have I done?"

"You're happy," she said.

"Yeah, I'm happy. This is awesome."

"You want there to be action?" she asked with an incredulous look on her face.

"Yeah, I want action. I'm a soldier," he stood upright, puffing up his chest, his muscles flexed.

"A good soldier never wants action. They're prepared for action. They don't want it. They don't actively seek it out," she said.

"If you didn't want action, why did you join what is technically the army?"

"I had a plan," she protested.

"Come on."

"This is where you get the best tech training in the world. Sponsored. I was going to do this for ten years. Get a plush quasi-government job somewhere or be employed by a company like Hamilton InfoSec. Spend the next ten years developing software. I'm a millionaire by the time I'm forty. Easy."

"You knew there was a risk. When you signed up—you knew."

"The risk was there, but it was small. Small enough to make a justifiable gamble." She looked away from him.

"You cannot be serious," he said.

"You may be looking for trouble, but I'm not. If you look around, you'll see that you're in the minority. No one else thinks like you," she whispered in a hiss.

"We are soldiers; going to war is what we do. You're on the tech track anyway."

"Do you hear yourself?" Her voice was raised. "You're the only individual in the world who wants last night to have actually been a terrorist attack."

"I just don't think you should believe everything they tell you on the news."

"Insufferable." Natalia finished cleaning her boots, threw them into her locker and stormed out of the room.

Massi was not unhappy that he had upset her. He felt excited, not just by last night's events but also at the thought that he had pushed Natalia's buttons at last.

###

Natalia headed back to the girls' barracks. There were no more classes that afternoon, and she felt exhausted. Her sleep the night before had been troubled. As she walked, she wondered why she spent so much time with Massi. When she got to her bunk, she remembered. The other female cadets were gossiping as they went about their chores. They did not even look up when she entered the room. She was not like them, and that was out of her control. Massi, for all his faults, was good company. He was also easy on the eyes. She had sometimes found her mind drifting to his muscular forearms and the broadness of his chest under his uniform. She turned onto her side to get the uncomfortable, inconvenient, illicit thoughts out of her mind. It was supposed to be the other female cadets who were shallow and vain. Natalia felt different from them, but she could never articulate why. They were glory-seekers, a trait she found unattractive even in Massi. She needed to be challenged. She wanted to be back in the lab, lost in the net with the mysterious Corio. He was the only one who presented her with real stimulation—the only other person she knew who inhabited the same intellectual space as she did. She pictured him as a shy computer geek who was secretly in love with her. Her current daydreams consisted of meeting a man who turned out to be Corio and being delighted that he was better looking than she thought he would be. Her nightmares involved Corio too. Perhaps he was just a foreign hacker who communicated with her because he already knew she was a cadet at the Academy? That could not be true, she assured herself. She had been so careful never to reveal any personal details online. She tossed and turned in her bunk, trying to retrace her cyber steps until she was certain she had not left so much as a hint. Only then could she finally rest.

Hackett and Manning trailed behind Sandy as she walked towards the main operation control room in ICHQ. The room was swarming with serious faces, all eyes trawling through data. Muro was poring over several files and glancing at various screens that relayed information. Digital maps of the East Coast with weather patterns moving across them. Time-lapse videos showing when the power had cut out in each city and following the darkness as it spread across the continent.

"About time. So, what do you think?" Muro was still staring at the report. She was visibly wound up. Her hair had a slight frizz to it.

"Are you talking to me?" Sandy regretted her tone the minute the words left her mouth.

Muro looked up sharply. "Yes, Lieutenant First Class, I am addressing you. I am your direct commanding officer, and I am addressing you."

"Yes, ma'am," said Sandy, chastised.

"So, what do you think? An accident? An attack? An infrastructure fault? A deliberate infrastructure fault?"

"How many died?" Sandy asked.

"I beg your pardon?"

"How many deaths occurred as a result of the power failure, ma'am?"

"As a direct result?" Muro looked at the report. "None, actually."

"On those grounds, calling it an attack, even an attack purely on our infrastructure, is probably unwise, ma'am."

"Yes." Muro's face softened. It was the reassurance she needed, and only Sandy could give it to her.

A nerdy-looking engineer who was standing behind Muro chimed in: "In fact, fewer people died than the statistical norm. The freeways shut down, so only a few non-automated cars were on the roads. Everyone stayed in."

"Thank you, Gerald." Muro turned back to Sandy. "So, what do you think it was?"

"A joke, ma'am."

"A joke?"

"It was a joke, ma'am." Her heart was beating so hard she could feel every thump. This was it; she would confess. She paused and thought carefully about her next few words. "Or a disgruntled employee. At the grid."

"What exactly are your reasons for thinking this?" asked Muro gently.

"Ma'am, I think this, because I don't see how it could have not been deliberate. The infrastructure of this city is superior, secure and sound. Since no one died, the individual or organisation responsible was not aiming for loss of life. With the level of security access they would need to have or infiltrate to do this, they could have caused many deaths. Easily. The timing of the incident, late at night, suggests they were not aiming to do mass economic damage, although inevitably some did occur. The fault was easily resolved. One can only conclude that with the access required to shut down the grid, even for a few hours, whoever is responsible would have also had the ability to do permanent damage. They either made a choice not to or never had any intention of doing so."

As Muro took in Sandy's words, her face looked as if it were aging backwards. Her eyes began to relax, and the fine lines around them ironed out. Her face flushed with colour once again, and she began to breathe more calmly.

"Yes, of course," said Muro. "Thank you. My office, please."

###

Muro pushed back in her chair and lifted her highly polished boots onto her desk.

"I knew it wasn't terrorists. I knew, but I couldn't be sure." Muro's voice sounded softer than usual and unsettled.

"Yes, ma'am," said Sandy.

"Speak freely."

"Yes, ma'am."

"I was scared," Muro confessed. "I was scared."

"Me too," said Sandy.

"There's been nothing. No intelligence whatsoever. Not even an uprising or a skirmish. No power struggles between desert warlords. Nothing. No terrorists. Nothing. Nowhere." Muro looked at Sandy, her intense stare making Sandy shift with discomfort in her chair.

"Peace and quiet," Sandy replied.

"Yes. We killed them," said Muro smiling but not meeting Sandy's gaze.

"We killed them all," said Sandy, nodding, the corners of her mouth turning upwards.

"Do you like it?" asked Muro.

"What?" asked Sandy, worried she was being played with.

"The silence?" Muro's face looked emotionless.

"I can't remember what it was like before." Sandy shook her head and looked at the floor.

"Me neither," said Muro, almost in a whisper.

They sat in silence for a short moment. Just enough time for them both to breathe deeply.

"I saw you get into Lyndon Hamilton's limousine last night," said Muro, her voice changed back to its normal, sultry calm.

"Yes," Sandy acknowledged dryly.

"Lift home?"

"He wanted to discuss the Veterans of the Long War Memorial Project," she lied.

"Of course. Nice of you to finally take an interest," Muro said derisively.

A wave of hot shame spread across Sandy. "May I be excused, ma'am?" she asked timidly.

"Yes. Yes, of course."

"Thank you, ma'am." Sandy stood to leave.

"Sandy?"

"Yes, ma'am?"

"I'm glad you're safe. I was concerned. I know that this...situation isn't ideal for you. I hope you know that I'm not doing it out of spite." Muro sounded sincere.

"Thank you, ma'am," Sandy acknowledged, although it felt like spite.

Sandy left Muro's office. At least she was sure now that Muro did not suspect her involvement in the incident. Something else was different, though. Sandy had never seen Muro so vulnerable. The relationship between the two women was undeniably, inexplicably changed.

Back at her penthouse, Sandy released her uniform at the neck and sat down at her computer. It took her three minutes to hack into Intelligence Command's incident logs. The report had just been updated, and the power failure had been recorded as an infrastructure fault.

She walked to the living room and slumped onto her sofa. It was only then that she became aware that she was wet. Soaked through, in fact. She had been aware of every throb of her heart, but she had not realised how profusely she had been sweating. She turned on the news and began peeling her uniform away from her skin.

Commander Muro was back to her usual strident self and giving another press conference. "After investigating last night's power failure, Intelligence Command has closed the case. There was not a shred of intelligence to suggest that this was an act of terrorism. I understand that this incident has created anxiety, but rest assured—our people have never been more secure."

Sandy walked to her bathroom without switching off the TV. She turned on the shower and ran the water as hot as it could go without scolding her. She sluiced the water over herself, trying to purge her body of all the stress and agitation of the day. The perfume she had worn to the ceremony still lingered on her hair and neck from the night before. Its scent was making her feel nauseous.

Sandy's white phone rang, interrupting her cleanse. She dashed out of the shower and, grabbing a towel, walked, still soaking wet, back to her living room. She switched the TV to mute and answered it.

"Sandy speaking."

"Good evening. Interesting day?" the smooth masculine voice asked.

"The best, Lyndon. How are you?"

"I'm well. I was just calling to check if you had any allergies. My chef is just about to start preparing dinner."

As he spoke, the ticker across the bottom of Sandy's TV scrolled to the left.

It read:

A PREVIOUSLY UNKNOWN TERRORIST GROUP HAS CLAIMED RESPONSIBILITY FOR LAST NIGHT'S POWER CUT.

"Sorry about this, but something's come up," she told Hamilton. "Can we reschedule?"

"Of course," said Hamilton, startled.

She hung up on him and unmuted the TV.

The newsreader explained, "A disturbing turn of events this afternoon, as a previously unknown terrorist group has claimed responsibility for last night's assault on the nation's infrastructure. We now have further evidence to support this claim. The terrorists have released this video. Viewers are warned that the following footage contains disturbing content."

Stunned and horrified, Sandy watched as the poor-quality footage showed three masked terrorists claim responsibility for the power cut. *My power cut*, she thought indignantly. *How dare they?* Sandy felt the muscles in the back of her throat tense in sheer dread. She scolded herself for being such a fool. Why had she thought this would be seen as some sort of technical anomaly? For a moment, she was physically paralysed, but she thought fast. Her eyes flicking across the screen, she made a mental note of every detail in the video. She cursed her hubris once more, then sprang into action.

"Are we safe?" the newsreader said. "That's the question everyone is asking tonight. How could Intelligence Command have got it so wrong, and is Claudette Muro still fit to lead?"

CHAPTER FIVE

Sandy raced down the hallway and scrabbled at the wall near one of her paintings. *Damn,* she thought. She could never remember quite where it was. A few moments later, a hidden panel yielded beneath her hand.

The small panic room contained a powerful bespoke machine that she had designed and built herself. The large monitor in front of her clicked on, and it took her mere moments to hack the news channel's system. She raced back to her bedroom, opened the closet, and flung her towel onto the floor. In a secret compartment at the back of her wardrobe, a black suit hung limply, looking like a dark ghoul. She took a deep breath as she pulled the suit on. A familiar second skin. In the mirror, a circular fleck of flesh peeked out at the side of her neck. She could remember exactly how she felt the day the bullet-sized hole was made. The pain had been excruciating.

When she went back to the panic room computer, the exact origin of the leaked terrorist footage blinked on the screen: a modest city townhouse in the Low Streets, an eccentric but affluent nearby suburb. *How curious...* She tapped the address into her wrist device and pulled her mask and visor over her face.

The cadets were seated in rows in the bright-white academy cafeteria. Instead of consuming their evening meal, they were motionless, eyes transfixed on a screen normally reserved for announcements and general information. A decision had been made from higher up to let them find out the way everyone else was finding out. They were not touching their food, and their faces were full of fear. Each one of them was aware of how few soldiers had come back alive and able-bodied the last time.

Natalia looked terrified. Massi moved his hand and touched hers lightly under the table. She pulled away and left the cafeteria. He followed her into the corridor.

"Hey! Hey!" Massi cried out to her.

"That's it. It's over." Her voice started to break.

"Don't talk like that," he said.

"I thought we were safe."

He pulled her into him. "You are safe."

"How can you know?" she asked.

"As long as I'm alive, I'll find a way to save you."

"It's usually me saving you, remember?" She joked and managed a small smile.

"We could save each other," he said and, forgetting where they were, leant in to kiss her.

She pushed away from him. "We can't do this here."

Sandy made her way through the city to the Low Streets. She had taken an autocar for a short distance and was now on foot. Her black-ops suit, when switched on, made her undetectable from surveillance cameras. The field uniform of Intelligence Command was not armour—it was more like a mechanical membrane. If you zoomed in on it, you would see that the suit was not fabric but small mechanised scales. Each link in the suit would mimic the colour of its immediate surroundings. Unless she was moving fast, the suit made her nearly invisible. Her form would appear blurred even in close proximity. The suits were not perfect, but they were good enough to have made so many other elements of tradecraft obsolete.

Her visor picked up the infrared signature of pedestrians, whom she needed to avoid, but the streets were dark and quiet. She crept up to her destination and peered through a small window. Inside the townhouse, she saw three grubby-looking post-adolescents—two men and a woman in their early twenties—sitting in a circle and passing a joint. Pulled down around their necks were the same masks the terrorists from the video had been wearing. Sandy observed them for a moment, listening to their conversation.

"They can't trace the footage. I encrypted it on a level they're not even functioning at," said the first hoaxer, an oddball, weasel-faced nerd with scarlet hair and a goatee.

"Is it tight?" queried the second hoaxer, a chubby brown-haired wannabe wearing a vintage tie-dyed shirt.

"It's about five years ahead of IC. Their tech is weak in some places and not in others. I can't quite hack it yet. The security surrounding their operating system is pretty good, but it's ahead of their mainframe."

"What are you going to do when you get in?" asked their female friend, a slim woman with facial piercings. One side of her head was shaved clean.

"I'm just going to play with their heads a little," said the first hoaxer. "Everything they say is so—'we must have order'—bullshit. They want order. I'm going to give them disorder."

"Everything they say is 'ganda," said the woman.

The first hoaxer spoke again. "You can't trust any of their statements. The tech fault or whatever it was just proves that this world isn't as perfect as they say it is."

"Frowning upon our immorality and chaotic lifestyles—say it ain't so?" mocked the second hoaxer, cackling.

"Yeah, we're filth," replied the first.

"You are filth," announced a distorted voice from above them.

The three hoaxers looked up in terror at all they could see of Sandy. It took her mere seconds to immobilise the stoned trio. Minutes later, they were tied back-to-back, bruised and whimpering. They sniffled through their bloody noises. Sandy grabbed the first hoaxer by the face.

"This is what's going to happen," Sandy said through the voice alternator built into her mask. "I'm going to call Police Command. Because this is a terrorism issue, they will take you to ICHQ. When you get there, you will confess, and you will grovel at the feet of Commander Muro and beg for her forgiveness. You will tell her this was a hoax. You will tell her team that you came up with the power outage, because even though little nobodies don't know how to switch off an entire city at the flick of a button, I'll let you take the credit. If you do not do what

I say, I will find you in whatever prison they send you to, and I will do unspeakable and remarkable things to you. Do you understand?"

The hoaxers nodded rapidly. Sandy felt relief that she had finally gained back control. Her sense of peace had been restored. Sandy tapped a few keys into a phone belonging to one of the hoaxers to summon the police but exited through one of the larger windows long before they arrived.

###

The next morning over breakfast, Sandy watched Commander Muro's latest press conference.

"Last night's so-called terrorists were nothing more than a sorry group of degenerates who are being held at separate penitentiaries," she began. "Anyone doubting my leadership should note that they were identified and taken into custody by Intelligence Command less than an hour after they released the hoax footage. Footage that they believed could not be traced. Behaviour that causes fear and alarm will not be tolerated. We found you this time, and we will always find you."

Sandy breathed a sigh of relief and turned off the TV. She sat, eating cereal in silence, until her white, encrypted phone rang.

"Good morning!" The deep, assured voice of Lyndon Hamilton resounded at the other end.

"Good morning, Lyndon. I'm sorry again for cancelling yesterday."

"That's quite all right. I saw the news. It must have been a busy time at Intelligence Command. Are you free to come over tonight?"

"I am," she said.

"Excellent. We'll be having a classic coq au vin."

"Sounds delightful. And thank you," Sandy smiled, "It's been a very long time since I was last wined and dined."

###

A group of sullen cadets, including Massi and Natalia, listened intently as Colonel Mathers spoke freely with them in a classroom.

"If you felt fear yesterday, don't make the mistake of thinking you're weak. Fear is natural. You cannot control what you feel. What you can control is how you react to those feelings. Being overwhelmed is a choice. If you're ever sent to war, you'll experience fear like none you have ever experienced before. The solution is to use it. Make fear your ally. Turn it into energy, adrenalin. Harness it. It may save your life." He turned to a blonde female cadet. "Cadet Andrews. How did you feel when the lights went out?"

"I felt fear, sir."

"And how did you feel when you learnt it was just a fault at the grid?" Mathers coaxed gently.

"I felt relief, sir."

"Cadet Sanghera. How did you feel last night when you thought there had been a terrorist attack on our great nation?"

"I felt fear, sir," Natalia replied.

"Cadet Moretti. How did you feel this morning when the terrorist attack turned out to be a hoax?"

"I felt pride, sir."

"Pride? Didn't you feel anger?"

"I did initially. But we caught them. We wouldn't have known it was a hoax had it not been for IC. At first I felt anger. How dare they make people scared? But then I felt pride. We achieved justice. People aren't scared anymore. I'm proud that I'm on the side of justice. I felt proud to be a part of Intelligence Command."

"I'm glad to hear that. What we're doing here is not just training individual soldiers. To be a soldier means that you're part of a unit. That unit must be strong. Even a unit in which some of the parts may be weak—or weaker than the others—can be strong. Even a unit where all of the parts are weak can fit together and make something stronger, something greater than the sum of its parts. And a unit where all the individual parts are strong can still be weak if the parts don't fit together."

###

Claudette Muro sat in her office, writing a report. Her eyes showed the stress of the past forty-eight hours, even if her flawless countenance did not. High Commander Drummond entered her office.

"High Commander!" Muro jumped to her feet and saluted while still holding her pen.

"Claudette, how are you?" Drummond returned the salute. The gold embellishments glimmered on his red uniform.

"I'm well."

"Good…good," he said, nodding.

They sat down.

"I'm sorry you felt you had to come down here, Christopher," said an exasperated Muro very fast as she shuffled the papers on her desk into neater piles, "but the threat was entirely false. They've already admitted to causing the power outage. The perpetrators of the hoax are at correctional facilities already. They said they wanted to pretend that it was a terrorist attack. Some people think that's funny. They will be receiving stringent re-education—"

"I'm going to stop you there." He held up his hand firmly.

"Sir?"

"I'm not here to reprimand you, Claudette." Drummond's voice was fatherly and comforting. "In fact, I think you handled yourself perfectly, considering the circumstances."

"When I saw the footage, my heart sank. There was no intelligence. Nothing. But there was no intelligence because there was no threat."

"There was no threat. That's all that matters," said Drummond.

"You're right—you're right," said Muro nodding.

"The threat was non-existent, and the hoax was neutralised. Although it may not have felt that way, this was a best-case scenario."

"I can't help feeling that maybe there's something more," Muro said, lowering her voice to almost a whisper. "That perhaps I'm losing my touch."

"No," he said, shaking his head with authority.

"No?"

"No. Claudette, this is what this job looks like in peacetime. Faults and hoaxes but no real threats."

"You always say the right thing," she said, not quite believing his words.

"I came here to congratulate you on a job well done. Especially with regard to the media."

"Thank you," she said and smiled sweetly.

"It's my pleasure," he said, smiling back.

"And when I next see Commander Nichols at Police Command, I will thank him for tracking the hoaxers. I don't know how his techies did it. My team was hours away from decrypting the source of the footage when we got the call. I didn't think their software was anywhere near as powerful as ours—"

"It's not," he said. "They got lucky. It happens sometimes."

The two commanders saluted each other, then Drummond left the room.

He waited until his car was moving away from ICHQ before making the call.

"Lucy, hello. Can you look into something for me? Commander Muro is under the impression that one of Commander Nichols's teams traced and apprehended the hoaxers. Nichols seems to be under the impression that the hoaxers were traced by IC, who then alerted the police. Can you double-check this for me?"

###

From the outside, Lyndon Hamilton's townhouse looked large, though otherwise unassuming. Compared to the other opulent townhouses on the same street, it was very plain. On the inside, it was a high-ceilinged, geometric palace decorated without frills in metallic greys and striking whites. There were few curved lines and no odd numbers in the decoration. If there were ornaments or vases, they were in pairs, never in threes. Two or four hanging lights. Never three or five. This had the effect of being slightly harsh on the eye. It was as if the interior decorator had intended to make visitors feel just a little prickly. Sandy liked the décor in an abstract way; she was impressed by it but would never choose it for herself. While Hamilton's home was charismatically austere, it lacked many of the domestic comforts Sandy craved.

Sandy and Hamilton ate dinner at an unnecessarily long dining table. Sandy had to raise her speaking voice to be heard clearly. On the table were four splendid silver candlesticks for decoration, and that was all. Hamilton's wine, the best red Sandy had ever tasted, was topped up by Farlow, who then disappeared back into the butler's kitchen.

"This wine is excellent, by the way," said Sandy.

"Thank you, Sandy. Would you believe it's non-alcoholic?"

"I would not have guessed. It tastes great."

"The coq au vin is cooked in it too. I don't consume alcohol myself. This delightful beverage was sourced by my chef."

"My compliments," said Sandy.

"I enjoyed your little stunt." He swirled the wine around the glass pensively.

"I enjoyed it too. I cut it a little close, though." She remembered the fear in Muro's eyes when she had been called to ICHQ. Sandy had not anticipated the scale of the panic she had caused.

"I can imagine."

Her tone became more sombre. "I didn't realise how fresh the fear still is."

"The fear isn't so fresh. The thought is always worse than the event itself," he assured her.

"I remember once when I was a teenager, it was the beginning of summer, and we were driving away from the Academy to go back to my aunt's. As we passed through the gates, we saw a bunch of conspiracy theorists protesting. They were holding up signs that said, 'Intelligence Command is behind the Soft Terror'. I remember thinking—even if that were true—I would rather believe a lie for a hundred years than know for certain just for a second that I lived in that kind of world."

He took a moment to consider her words. His mouth twitched, piqued by the perverse type of lawlessness she had just described.

He then said, "Are you happy with the terms of our agreement?"

CHAPTER SIX

Sandy sobbed into her arms. Enveloped by self-loathing and guilt, she was curled up in a near-foetal position in the back of Muro's limousine.

Muro looked at her in disgust.

"Don't make me," Sandy cried. "Please don't make me go in there."

"Get hold of yourself. You're acting like a child."

"I can't. I can't."

"Get yourself together. I have to deal with this. You have to deal with this."

"I don't want to. I don't want to. I don't want to."

"Pathetic," Muro said with undisguised disdain.

The limousine pulled up outside a residential care home on the edge of the suburbs.

"Get out," Muro barked at Sandy.

"I can't. I'm a coward. Leave me. Leave me. I'm a coward. I don't want to go."

"My patience for tolerating your childishness and melodrama is wearing exceptionally thin," said Muro in a voice that was close to a yell.

Muro got out of the limousine and walked around to Sandy's side. She opened the door, grabbed a fistful of Sandy's hair and yanked her clean out of the car. Muro then pushed Sandy into the building and dragged her to the elevator. By the time they reached their floor, Sandy had composed herself fully. Not a single hair was out of place. There was not a hint of the wreck she had been just moments earlier. The two women steeled themselves and walked into the ward.

Propped up in chairs and sitting upright in beds were some of the last remains of Sandy's comrades and former Academy classmates. The wounded soldiers in this particular ward were mostly the victims of a particularly nasty gas attack that had damaged their nervous systems. Most of them still had all their limbs but had lost the ability to use some or all of them. Medical science had most of the answers but not all, and the recovery process was long and expensive.

As Sandy walked past the wounded veterans, a hand reached out and gently gripped hers. Startled, she looked into the patient's soft eyes. Her hair was greying, and one of her arms was withered. Sandy did not recognise her. She had to look at the name on the wall above her chair.

"Britney?" she asked, uncertain.

The woman nodded.

Sandy's face relaxed. "It's good to see you again, old friend."

Sandy stayed with her for a while, not letting go of Britney's hand. She let her mind drift to better times, to when she was a young cadet, thriving—if not always happy—at the Academy and surrounded by friends. She could not truly say that she was glad she had come, but neither could she ease her guilt at not coming more often.

Afterwards, she approached Commander Muro, who was wiping dribble off the chin of a male patient, saying, "That will have to do for now, darling. Sorry it's been so long. Mummy has been awfully busy."

The name above the bed read, 'Martin Muro'. Claudette's son had been at the Academy at the same time as Sandy. His body did not move anymore, but his eyes stared at Sandy, hard and resentful. Claudette planted a long, gentle kiss on his forehead before leaving.

Muro and Sandy walked out into the care home's courtyard garden. High Commander Drummond was sipping tea and chatting to the veterans' families.

"Claudette!" Drummond saluted, then kissed Muro on both cheeks. "Lieutenant," Drummond said and looked Sandy straight in the eye, "I believe you know many of the families here already. It would be good if you could circulate."

"Yes, sir," said Sandy, taking the hint.

Ah, a garden party. An introvert's dilemma made all the more excruciating by the judgmental glares of the other veterans' families. Some resented Sandy for not being broken and damaged like their own children were. Some pitied her for being left alone. Some wished her dead. If none of them came to talk to her, she would not go out of her way to talk to them. She tucked herself under the shade of the catering tent and stuffed her mouth full of teacakes and coffee. Nodding politely at the Lyles and the Thompsons, Sandy felt a spasm of jealousy slither up her neck. Why did they hate her so much, when, at the same time, they adored Drummond and Muro? Drummond had an easy charm despite being a serious man, but he had also sent their children to die in far-flung places. Muro's polished femininity masked an obstinate lack of humanity. Sandy had fought alongside these people's children. Only she knew their true stories. Perhaps the families found comfort in authority. Like a form of Stockholm syndrome.

Drummond stood in the centre of the courtyard and thanked the guests for coming. Sandy's life had become an endless parade of ceremonies, fundraisers and security theatre. She had pledged a small part of her personal fortune to the Veterans of the Long War Memorial Project over the years, an act that was being acknowledged by Drummond at that very moment. It did not make her feel any better. After being thanked for her donation and receiving polite applause, Sandy tried to return to her hiding place by the scones but was stopped by an elderly woman with red hair. She was Lauren Byrne, Britney's mother.

"Sandy. Good to see you."

"Good to see you, Mrs Byrne."

"How are things with you?" Mrs Byrne queried in a warm and motherly tone.

"Er, I'm getting by." Sandy was surprised by the heartfelt question. Mrs Byrne genuinely seemed to care, and it was as though an ordinary answer would not suffice.

"You always do. You always make it through. I like that about you. I've always liked you."

"Some days, like today, are harder than others," Sandy began and wondered for a moment if she should be open with Mrs Byrne. She felt an overwhelming desire to unburden her soul. Perhaps she should tell Britney's mother about all the things that made her feel sad and the things she thought about at night when she could not sleep. If not here then maybe she should go for coffee with Mrs Byrne and just talk. To just have someone to talk to.

"I know. I know." Mrs Byrne replied and paused. "Have you moved on, Sandy?"

"Umm, to be honest..."

"Be open to finding someone. It'll happen sooner than you think."

"I'm sure I will know him when I see him," said Sandy.

"There's a nice boy out there for you. You'll find having a family very healing. I'm sure of it." She gave Sandy's arm a comforting touch and walked away.

Sandy closed up again. Mrs. Byrne's words were so kind, so warm, so well-intentioned—and so unwelcome. Although they were not nearly as unwelcome as her exchange with Robert Patel, the next person to approach her.

"Hello, Sandy," he said.

"Mr Patel?"

"That's right," he said, nodding.

"How's...er..." Sandy looked blank.

"Jay. Our son is Jay," Mr Patel said, prompting her.

"Ah, yes. How's Jay?" said Sandy, looking sheepish.

"He's better. He was friends with Luca, you know."

"I remember. He's not the same age as me, so I can't recall exactly..."

"There was barely a difference between him and Luca at the Academy."

"Yes, I remember now. He was a good soldier."

"Absolutely. The difference now is that if Jay had access to Luca's level of treatment, he'd be back to full health. This time you gave only three million dollars to the other veterans. That's a drop in the ocean."

"Hey, I could have given nothing. If my donation was unwelcome, I'll take it back," said Sandy, visibly irked by Mr Patel's suggestion.

"You think you've been generous, but I know how much you earned from that gym gear commercial. You're giving chump change, and it's time you pulled your weight."

"Okay, well, here's another difference between your son and Luca. I don't care about your son, and I have no reason to. We weren't friends. We weren't even in the same grade at the academy. Good-bye, Mr Patel."

Sandy excused herself from the conversation. The garden party soon came to an end. Drummond's car arrived first.

"I hear you're going to your cousin's wedding, Sandy. Have fun in the South," he offered.

"Thank you, sir." Sandy faked a smile.

"Claudette, I'll see you this afternoon," he said, getting into his car.

"Yes, sir," Commander Muro replied.

The two ladies got into Muro's car just as they had when they arrived, but Sandy thought Muro seemed different. Her face was sunken and more lined. She was looking the age she actually was, for once. The car pulled away.

"So, that wasn't so bad, was it?" Muro said.

"No, ma'am," Sandy lied.

"The thought is always worse than the actuality, don't you agree?" Muro asked, rhetorically.

"Yes, ma'am."

"Drummond always plays these types of events just right. He really is one of the greats."

"Do I detect some chemistry there, Commander? Drummond always looks rather dashing in his upholstery and horse brasses."

Muro stared straight ahead as she spoke in slow, splintered sentences. "So much wasted talent and human potential in that ward. My son. Squandered." She muttered the last word under her breath. "A room full of broken soldiers, and the only one who came back was you. I never would have put money on you. I've always wondered how it is that you're here and they're not. Yet you always surprise me."

Over the day, it appeared that Muro had absorbed the resentment the other families felt towards Sandy. Sandy just swallowed and said, "I guess I'm just surprising."

Muro smiled. "It's not that life isn't fair—it's that death isn't fair either."

Sandy was dropped off at home by Commander Muro; neither of them had spoken another word for the rest of the journey. Sandy changed into jeans and a plaid shirt. She had hired a flight pod, a small plane with room for just her, for most of the trip. She parked it at the closest airport to her aunt's house, but it would still take a while to get to her childhood home.

Her cousin William picked her up from the airport. It seemed ages since she had been in a car (or, in this case, a truck) that someone actually had to drive. Rural areas lacked the tracks and sensors that the autocars in the cities ran on. The air was sweet and crisp. Light shone through the trees and made dappled patterns on the dashboard.

"You'll just love Caroline's dress, Sandy. She looks so beautiful in it. I almost cried when I saw her try it on," he said.

"I can't wait. She seemed very happy the last time I spoke to her. Obviously, I haven't seen her since she got engaged."

"You should come visit more," said William.

"I would, but they keep me busy at work."

"Make time for family, Sandy. No one goes to their deathbed wishing they'd spent more time in the office."

"So they tell me, Billy. So they tell me."

Ten minutes in, and the folksy advice had already started.

###

"Commander, we have a major problem." Drummond stared intensely at Muro, whom he had summoned to his offices. "Police Commander Nichols here is under the impression that you sent a black-ops agent to thwart the perpetrators of the recent terrorist hoax, while you are under the impression that it was Commander Nichols who traced and apprehended the hoaxers."

Muro and Drummond stood alone with Commander Everet Nichols and looked down at an operations map of the city. Nichols was a slight, sharp-faced man with spectacles and thinning brown hair. Whereas Muro's job was identifying and neutralising international threats, Nichols was the man in charge of maintaining the domestic rule of law.

"When we interviewed the hoaxers, they said they were incapacitated by 'a moving blur they couldn't really see'—that's a black-ops suit," Nichols said.

"That can't be possible," Muro snapped defensively. "I didn't send anyone. We didn't even know where the hoaxers were located when they were picked up by police."

"A distress call was made to the police from the hoaxers' location. They were tied up before we got there. The hoaxers are just a bunch of kids. But there were three of them." Nichols added, "To apprehend all of them so easily and at once would require skill."

"It could not have been one of mine," Muro declared gravely. "We weren't even close to tracing them. I had my tech team interview them. The leader is some sort of encryption prodigy."

Drummond spoke slowly. "Yes, I'm giving him amnesty on the condition he spends the next ten years of his life helping us instead of hindering us."

"So the person who apprehended these kids not only had the military training to physically restrain them but the tech know-how to trace them," Nichols continued. "And a black-ops suit."

"Are all your black suits accounted for, Claudette?" Drummond asked.

"Of course, they are," said Muro, looking offended.

"There's one that you haven't accounted for," Nichols asserted.

"Sandy's? I haven't accounted for it, because it's several years out of date, and it was heavily damaged. It's practically pyjamas."

"Why on earth did you let her keep it?" asked Nichols.

"It was the one she was injured in, and since it's obsolete, I didn't think it mattered. Sandy is technically still active military personnel and entitled to one. I let her keep the old one as a compromise."

"Is its masking mechanism still intact?" Drummond asked.

"I have no idea what the functionality of that suit is now," Muro responded.

"She could have repaired it," Nichols offered.

"She doesn't have that type of skill set," Muro countered. "And a black-ops suit is not something you can just take somewhere and get fixed."

"She managed to trace the hoaxers before you did," said Nichols.

"We don't know that it was her. She doesn't have that type of skill set, either." As soon as the words left Muro's mouth, she became unsure of them. "At the Academy, she took the field-agent track. She never did any tech. Although…the Academy's teaching didn't help my team trace the hoaxers either," Muro added.

"It is not implausible that she attained these skills elsewhere," Drummond suggested. "The truth is we don't know what she knows."

"We checked the surveillance cameras. There's no sign of anyone entering or leaving that house. They were either apprehended by an individual wearing a military grade suit with full masking capability, or it was magic," Nichols sneered.

"There's something else," Drummond added. "The newly elected president of the Central Arabian Republic is keen on having a deeper inquiry into what happened at Hazirat."

"How keen?" Muro asked, a slight panic rising inside her at this news.

"It was one of his manifesto pledges. I have been asked by the Ruling Council to make preparations in the event that he pushes another inquiry," said Drummond.

"That will bring Sandy back into the spotlight. And not in the endorsing-soda kind of way," Nichols said.

"She's not resilient enough." Muro stared at the two men. "She wouldn't last under that type of scrutiny."

"We don't know that," countered Drummond. "There are now questions about her psychological fitness, her physical fitness and her technical knowledge."

"Right now, it looks as though she's not doing too badly on any of those fronts," said Nichols. "If she tied those kids up, she's fitter than we thought she was. If she was the one who traced them, then she possesses a tech skill set we never even thought she had. And as for her psych levels, frankly, she's always seemed crazy to me."

"That's not quite fair," Muro protested.

"Just admit it, Claudette, you have no idea what her capabilities are," said Nichols.

Muro's grimace revealed her discomfort. She did not like the idea of Sandy being an unknown.

"We need to devise a test," said Drummond. "Something that will show us what she knows and what she can still do, but she can't know she's being tested, especially if there's the possibility she's a rogue agent. Claudette—think of something."

###

Caroline's wedding was a modest, beautiful and charming summery affair. The venue was a white wooden church. The dress was pretty, and the groom was handsome. Caroline's bouquet was made of orange lilies, yellow sunflowers and white roses. Sandy sat behind Caroline's mother, her aunt Cora, and had to lean slightly to one side to see the couple exchange their vows from behind Cora's enormous, lilac mother-of-the-bride hat. The reception was held in Cora's home, the house in which Sandy had grown up. Everyone there was on a first-name basis with everyone else, and there was a large cake with the white buttercream frosting Sandy loved. Guests came up to Sandy and thanked her for her service, and she accepted their remarks gracefully.

As the sun set, the wedding party waved the couple away on their honeymoon. They sped off in a cloud of dust whipped up by the groom's decorated Corvette. Sandy went back inside, helped herself to another slice of cake and went to spend some time alone in her favourite room of the house. The kitchen was warm and always smelt of apples. She scraped every last bit of icing off the plate with her fork and let the sugar melt on her tongue.

Cora entered the room and sat down at the table. "Finally, a seat." She removed her hatpin, placed the large lilac hat on the table and kicked off her shoes. "You're looking well, Sandy."

"Thank you. I had a really good time today. The ceremony was beautiful. Good vows, too."

"Yes, I told Caroline the most important thing was the vows. That is the promise, the contract you make with the other person, after all."

"She seems very happy with him. They suit each other well."

"Yes, he's ideal for her," Cora said with satisfaction.

Sandy smiled politely, still holding the plate and fork.

"Your sister wasn't able to attend. I am disappointed in that," Cora continued.

"Ah, yes, well, you know she's doing her own thing."

"You two don't talk these days, then?" asked Cora.

"No," said Sandy, "Does she talk to you?"

"No, she does not. I did try to get in touch to let her know she was invited and welcome to return home. I'm not sure she got the message. I'm not even sure where she is."

"Pretty sure she's still in Tibet or Nepal or wherever," said Sandy, shrugging and ignoring the hurt evident in Cora's voice.

"Maybe she just has no signal," said Cora, refusing to believe any other scenario.

"She does check her email occasionally—every month or so. She just doesn't want to be in a place where she can be contacted at any time of the day." Sandy was also hurt but more accepting than her aunt. "That's the point. I'm sure she's happier wherever she is than she was here."

"Yes, I suppose you're right. Those types are always happier with a certain lifestyle. How's Luca, by the way?" Sandy's aunt spoke the two sentences so quickly that Sandy did not have a chance to evade the new topic of conversation.

"He's the same," Sandy answered reluctantly.

"No improvement?"

Sandy looked at her feet and shook her head.

"It's always good to see you, Sandy, and you know I love you. I absolutely love you. But what you're doing to that boy is wrong," Cora said solemnly.

"Stop!" Sandy knew an ambush when she saw one.

"You're keeping him alive for you. Not for him. There's no life of any quality for him. It's so <u>inconsiderate</u>."

"I lose everyone I love," said Sandy, distraught.

"There are always more people to love," Cora offered, pleading.

"I don't want love from anyone else," Sandy whimpered.

"Keeping someone hooked up to a bunch of wires like a potato clock sure as hell isn't love."

"What am I supposed to do?" asked Sandy.

"Let him go. It will make room in your life for someone else. When relationships that aren't working—or are dead—are removed from your life, new ones enter. Let him go. It's immoral."

"I can't. It's not fair. I owe him," said Sandy, looking downwards and shaking her head.

"You can, and you will," Cora urged.

"I don't think I can."

"Of course, you can." Cora paused. "I've had your bed made up. Pancakes tomorrow morning."

Sandy was overwhelmed and turned away from her aunt. She then threw the plate into the sink, almost cracking it, and stormed out of the room. Cora shook her head, then gathered herself up and returned to her guests.

CHAPTER SEVEN

There were only a handful of venues at which Muro could stage a full-capability test without getting anyone killed. Guns, even though legal, were not widely owned due to the absence of crime and violence in the city. There were, however, zones and buildings where traditional firearms were prohibited. One such zone was a vertical farm complex about a twenty-minute drive from ICHQ. Using a gun on anyone here would be suicide. The complex was a heaving maze of pipes carrying carbon dioxide in and oxygen out—not to mention huge stockpiles of nitrogen, phosphorous and potassium. One building in the complex was a multi-storey aquaponics system that looked fragile to Muro. After a brief, congenial meeting with the complex's owner—and the transfer of a large sum of money—the stage was easily set.

It was one thing to test Sandy's physical abilities, but assessing her mental aptitude and emotional resilience was another. It was there that Muro became stuck. The Academy typically monitored cadets during tests by attaching small monitors to the temples and chest. These monitors scanned the brain and recorded how quickly the cadet's heart rate recovered from various shocks throughout the test. They also took saliva samples during various stages of the assessment to monitor adrenalin and cortisol levels.

It was late in the day, and she was feeling despondent. She had given instructions to her team to come up with something—anything—to test Sandy's aptitude and emotional resilience, and every one of them had drawn a blank.

Muro was sitting in her office in a contemplative silence. It had been a long time since she had last felt insecure in her job. She thought about how she had managed Sandy since the armistice. She was fond of Sandy in her own way, but she was also frustrated by her. She knew Sandy resented her. Muro had tried to communicate to her that the rules in peacetime were different from the rules in war. It was also hard to give Sandy a desk job when she was too busy swanning around doing commercials. But Muro did not lack empathy; she, too, felt the living loss of Lucian Scott and, of course, her own son, acutely. The world had moved on, yet Sandy had not. Muro felt that there was nothing she could do about that. The possibility of Sandy being a rogue agent, however, was something Muro had not considered. Sandy had been steadfast and faithful to IC during the war. Muro had even noticed how much she admired High Commander Drummond, even though she did not seem to like him. Sandy's respect and loyalty had never been in doubt—until now.

A sharp knock at the door disrupted her thoughts.

"Gerald," she said, "unless you have something constructive to say to me, remove yourself from my office, never to return."

"I think you'll like my idea, ma'am," he offered.

"I had better."

"No two individuals are exactly alike, but I've been playing around with the Academy's psych tests to see if there is anyone like Sandy. Obviously, that answer is no. However, there is one cadet at the Academy who is emotionally very similar to Sandy and another who is intellectually very similar. My idea is this: we bring them in, hook them up to the relevant monitors and have them experience what she's experiencing."

"Go on," said Muro.

"If we create a situation that makes them believe they're undergoing the same stresses and challenges as Sandy, then they can explain what they are thinking and feeling so that we can piece together what Sandy is thinking and feeling while she's in the simulation. We can do this by modifying Sandy's balaclava so that it includes a discreet camera at the neck and a monitor across her mouth to test the saliva in her breath."

"Gerald, some days I wonder why I pay you. Today is not one of those days. Well done."

"Great! Can I have a raise?"

"No," said Muro.

###

Sandy had been itching to return to work on Hamilton's model. Instead of going straight home from her aunt's, she parked her flight pod on the landing pad of the Hamilton InfoSec building. The model was already looking healthier. Sandy had programmed her own algorithms to identify the gaps in the model and harvest what was needed to plug them. The model was building itself up, but in some places Sandy had to intervene. Whoever had been working on the project before her had left bugs in the software that needed fixing.

Sandy would not need much to complete the project. She would build up the map from clues. For example, a pharmaceutical company that makes a certain medicine must have the formula for that medicine. In order to get medical formulae, that company must employ, or have relationships with, medical research scientists and the research institutes they work for—not to mention chemical suppliers, the pharmacies that sell their drugs and the public relations networks that advertise them. There are relationships that simply must be present in order for the pharmaceutical company to have the output that it does. By looking at a company's output, Sandy would create an algorithm that would work backwards to map the relationships between the data that each company used and the people who had created it. Sandy was becoming confident that she could create a living map to anyone.

The only obstacle Sandy could predict was the matter of information deliberately kept off the Web. One of Hamilton InfoSec's main competitors was a firm called Ingham & Williams Information Security Experts, more commonly known as I-WISE. They kept large swathes of data in huge warehouses full of filing cabinets. If it was not on the Web, it could not be hacked. For this reason, I-WISE was a favourite among companies that needed to store things like secret recipes and patents. These warehouses were like fortresses. Sandy had identified one significant weak spot, however: the CEO of I-WISE's party-girl personal assistant.

###

Massi and Natalia did not know what to make of being pulled out of their classes for the day. It was hard enough to miss class when they were genuinely ill. They were not told where they were being taken, but they were assured they were not in any trouble. When it became obvious that the car was taking them to ICHQ, they both began to feel as though they were about to be a part of something bigger than themselves. Natalia's quick mind made an imaginary list of all the possibilities. Perhaps they had been in the vicinity of a crime and would be asked if they had seen anything. Perhaps someone close to them at the Academy was suspected of being a counteragent. Perhaps they were being awarded for outstanding performance. She dismissed that notion as soon as she dreamt it, as that hypothetical situation could only apply to herself. She was fond of Massi, but he was not an excellent student. Before the spate of bullying he was enduring began, he was, on a good day, an above-average student. Nothing more. His physical prowess compensated for his intellectual performance most of the time. Now, however, his academic performance had understandably taken a dive, as the bullying had gone from teasing to something much more sinister. Natalia secretly hoped he would pull himself together and deprive the bullies of the satisfaction of seeing him fail. *Perhaps I should tell him this*, she thought…but then left her thoughts unsaid.

The car pulled up to the entry of ICHQ. Massi and Natalia were led through warrens of corridors. Muro's office was a full fifteen-minute walk from the front door. Massi was sure this was by design rather than coincidence.

Finally at her office, the two cadets stood before Muro while she looked them over, not uttering a single word. Muro reminded Massi of Natalia, her sharp mind working quickly behind her dark eyes, constantly processing information at a furious rate.

"My apologies for disrupting your studies, cadets. Obviously, I would never do this were it not of the upmost importance." Muro spoke fast and formally. "Our intelligence has revealed that a terrorist attack will take place tomorrow at the Obsidyne Farm Complex. The attack is being carried out by a group of Luddites who seem to think we should all go back to growing food in the ground, as if it were still the dark ages. They're just a bunch of losers. They will be easily vanquished. Instead of preventing the attack outright, we thought we would use this opportunity to assess the effectiveness of one of our operatives. Do you understand?"

"Yes, ma'am," they said together.

"Excellent. You should never let a good crisis go to waste. Remember that. No real guns can be used at the farms, or they'll blow the entire complex sky-high, so this will be a test of more than just firepower. Our intelligence suggests that the ecoterrorists will be using a type of stun gun similar to the ones you use when playing paratag."

The cadets stood in silence.

"Ah," Muro continued, "I imagine you're both keen to hear how you're involved. I think you'll enjoy this. As you know, the Academy tests every cadet psychologically, but we also test your emotional traits, as well. How you react to stress, for instance. But also what gives you pleasure, what art moves you, what games you enjoy, what temptations you find less resistible than others and things like that. Cadet Sanghera, intellectually you are very similar to the operative we are assessing. If anything, you are superior to this individual in many respects. But it's not about test scores—it's about the paths your minds take to reach their conclusions. Cadet Moretti, you are emotionally similar to our operative." Muro smiled to herself. "With the two of you, I have one whole replica, or rather, one as similar as I can find on such short notice. Tomorrow, you will have standard psych test monitors attached while our operative neutralises the terrorists. You will be able to have a first-person view of the action via a body cam attached to the operative so we can get a fuller picture of how this individual tackles challenges from their perspective. Any questions?"

The cadets stood in silence, overwhelmed by the information they had just heard. After a moment, Massi spoke.

"Do we get to know who the operative is, ma'am?"

Muro smiled but did not answer.

The cadets were led away. They were hustled into the empty ICHQ canteen, where they ate their evening meal in silence. The majority of the HQ staff had gone home by that time, but Massi and Natalia were informed that they would be staying in a suite within the ICHQ compound. After dinner, they were led back to the suite, which comprised a large room with a kitchen and living area and a bedroom with two single beds.

Natalia fell asleep in an instant. Massi lay awake with his hands behind his head. His body was aching and tired, but his mind was racing. He wanted to move and pace around the suite. He had to physically stop himself from fidgeting and making noise. He did turn and look at Natalia, though. As he stared at her, he tried to stay calm while she slept soundly in the bed next to him. It was so quiet that he thought he could hear her heartbeat. Her breath was soft, and her face, now perfectly relaxed, had become more beautiful than ever. He may never have another chance. *Perhaps*, he thought, *I should wake her and tell her how I feel about her.* Life had seemed unpredictable lately.

He did not wake her.

He let her sleep, and soon, he was asleep too.

Sandy walked into the club with an intense sense of entitlement found only in the young, rich and beautiful. Most days she forgot that she was all those things. She wore tight blue jeans, a black blouse and a black waist clincher. Her hair was straight, and her make-up light. Her long sleeves obscured her WristWatt; the military model would have looked out of place on a night out.

She located her vapid target easily. Sheila-Marie was dancing with a group of friends, and Sandy watched her discreetly from the club bar. She waited patiently.

"Hey, there!" She turned around, startled by the unexpected attention. He was tall and handsome. Sandy's type, in fact. But he was a hindrance.

"Hello," said Sandy, surprised.

"May I buy you a drink?"

"No, thank you," Sandy said with a smile. "I'm teetotal."

"Oh, well, may I buy you a soft drink?" he persisted.

"Okay, I'll let you buy me a drink, but would you be so kind as to do me a favour?"

He returned her smile. "For you? Sure thing."

"See that girl over there?" Sandy pointed to Sheila-Marie. "She's my friend. She's just come out of a nasty breakup, and she's out on the town to cheer herself up."

"I get ya," he nodded.

"Do you have any friends who would buy her a drink and just make her feel special? I think a bit of male attention is exactly what she needs," said Sandy flirtatiously.

"Oh yeah, I'm here with friends who would love to buy her a drink. She looks like a super nice girl."

Polite, charming and eager to please, Sandy thought. Heading back to his friends, the man pointed to the dancing girl. They did not need much persuading.

When the man's friend approached the bar, his new arm candy in tow, Sandy swished her drink around in her glass and looked in the opposite direction. After a minute or so, Sheila-Marie and her new catch began making out, and Sandy had the opportunity to slip a pill into her drink. Just as she made a move for the cocktail, her own new friend accosted her at the bar.

"So, can I get a kiss for all my hard work, too?" he asked, grinning.

"Sure," said Sandy, playing suggestively with his shirt. She kissed him passionately while simultaneously sliding a pill into his beer. When they came up for air and he took a swig, Sandy only had to make small talk for another five minutes before he excused himself and rushed to the restroom. Sandy had brought only a few of the pills, so before she lost her only chance, she quickly slipped a second into Sheila-Marie's cocktail while the young woman was occupied.

Minutes later, Sheila-Marie became violently ill and excused herself to the ladies' bathroom. Sandy waited for a woman who was washing her hands to leave, then looked under the door of Sheila-Marie's cubicle. She snatched her target's clutch, removed the phone and inserted a small disk into it. With a few taps on her WristWatt, all of Sheila-Marie's personal and professional information was copied straight to Sandy's hard drive at home. Sandy removed the disk, put the phone back into the clutch and slid the bag back under the cubicle door next to its convulsing owner.

Sandy strutted back onto the dance floor feeling pleased with herself. The nightclub was a three-storey building, with each floor playing a different type of music. Enjoying herself and her surroundings, Sandy worked her way back towards the exit. She danced a little as she moved through the heaving mass of people.

Without warning, all around her the clubbers became consumed by seven-foot flames. The fire lapped at the walls, and the music became drowned out by screams of bloodcurdling terror.

Sandy scrambled to a wall. She turned around and saw that the dance floor was still a pool of fire. She tried to catch her breath, but the air was thick. After a few minutes of heavy breathing, she located her faux lipstick in one of her back pockets and consumed a tab to put her straight. The club patrons transformed back into their smiling, revelling selves, and the music became muted and more pleasant. Sandy walked around the club in a blissful state but uncertain if she was walking in the direction of the exit. The powerful drug careening through her veins had cancelled out her panic. She continued walking, yielding to the force of all the moving human bodies around her, until she felt the strong hand of a large bouncer grabbing her by her collar, pulling her so hard her shirt almost ripped. He had spotted her heavily dilated pupils from the other side of the room, and, after lifting her effortlessly out of the crowd, he tossed her out of the club and onto the sidewalk. She landed limply and flopped like a fish on dry land for a few seconds. Her limbs were so relaxed she did not feel a thing. She moaned, lifted herself off the ground and stumbled into a nearby autocab. She swiped her wrist device at the cab's console and muttered the word "home" before collapsing on the back seat.

CHAPTER EIGHT

Sandy woke with a jolt. A splitting pain flared through her head, and she thought for a moment that she could hear gunshots. But they were not gunshots; they were several loud, aggressive knocks at her front door. Pulling herself out of bed, Sandy grabbed her robe and, desperate to make the noise stop, limped to the front door. Every knock pierced her skull and made her whole body ache. She wrenched open her front door, almost pulling the door handle off with it. Hackett and Manning stood on the other side.

"You again?! What do you want now?" asked Sandy.

"You wanted a job, right?" Hackett barked.

"Get lost," she hissed.

The two men asserted themselves into her front hallway.

"Muro wants you and your black-op suit out there now," said Hackett.

"Is this a joke?" asked Sandy, now with genuine alarm.

"It's an order, soldier," Manning affirmed.

The two men loomed over her. After she scrambled to her room and pulled on her suit, Hackett and Manning frog-marched her down to a waiting car.

"This better be serious," she said as she climbed into the car. "Today is not a day I can stomach another awkward conversation with Muro."

"Now that's a shame, Sandy. I do so enjoy our chats." It was Muro, waiting for her.

"Oh. Er... Sorry, ma'am."

Hackett and Manning slid into the car, sitting on either side of Sandy as if she were their prisoner.

"No offence taken," said Muro. "We have an incident. A group of ecoterrorists calling themselves 'Return to Earth' have occupied the Obsidyne Vertical Farm Complex. Are you familiar with it?"

"The buildings on 54th?" asked Sandy.

"That'll be the place. The Return to Earth group wants the usual. Typical Luddite manifesto. Natural food, save the whales, turn your back on life-saving medicine—blah, blah, blah. The difference is that this group got through security by hiding plastic paraguns in farm worker overalls. The complex's security screening only tests visitors for metals and doesn't frisk their own workers every day."

"That seems like a rather wide gap in their security," mused Sandy.

"Quite. The complex is a twenty-four-hour facility," said Muro. "To screen at every staff shift change would make the operation considerably more expensive."

"You didn't have any intel on this group before now?"

"Before today, they were indistinguishable from any other group of unwashed hippies with a badly written manifesto on the Internet," replied Muro.

"Okay."

"These are not sophisticated terrorists, Sandy. I'm sure you'll make short work of them."

"You couldn't get Field Command to take care of this?" asked Sandy.

"Conventional weapons will blow the complex sky high. It has to be a black suit, and since you've been begging me for a job, I thought you'd be jumping at the chance."

"What weapon will I have?" Sandy rubbed her head. It still throbbed with pain.

"A modified paratag gun," she said, pulling the gun from its spot under her feet and handing it to Sandy. "This could kill a person with a weak heart, but it will immobilise a healthy adult for a few hours. It's more powerful than the ones Return to Earth have. You'll make short work of them, I'm sure," Muro repeated, and Sandy thought she detected a slight sneer in her voice.

Sandy held the gun in her hands and gulped. *Am I ready for this?* The thought flickered through her mind. *Why did it have to be today?*

"We need to quickly make some modifications to your balaclava," Muro said, and gestured at Hackett. Still looking at Muro, Sandy handed her hood to Hackett without question. Hackett then discreetly attached the camera to it at the neck, placed a small flexible square device in the balaclava opposite where her mouth would be and handed it back to her.

"It has a transmitter, and it'll monitor your breathing. It should be kept it in contact with your mouth at all times," said Muro.

Sandy pulled on her hood. "What if I need backup?" she asked through the alternator.

"You won't," said Muro. "But if you do, we're monitoring the situation from ICHQ. The complex has a comprehensive system of security cameras. We've already taken remote access control. We'll be watching you very closely."

###

Massi's heart was beating so hard he thought it would burst through his sternum at any minute. He was being hooked up to several different machines. One sensor was on his finger, presumably testing his pulse; another was in his mouth, measuring his adrenalin and cortisol levels. The chair he was sitting on was not uncomfortable, but his arm, with a cannula inserted into it, felt cramped and awkward. Periodically, a droplet of blood would travel from that arm, down the tube and into a machine. Though he overheard a technician mumbling instructions to a colleague, Massi could not discern what they were measuring. He looked over his right shoulder at Natalia; she looked calmer than he felt. He never could tell what she was thinking; she was always so serene. The technicians fussed over both of them for about twenty minutes, eventually hooking them both up to an earpiece and microphone. They had been told to watch the screens in front of them and to say the first thing that came into their minds. Massi thought it was odd that neither he nor Natalia had seen Commander Muro that day.

The screens flickered in front of them, although no clear picture came through. Massi looked again at Natalia. This time she was looking back at him. Her eyes, with their anxious glare, contrasted sharply with her cool demeanour. A short-lived screech snarled through their earpieces, jerking them both upright. Then the screens in front of them came alive. The IC technicians were observing other monitors behind them, but Massi and Nat could only see one perspective. That is when the two cadets found themselves staring at Commander Muro seated in a car. She looked stern. When the car stopped, whomever the body cam was attached to clambered out of it.

###

As the car sped off behind her, Sandy stared up at the tall buildings. The ultra-modern complex appeared to have been made of floating glass. A wave of insecurity washed over her. She did not have her tabs with her. She tapped at her WristWatt, turning her suit on, and walked straight through the building's gates and towards the abandoned security checkpoint. The alarms screeched as she passed through it, and she arrived at a deserted courtyard. Police and Field Command had cleared the streets within a five-block radius, and the air was still and silent. Sandy paused and crouched behind a decorative water feature. She took a moment to calm herself. Before she went into the building, her mind had to be exactly where she needed it to be. She readied her gun and took a deep breath.

Sandy walked through the front door and into the lobby, which was really more of a fancy, high-ceilinged echo chamber. It seemed too corporate to belong to a farm; it looked as if someone, somewhere, was overcompensating for something. *What a curious start to a mission*, she thought. She almost laughed to herself when she recalled the times she had begun missions by parachuting into jungles or decanting onto foreign beaches guarded by mines and armed guerrillas.

She reasoned that if the terrorists had not taken a shot at her in the courtyard, there was no one on the ground floor, which suggested there were not many of them—and that they were not expecting her. Or they had set a trap. A flicker of movement caught in the corner of her left eye sent her diving for cover behind a security desk. She scanned the reflective surfaces around her for hints as to where her assailants might be located, but she found nothing. When she peeked her head over the desk, a round of paragun shots were fired in her direction. These pulsating waves dispersed. She huddled beneath the desk until she was in the clear. She then moved quickly, firing off two shots, both of which nailed her panicked targets. She darted to their positions and tentatively made sure they were immobilised before continuing to the next level. As in all emergencies, the elevators had been shut down, so Sandy ascended the stairs. As she emerged from the stairwell onto the next floor, she found three startled assailants, who fired rapidly but inaccurately in her direction. She took them out one by one and made her way over to an evacuation sign. She looked at the map, committing the relevant markings to memory. She also looked at the terrorists, writhing on the ground in their stolen farm-worker overalls. They were so young. But at their age, she had already been sent to war.

Massi and Natalia watched the soldier take down the terrorists. Both of them were now hyperaware of the blood that was coursing through their veins. They thought about which physiological values ICHQ could be monitoring. Their adrenalin was certainly raised. Massi could not help but feel on a high. He was an adventure seeker, and this was the ultimate thrill—to experience what combat really felt like. They were meant to be reporting back verbally, but neither of them had said a word.

The anonymous soldier whose first-person view they were seeing stood for a long time in front of the evacuation map, prompting Natalia to speak. "He's memorising the map. He doesn't want to back himself into a corner."

"Anything else?" Claudette Muro had entered the room without either of them noticing.

Natalia continued, "He's going to go the long way up. Up through the farm. Not back into the stairwell, because he'd be too vulnerable. The place looks like it has some sort of main office from where the farm environment is controlled. There in the centre. That's where the terrorists are most likely to be. That's where he's going to go."

"Excellent. How are you feeling, Moretti?" Muro enquired.

"Thrilled." He exhaled the word with excitement.

The next room Sandy entered was humid and housed several thick plants. Various rubber pipes ran all around the ceilings and walls, delivering carbon dioxide to the vegetation and removing excess oxygen. There were no windows, just mirrors reflecting light around the room. When she heard a rustle in the leaves, she did not immediately consider the prospect of being attacked. Instead, the sound led her back to a jungle in her memory, but she stopped herself from going down that track. Surprisingly, she was able to stop herself from another flashback and the corresponding panic attack. Perhaps there was still something left of the drug in her body from last night. She could not see where her assailants were. She scanned the reflective surfaces, looking for hints.

Sudden movement.

There was more than one other person in this room with her. She felt as though she were being watched, which, as she knew, was a feeling that no spy liked. Sandy realised that the terrorists might not know exactly where she was. After all, if they knew, they would have fired at her. Glancing up at the mirrors on the ceiling, she saw a leaf ripple. Sandy took aim and fired at the mirror, knowing the waves from the paragun would ricochet like a wave of light as though she were a master snooker player easily performing a trick shot. A deep grunt told her she had nailed her opponent. It unsettled the other terrorists in the room—two of them—whose nervous movements betrayed their positions. Sandy took them out within a moment of each other.

Sandy proceeded to the next room. The opening mechanism of the door leading to the next storey had been ripped apart, and its security features meant that the door was now locked by default. She needed a specific part to open it. It had to be close by. It was a heavy piece of equipment that had an encryption key and latched onto the outside of the door.

This particular room was filled with two large aquaponics tanks. Both of them were about twenty metres deep and stretched to the storey below her. She looked them over, seeing exactly what she needed. The 'key' was on the bottom of the tank to her right. She had to swim to the bottom and fetch it—without drowning in the process. Looking up again, she climbed onto the large metal hatch of the tank.

She pulled a stretch of narrow pipe from the wall that was marked with the symbol 'O2' on the side and made two holes in the rubber with her thumbnails. She clambered into the tank, leaving her gun next to the hatch, and took a swig of oxygen before tucking the pipe into her suit. Sandy dove to the bottom of the tank and grabbed the metal lock. She was surprised by the weight of the object, but it was not immovable. She heaved it up a few feet before her lungs ached for more oxygen. She rested, gripping a plant at the side of the tank, and managed to get the pipe into her mouth for another hit of pure oxygen. Pushing the pipe back into her suit with one hand, she grabbed the key and hauled it to the surface of the tank. The hardest part of the whole endeavour was getting the key—and then herself—out of the hatch and onto the top of the tank.

Once out of the water, she lay on the cold, hard floor, conscious for the first time that she was not as young as she used to be. She lifted herself to her knees and examined the enormous key before latching it into place. Next to the door was an electricity box with plastic casing, which she ripped off. She thought she might be too wet to be playing with wires, but it was the quickest way through the door. She rewired the lock, almost shocking herself, but the door eventually opened.

The next room had a ceiling that was three stories high. The crops—raspberry bushes—were on moving platforms that reached to the crystal skylight above. They were circulating in clusters on a larger rotating mechanism as though they were taking a ride on a white, clinical Ferris wheel. The machinery hummed as the platforms rotated, moving the plants from the ground level all the way to the high ceiling, ensuring that they got the light and air they needed.

Sandy could walk to the other side of the room, through the door and up the stairs, but that would be taking the long, easy route up. There were bound to be more assailants in the stairwell and outside the control room entrance. Some considerable way up the wall on the other side of the room, however, was a ventilation shaft. Having memorised the map, she knew that the shaft would take her up above the main control room. She climbed onto one of the platforms and began her ascent. Her weight slowed the platform, and she had to judge her leap to the next level with great care.

So far so good, she thought—until a wave rocked a bush from its platform just above her.

CHAPTER NINE

Sandy just managed to miss the falling raspberry plant while staying on her platform. The plant's rigid pot was made from some type of fibreglass or hard plastic, and the noise it made when it crashed onto the floor dissipated in a lingering echo. She had not noticed that she was not alone. Every other time, she had known. Her body had ached all morning, but that was not the problem. The problem was that her mind had begun to tire.

She looked for her assailant. He was standing on another platform about thirty metres away. He shot again. She dodged the wave, fired back and missed. Sandy had failed to account for the movement of their respective platforms. She hopped to another platform and crouched to steady herself, taking her position behind the plant so that the terrorist could not see her. She waited for her assailant's platform to move into a position she could hit.

###

Massi felt his gut lurch every time he caught sight of the ground on the screen in front of him. The camera swayed with the soldier, who was now standing on a moving platform. The terrorist was concealed on a nearby platform that had moved out of view. His eyes flicked to Natalia before finding their way back to the screen. She looked calm, almost serene. It was as though he were watching a horror movie that left her unfazed. She was back to her steely ice-queen persona. When they had both been strapped to the chairs, he could have sworn she was just as tense as he was. Maybe she knew something he did not. Or maybe she was just made of different stuff.

Muro paced behind their chairs, making Massi more anxious. Her team of technicians seemed to want something from them. Massi did not know what to say.

"He has to time this just right," Natalia offered.

Sandy waited patiently. Her weight had changed the platform's speed, but the same was true of her opponent's platform. In her mind, she processed a thousand calculations at once, trying to determine the precise moment to fire her gun. She peeked from her hiding space momentarily, then aimed and fired. The blast was not good enough to hit her assailant, but it did rock him off his platform. He grasped another platform on his way down and clambered onto it, saving himself from a fall that would have been injurious, if not fatal. His gun had fallen to the ground. Sandy watched as it dropped to the floor with a CLANG before she scrambled to a higher platform. She had gained enough time to make her way unimpeded to the ventilation duct halfway up the wall.

The duct was huge, but the air inside it was so dry that when Sandy breathed in, her throat was instantly raspy. She rested to catch her breath for a moment, then flung the gun onto her back and crawled on her elbows, making as little noise as she could manage. It was not long before she was on top of the ventilation grate over the main control room of the entire farm—the humming heart of the complex, where all operations, such as temperature, humidity and oxygen levels, were monitored and regulated. Sandy peered down into the operations room. Years of combat had taught her that patience and sharp observation skills were worth more than even the most powerful of weapons.

The remaining ecoterrorists had not come to find her. As she watched them, she noted that they were not relaxed but passive. They kept looking at the door, assuming she would attempt to breach their position by that means. Sandy thought back to the map. She could have taken a path through the farms that would have led her to that door, but she had decided to go through the vent instead. She thought back to her time in the Academy and recalled how much she hated being told that 'there were no wrong answers'. There may have been no wrong answers, but there were always some answers that were better than others, and in war, some decisions got you killed and others did not. That, at least, was an objective measure. Being judged on one's subjective preference made things personal.

There were five terrorists in the operations room. Four bored-looking individuals were positioned in and around the control desk, which looked like a giant bejewelled ring in the centre of the room sparkling with coloured buttons, dials and screens. The fifth terrorist was milling in front of the door, looking through its panelled windows for any signs of movement. Sandy aimed the nozzle of her gun at this individual first and fired. With a guttural grunt, he fell to the floor. The other four terrorists panicked and ducked for cover while facing the door, their backs exposed to Sandy. She let loose two more rounds within quick succession of each other, taking out two more of the terrorists.

The remaining two realised that the shots were not coming from the door and moved out of sight, disappearing behind the far side of the circular control panel. She punched downwards, throwing open the ventilation grate, and dropped feet first into the control room. She landed in a crouched position, her gun at the ready. She could hear her two opponents shuffle away from their initial positions, but the noises came from opposite sides of the room and confused her senses. She decided to hold tight and let the others do her work for her. They would reveal themselves eventually. She waited for what seemed like too long until one of the terrorists made a small movement. She saw a sputter of action from the corner of her eye and ducked. A terrorist had fired and missed. She darted to his position and punched him straight in the face, knocking the gun from his hands. She shot him at point-blank range, stunning him, then dropped onto the floor next to where he had been left unconscious. She moved around the space, her position now hidden by the circular control panel. The last remaining terrorist was doing the same, but Sandy was quicker. She crept around the panel, travelling almost all the way around the room until the terrorist's feet came into view. Sandy stood up and shot her opponent just as the frightened girl turned her face upwards to meet Sandy's resolute glare through her balaclava visor.

Her opponents now nullified, Sandy moved to the control panel in the centre of the operations room and tried to make contact with IC.

Just as she began tapping the dials to complete the call, a THUD startled her. She swivelled around while throwing herself sideways. The terrorist from the room with the moving platforms had retrieved his gun and had followed her through the vent. He missed his first shot, but Sandy was now separated from her weapon, which she had put down to phone IC. In an instant, she moved forward, tackling the male terrorist and flinging him backwards. His gun flew into the air. While he squirmed on the floor, Sandy was able to get several punches to his gut. She was tired, and he was young, and she knew if it came to a pure test of strength, he would be the victor.

One of the incapacitated terrorists lay nearby, and Sandy spotted his gun. In the split second it took her to reach for it, her assailant managed to find his footing and thrust his hand around her neck. He stood, dragging her upwards and away from the weapon. That is when Sandy pulled a gun, a real gun, from the concealed strap around her right ankle.

"Enough," she said.

The stern-faced youth froze; his hand was still wrapped around her neck.

She continued, "You may value your life, but I don't value mine, not anymore. If you do not desist, I will take you, me, your friends and this entire forsaken compound down with one bullet to that oxygen pipe."

She gestured at a pipe that ran around the ceiling of the room. It was marked 'O2'. The terrorist released her neck and raised his hands in surrender.

"Silly boy. You should have shot me while you were still in the vent. You were impatient. That's why you lost." The youth lowered his eyes in shame at her words. It seemed so obvious to him now.

Muro fumed in silence as she observed the sorry surrender. The 'terrorists' were some of her best junior officers. She had handpicked them. She had chosen them based on the fact that they looked younger than their age, which, she assumed, would have caused Sandy to underestimate them. Muro had hoped they would have put up a better fight.

"Well, that's that," Gerald said dejected.

Muro's team seemed unsure as to exactly what had happened.

"What do we know?" Muro queried.

"The operative had a real gun," Gerald offered. "They laid down their arms." "What can you tell me from the tests?"

"The operative's adrenalin was high the whole way through. They coped with it well. Like they were enjoying it."

"Typical!" said Muro.

"The operative's adrenalin levels were similar to Cadet Moretti's, in fact. Cadet Sanghera, your cortisol levels dropped after the soldier left the second room with the large plants. That's not what we would have expected to happen. Do you have any idea why that was?" Gerald enquired.

Natalia began to mumble something but was caught in Muro's icy glare. "Because," she said, "they're not real terrorists. They're not, are they?"

Muro's team looked at her in a stunned silence.

"How did you know that?" Muro barked. Massi stared at Natalia in disbelief.

"Because at the Academy, all advanced cognitive tests follow the same pattern..."

"Go on," Muro urged sternly.

"First you lay an ambush to see if the test subject can deal with panic. That happened in the lobby and the first room. Then the soldier had to memorise the map of the complex to know where to go—a simple memory test. Then the soldier couldn't see into the next room, so they had to use reflective surfaces. This was a spatial reasoning test. And target practice, of course. The tank was a situational judgment test. The moving platforms were a mental chronometry test. Then the ambush at the end, another stress test to see if the subject could still function when mentally and physically tired."

An uncomfortable silence fell on the room.

"It was a good test. Whoever designed it was obviously a pro, but if you know where to look, you know it's a test." Natalia had been hopeful that her comments would elicit the approval of her superiors, but their faces did not change.

"Thank you, cadet." Muro tried not to sound as angry as she was. Instead, she turned to Hackett and Manning. "Please escort these two back to their suite. They'll be debriefed this afternoon."

The two cadets were led out of the situation room. Muro's team looked on in a flummoxed silence.

"Commander?"

"Yes, Gerald?"

"Cadet Sanghera. Her cortisol levels dropped at the same time that Sandy's did. Sandy's didn't drop as much, but I imagine it was for the same reason."

"I see." Muro looked pensive. "I'm heading over to retrieve our little soldier now. Please modify the debrief we had planned for the cadets to accommodate our new information."

He nodded.

Sandy was slumped in a chair in the centre of the upturned control room when Muro sauntered over to her. She was exhausted. The faux terrorists she had defeated were recovering, groaning and sitting upright. The youth she had pulled the gun on was sulking in a corner, avoiding eye contact with her. Several armed male officers accompanied Muro, flanking her as if they were her own personal bodyguards. This was unusual.

"You know us better than we know ourselves," Muro said, looking down at her.

"It would seem that way," Sandy replied without looking up.

"You're the type who'd bring a gun to a knife-fight."

"Yeah, that sounds like me." Her voice was quiet but harsh.

"Where's your honour, soldier?" Muro derided.

"I lost it in Indashin."

"Is that so?"

"I don't ever go into a fight without having the upper hand first," she said.

"How are you feeling?" Muro asked.

"Still a little hungover, to be honest." Sandy's face changed from jovial to staid. "And rather insulted that after all my years of service—the things I've done—you felt the need to test me." Her voice had risen almost to a shout.

"I see." Muro leaned back. The guards around her tensed ever so slightly.

"Do you doubt my loyalty?"

"Certainly not. I simply wanted to make sure you were combat-ready. You haven't been on any missions lately. I was worried you were rusty."

"Whose fault is that?" Sandy stopped herself. "So what now, then?"

"Hmm...I see that you're as sharp as ever. Here's a uniform." Muro handed a white bundle to her. "I'll be taking your black-ops suit with me now. It needs to be repaired."

Sandy began to strip, then handed her black suit to Muro without looking at her. Both women knew Sandy would not be getting the suit back.

CHAPTER TEN

It had been a while since Natalia and Massi were on the same page. As they were driven back to the Academy from ICHQ, they both had the same feeling: the uncomfortable, cloying unease that they had just been used. Neither of them knew what for. They had both sat through a vague debriefing. They had been thanked for their time and had received an apology for having had their studies interrupted. They had just assisted ICHQ with monitoring the vitals of a soldier during a test. But who was this soldier, and why did Muro have to test him without letting him know?

Massi caught Natalia's eye. His lips parted as if about to speak, but Natalia snapped her index finger to her lips to silence him. Best not to talk about what they had just experienced in one of ICHQ's complimentary cars, even though they were alone.

It was night by the time the autocar deposited them back at the Academy. The school seemed quiet, and there were no other cadets around the front of the building. Natalia exited the car first and made a beeline for the computer lab. Massi hesitated. He thought about going straight back to the barracks, but he could not help following her instead.

"Why aren't you going straight back?" he asked breathlessly, running to keep up with her.

"I'm behind on my work," said Natalia.

"That's a lie. You're going to the lab."

"I'm behind on my computer work," she said, continuing to walk briskly.

"Stop! Wait!" said Massi, trying to grab her arm.

"Let me be," she said, and shook him off.

"You're going to hack IC's system, aren't you?"

Natalia stopped and looked at him in silent outrage.

"I know you can hack into them; I've seen you do it." His smile was accusing.

"What's it to you?"

"We were used by them. It's not fair that only you get to find out why. Tell me!" he demanded.

She shook her head. "The less you know, the better."

"That's not fair. I was there too."

"I'm not going to hack IC," Natalia lied.

"Yes, you are. I know that look on your face."

"Leave me alone," she said in frustration.

"There was a time when you and I were friends."

"Enough." She continued walking.

"What's your problem with me now?"

"I don't have a problem with you," she insisted.

"Yes, you do. Like everyone else in this place."

"Fine. I'll show you what I can find, but only if I can find anything at all," she said, reconciling with him. They were almost at the lab.

"You can always find something. I know you're miles ahead of anything they've taught. Why do you pretend that you're just the smartest girl in class when you're so much more than that?" he said, almost in awe of her.

"They don't need to know what I know."

"You know how to do things that would get you into trouble."

"Think that if you want." She entered the lab, dismissing his suggestion.

"What you do is illegal, isn't it?"

"Stop this," she said with a serious look on her face.

"It is illegal," said Massi.

"Don't be absurd." She held up her hand as if to push him away before sitting down and powering up her machine.

"Then why don't you show them what you can really do?"

"I'm not a troublemaker or a show-off like you," she replied haughtily.

"Then what are you?" He asked, thumping his hand down on one of the nearby desks.

She turned her face towards him. "I'm just curious."

###

Claudette Muro was enjoying a vodka tonic in her office. She had just finished debriefing Sandy. Muro had improvised her way through the debriefing badly. She had prepared a perfect explanation of how the ecoterrorists had come to find themselves in the vertical farms and was ready to articulate how aptly (or not) Sandy had neutralised them based on the outcome of the operation. Sandy, however, had forced her hand in another direction. Like the young female cadet, Sandy possessed the ability to transcend the situation and had looked upon it from the outside in, seeing it for what it was. Muro contemplated a new unknown: if she had underestimated Sandy's ability to know when she was being tested—or rather, when she was being played with—perhaps Muro had underestimated Sandy's abilities in every direction. Sandy's black-ops suit had been examined by Muro's team. It was not as badly damaged as Muro had presumed it was, despite the conspicuous hole in the neck. Sandy had done some basic cosmetic repairs on the suit but had chosen not to fix the hole. This struck Muro as odd.

It was then that Commander Nichols, Muro's rat-faced counterpart at Police Command, knocked on her door, interrupting her thoughts.

"Everet?" she asked.

"Vodka, Claudette? Has it come to that?" he asked, his voice snarky.

"Are you lost?" asked Muro, incredulously. She moved the bottle of vodka out of his sight, placing it on the floor by her feet.

"No. I have sought you out." He walked deeper into her office, sat down in front of her and crossed his legs.

"To what do I owe this honour, Commander?"

"I need to talk to you regarding a missing person." His voice had become serious.

"That's a rather domestic matter, don't you think?" Muro said flippantly.

"Not anymore. I have reason to believe that the disappearance of this person could be associated with a threat to national security."

"Who is this person?" asked Muro, sitting up to attention.

"Maria D'Souza, an information technology engineer of some significance within her field of expertise. She has disappeared, and her husband has taken their child and moved to the West Coast. He says he's living with his relatives, because his wife left him. The company she worked for says she just stopped coming to work one day and hasn't been in contact."

"How do you know she hasn't?"

"The company she worked for was Shaw Safe; they make security systems for high-net worth individuals and companies, as well as prisons."

"I've heard of them," said Muro, nodding.

"What they didn't tell me was that they hired a private investigator, a former colleague of mine, to find out where she went. Her disappearance has cost them a great deal. She'd worked there a long time and left a lot of loose ends and was in the middle of a large research project. She was also well-liked, despite the fact that I would consider her a very nasty piece of work."

"Oh? She sounds like 'Little Miss Perfect' to me."

"She's the member of a moderately aggressive purity cult, and I don't mean 'no sex before marriage'; I mean something much more sinister. When the private investigator looked into her case, he found that both she and her husband had been keen members of the Sun Circle Group."

"A cult?"

"Yes. A really bad cult," said Nichols.

"Is there such a thing as a good cult?"

"Well, no, but this one is more insidious. They preach a great deal of things that people would find positive. Good values. They value kindness, manners, being physically fit, dressing in a neat—if somewhat plain—fashion, being clean-shaven, no drugs, no drink, no unnatural-coloured hair dye and no tattoos. They frame their arguments in a way that makes them seem well-intentioned, and this tends to cover up for their inherent wickedness. They disapprove of not just being overweight but also of eating rich food or any more than you need. They hate activities that they consider decadent and indulgent; they disapprove of certain kinds of books, music, art. They're preoccupied with living not just a good life, but a pure life—without distraction, so human beings can be free to fulfil their potential. They even hate wallpaper. They think it's unnecessary and indulgent. They also have strict rules as to who should be able to reproduce and who should not. Members who do not meet certain moral or intellectual standards are discouraged from having children."

"Do they have many members?" Muro asked.

"About fifty thousand in America's megacities—a few million across the world."

"Surely they're just ascetics," said Muro, trying to play down his concerns.

"They're not ordinary ascetics. They're not religious, and they're not anti-wealth. They believe in using wealth to change the world into the one they want. They've become more…proactive recently."

"They must have strict rules about murder, don't you think?" asked Muro.

"Generally, it's frowned upon. But they're collectivists rather than individualists. They don't value human life in the same way. They believe in self-sacrifice."

"So you think Maria D'Souza was killed by another member of this cult?"

"Not just another member. Maria D'Souza was almost certainly murdered by Lyndon Hamilton." His voice was stern but calm, his face blank.

The blood drained from Muro's face.

"Have you gone completely mad? Everet, I really did hope your mental faculties would have held out for a little longer," said Muro, horrified.

"He did it, Claudette. He's only one who could have done it."

"What on earth could have led you to this belief?" she asked incredulously.

"My friend, the PI hired by Shaw Safe, brought this to my attention only after his contract was terminated abruptly. He was fired the very day after he reported what he had learned regarding Maria and her relationship with the Sun Circle Group. Shaw Safe never filed a missing person's report as he had advised them to do. A few days later, someone from Shaw Safe called him to let him know that Maria had been in touch and that she'd moved away but had left no forwarding address or number. I then had my team investigate the cult discreetly; its local members were genuinely upset by Maria's disappearance. Maria hadn't been in touch with a single one of her friends. Most of them are benign and fairly ordinary, even as cultists go. I thought about dropping the case until one of them called Police Command anonymously with a tip-off. This individual said they worked at Shaw Safe and ate with Maria almost every day. They heard Maria talking on the phone to someone called 'Lyndon'. I'm certain this was Lyndon Hamilton, because the cult used to receive small donations from Hamilton InfoSec in the past. I've seen acknowledgements of thanks on the group's newsletters—though that stopped a few years ago. He's a sympathiser, Claudette."

"IC has received donations from Hamilton InfoSec, as well," Muro said emotionlessly.

"That's because he loves the military. The uniformity. The discipline. He thinks soldiers live a pure life. He wants everyone in the world to be like that," he said, raising his eyebrows.

"I need more evidence to even touch this," Muro said, and shook her head.

"Shaw Safe did Hamilton's security system. For his home. For his offices. They knew each other, Claudette. I bet those donations didn't stop. I think they're being channelled through other companies or even charities to disguise just how big they are now."

"That is the most flimsy circumstantial evidence I've ever heard in my life," said Muro, struggling to digest the gravity of Nichols's words.

"The person who made Maria disappear without a trace can't be just anybody. This part of town has the best surveillance system in any of the megacities. I also have the best forensics department in the world," he mentioned, with a smug look across his face. "Anyone who can make a body disappear from right under my nose is not only exceptional but would have to have means. We're talking about a very dangerous individual indeed."

"Still, it's just too flimsy." Muro continued to shake her head, disbelieving. "If she was talking to Hamilton then maybe she was just touching up his security system?"

"Then why didn't Shaw Safe know about it? Why was she still in contact with Hamilton after her own company had finished working on his system? Maybe they were having an affair? If she wanted to leave him—that would give him a motive for killing her."

"We don't know that she's dead. Anyway, he's not the type of man who would have affairs."

"In my experience, when women believe that it means the opposite," he smirked.

"Oh, shut up." She rolled her eyes.

"All right, but because of her field of expertise, I have to refer this to you now, anyway. I'll tell you what—if you find her, then it's not an issue. If your team can't find her, then she's definitely dead."

Massi was pacing around the computer lab.

"Stop it!" Natalia said sharply.

"What am I doing now?"

"You're making me anxious," said Nat.

"Are you in yet?" he asked.

"This takes time."

Natalia typed speedily. She had mastered a language that Massi could not even understand. After a long, gut-wrenching silence, Natalia shook her head. "Odd. I can see where they arranged to pay the company that owns the farms. But I can't actually see the specifics of today's events."

"Why would they go through all that trouble?" Massi said, throwing his arms up in bewilderment and frustration.

"The expense was phenomenal." Nat sounded impressed.

"Do you know who the soldier was?"

"That's not on here. But it must have been someone of high value."

"Why was IC testing them?"

"There must have been serious questions about that person's abilities."

"Is that all?"

"There could also be questions about that soldier's loyalty to IC," replied Natalia tentatively.

"A traitor? That's extraordinary." Massi shook his head in disbelief.

"A high-profile traitor. Or maybe an enemy soldier who defected? This is highly irregular. And against all regulations. Even training exercises have to be logged. Something has been deleted or kept off the system deliberately."

"They screwed up. You knew it was a test. You embarrassed them." Massi sounded proud.

"But here's the thing. The soldier knew it was a test, too." Nat turned to look at Massi. "Muro was pissed."

"Thanks, Nat. You're brilliant."

"I was going to do it anyway," she admitted.

"How did you learn how to do that?"

"You just have to know what buttons to push."

"They can't track your hack, can they?" he asked, his brow furrowed.

"No, I've made sure of that." She turned the computer off and stood.

"How?"

"You'd never understand." She flicked her long plait over her shoulder and left him alone in the lab.

###

Massi walked back to the barracks. His mind was filled with the thought of touching Natalia's dark skin. He wanted to move his fingers down her naked back. He wanted to be alone with her somewhere other than the lab. He wanted to be close enough to her that he could whisper things in her ear. He wanted her to listen to him, to hear his whispers and laugh out loud. Their relationship had changed, and he could not pinpoint exactly when that had happened. He still wanted to be with her all the time, but that was not enough anymore. For years, just having fun together was enough. He had once been the only person she was open with. Not anymore. His hunger for her had changed how she saw him, too.

Almost all the guys had come back for the night by the time Massi entered the boys' barracks. Some of the cadets had gone to sleep even though the lights were still on. Most, however, were chatting or sitting up in bed reading. When Massi got to his own bunk, his heart sank. His belongings had been removed from his locker and now lay strewn across his bed. Nothing had been broken. It was then that he realised how tired he was. He would have to place every single object back in his locker before he could lie down.

Massi looked around. The other cadets were deliberately not making eye contact with him. He began putting his things back into his locker, and with every object he put away, his rage built. He was almost done when his hands found an unfamiliar object. It was a plastic name tag. All cadets were required to have their clothing and equipment tagged, but the tags were plastic and often came detached. The tag in Massi's hand clearly read, 'Henry P. Macey'.

Massi felt his fury rise up on the back of his neck like a searing-hot poker had been touched onto his flesh. He strode over to Harry Macey's locker and pulled it to the floor, spilling its contents across the barracks with an enormous crash. For a moment, Harry, who was sitting up reading in the adjacent bed, looked up in a speechless silence. The boys who had been sleeping woke with a start. Massi stood, surveying his damage for a second longer than he should have.

Within a moment, Harry Macey had leapt up off his bed and landed a clear, closed-fisted punch to Massi's face. Massi fell backwards but was caught by several cadets who had amassed around the pair. Massi was being propped up while Harry was being held back. Massi's eyesight was now a blur of light and dark spots. He staggered backwards as the other cadets tried to pacify Harry.

Colonel Mathers flung open the barracks door. The boys not involved in the altercation scattered back to their beds. By now, a trickle of bright-red blood was streaming from Massi's nose, making its way down his face and onto his chest. Mathers grabbed the youth by his arm and yanked him in the direction of the medical centre.

The nurse finished cleaning up the blood. Massi's eyelids felt like they were made of stone. He just wanted to sleep.

"He has to stay here tonight, in case of concussion," said the Academy's medic.

"Thank you, Nelson," Colonel Mathers replied. "I'll be off, then."

As Colonel Mathers left the white, sterile room, Massi leapt up and followed him.

"Why are you letting this happen?" he asked the older man.

Colonel Mathers turned around and stared back at him blankly while considering his words. "We're monitoring the situation."

Hearing the unsatisfactory response, Massi looked dejected.

"Why is this happening to me?"

"You're not really bonded to the other members of your team, I guess."

"We've been together in this unit since we were fourteen."

"Yes, you were a good team player—once."

CHAPTER ELEVEN

To Christopher Drummond, Ruling Council meetings were usually invigorating, but today's was not. Instead, it was laden with uninspiring discussions about the state's dry, mechanical processes. Years ago, the government had been forced to rethink the structure it had held during the Long War and had replaced the office of president with the Ruling Council. Executive power was now deemed too important—and too dangerous—to be left solely in the hands of one man. The creation of the Ruling Council was a tacit acknowledgement that the highest office of the land had been abused too many times.

There were five seats on the council. High Commander Drummond held one, which made him responsible for the New Republic's rule of law and its monopoly on the use of force. Intelligence Command, Police Command and Field Command reported to him. The other seats belonged to the high ambassador, the chief treasurer, chief justice and the chief of civilian affairs. The high commander and the high ambassador worked together on foreign policy, while the chief justice managed legal affairs, and the chief of civilian affairs worked on domestic policy. The chief treasurer informed them of what they could and could not afford.

After the meeting ended, Drummond's diplomatic counterpart, Clement Worther McCawley, pulled the high commander aside. High Ambassador McCawley was a portly, older gentleman with a greying moustache. Drummond, though he did not particularly like McCawley, did respect him. Indeed, very few denied that McCawley was good at his job. The high ambassador had handled the peace process at the cessation of the Long War so skilfully that he had gone on to win his re-election uncontested. Despite this, Drummond often felt that he could not trust

McCawley, though he had no rational reason to feel this way. McCawley, like a born-again convert, was fervently loyal to his country. Although Drummond never would have admitted it, his dislike for McCawley was simply a matter of taste. The military bluntness on which Drummond thrived was absent in McCawley, who managed to tell everyone what they wanted to hear while simultaneously never ceding an inch. This was what made McCawley a brilliant attaché but a lousy companion.

"Chris," said McCawley, "may I have a word?"

"Of course, Clement."

"You need to stop referring to the Federal Nusantara Republic as 'Indashin'. I can't stress this enough. Remove it from all official literature and speeches at once."

Drummond held his breath and thought carefully before responding. "Point taken. Until very recently the disputed islands didn't have a name, so, as per official guidelines, I was using the name that had been used in the past."

"A name derived from somehow bastardising 'Indochina', once used to describe the territories directly north of the disputed islands, Vietnam, Thailand and Malaysia—our valued and treasured allies who have painstakingly assisted us in this diplomatic process by cleaning up the mess left by the Long War. They're not happy about it. Desist immediately. There are new guidelines now."

"High Ambassador, I appreciate all of this, but..."

"Stop," said McCawley. "You just have to stop. The Australians are on my back about this too."

"What do they have to complain about? They're practically a superpower now."

"And yet, somewhat unsurprisingly, they're still not keen about having war on their doorstep." McCawley was both charming and sardonic.

"The new name was decided only three weeks ago," said Drummond. "We used the name 'Indashin' to avoid offending any of the parties relevant to the negotiations while the talks were taking place."

"So we offended everyone else instead?" A look of incredulity covered McCawley's face. "This insensitivity is typical of the disastrous foreign policy that led to the Long War in the first place. We're better at our jobs now."

"I will take every measure to cease the use of this name at once. It will be purged from all official literature, and any officer using it will be subject to disciplinary action."

"Ah, now, that's the correct answer, my son!"

Drummond winced at the familiarity. "Why were we using 'Indashin' as a temporary name in the first place? The borders of the Central Arabian Republic are still under dispute, but we were happy to name the new state almost immediately."

"That's irrelevant to this discussion. Just take the necessary action."

"Consider it as good as done."

The high ambassador paused. "That's another problem, by the way."

"The Central Arabian Republic?" asked Drummond. "What's wrong with that name?"

"Not the name—the peace treaty and settlement. They're still not happy, mostly because they think Lieutenant Attiyeh got off too lightly. They've got a new president, you must have heard? Al Khatem? I've talked them out of an inquiry into Hazirat several times now. I keep blocking it, but it just keeps coming back up."

"Why do they continue to rehash this?" asked Drummond. "She's already been pardoned. All is fair in love and war."

"Nothing's fair in love and war," the high ambassador chuckled. "There are those who are still bitter about it. Unfortunately, one of those is President Al Khatem."

"Those feelings may ease in time. Especially now that there's peace."

"Let's hope so. That's another can of crap we need to keep shut."

"Do you have a plan to deal with CAR if they insist on making further demands?" asked Drummond.

"I don't have a plan. I have managed the situation for now."

"Good," said Drummond, nodding as if to reassure himself.

"If it comes to it, however, I would happily throw Lieutenant Attiyeh to the dogs and let them tear her apart," he said plainly, "if that's what's best for the country, of course. I don't like feeling that this peace is fragile."

Drummond inhaled at these sacrilegious words. He straightened himself up to his full height, which was half a yard above McCawley's, and said, "Lieutenant Attiyeh holds an unrivalled reverence for this country. She has followed every order. She killed our greatest enemy. What's best for our country is to give her our unfailing loyalty."

McCawley looked into Drummond's dark stare and backed away slightly.

"Oh, Chris, I spoke in jest!" He cleared his throat and his face reddened. "It was a joke. I would never give a fine veteran and patriot, and a young lady for that matter, to those...folks."

Drummond softened, but the sense of unease did not leave him. The two men, their aides having flittered off to answer calls, now stood alone in a quiet corridor. Before turning to leave, McCawley gave Drummond a manly thump on the back, and they shook hands.

In the car on the way to his office, Drummond sat deep in thought. His two closest aides chattered in the back without noticing their boss's glazed-over eyes. Drummond's mind had drifted back to a painful place—his childhood. Back then, the world had been divided into those who wanted to live under the auspices of Enlightenment values and those who did not. Drummond had tried to swallow the high ambassador's comment about peace seeming fragile; still, it had shaken him. Drummond usually never wondered whether he would have joined the army had it not been for the Soft Terror. He had always taken for granted that he would have—he was just that kind of man. But a familiar voice, an infrequent visitor in his mind, now crawled back in, reminding him of the pain and distress of living under the Soft Terror. Memories of alarming news stories flashed in his mind. He remembered feeling that there was nothing surgical or precise about a drone strike and that the terrorists seemed to be getting better at hiding in plain sight as the strikes became more and more haphazard. That the mounting list of civilian deaths augmented the terrorists' ire. That every attempt to destroy the insurgency gave them new moral ammunition. That domestic terror attacks had become more common.

He remembered how the war abroad had seeped into every facet of everyday civilian life. Soft targets were now being routinely attacked by non-state actors. During his formative years, security checkpoints had become commonplace on roads and in shopping malls and offices—they were no longer a feature found only in airports and government buildings. When his mother had switched on the news, some talking heads lamented the lost land of the free. Others welcomed the change—it was justified, or so they said. Shortly thereafter, civilians could not go a day without being scanned, examined and probed in a futile show of security theatre that was both burdensome and expensive. Drummond remembered how everyone became scared and then irrational and skittish—after all, that was how scared people behaved. Charismatic charlatans took advantage of the feeble-minded and terrified. There were mass suicides to appease angry gods. Hysteria in the streets. Riots. Looting. People abandoned cities and made new homes in the virgin territories away from civilisation. Drummond remembered one particularly nasty incident in which travellers seeking respite had been ambushed by the very community they had hoped to join. Soon after, the travellers had been strung up in the trees, victims of the commune's paranoia.

While the world burnt, Drummond passed the Academy's entrance tests, graduated and progressed steadily up the ranks. As the Long War dragged on, he became increasingly disillusioned with the top brass, as did many young officers. The military was like any other instrument. The more it was used, the blunter it became.

Among the vivid memories that revisited Drummond was the time he was invited on a secret 'camping trip'. It was an August night when he and a fellow soldier had trudged through the quiet thicket of a northern Virginian forest. The humidity was oppressive, even after dark; still, the two men marched to a wooded clearing using only a small, rickety navigator to guide them. After what seemed like forever, their destination came upon them. Eleven sullen faces waited patiently, the whites of their eyes gleaming blue in the moonlight.

An aggressive senior officer, his face lit by a small torch, suggested that the only option to change the course of the war for the better was a coup d'état to remove the flailing generals. Drummond stood in front of them and declared that while he sympathised with their cause and wished them luck, he wanted no part of the treacherous act. After speaking, he turned on his heel and left without looking back. The men present were Drummond's age, and he'd known all of them since the Academy; in fact, some of them were his friends. They had eaten together, drunk together...and bled together. The next day, eleven of the men from the night before were marched out of their barracks, blindfolded and shot. The twelfth, the snitch, was given a comfortable desk job for the remainder of the war but never received another promotion. The generals in question, fearing more mutiny and conceding that their strategy was not working, resigned, but not before unanimously appointing Christopher Drummond to the rank of general, a position he had always wanted but never imagined he would attain at so young an age.

In exceptional circumstances, seemingly unexceptional men got the chance to prove their greatness. Drummond was Leonidas. Drummond was Hannibal. Drummond was Caesar. He had studied the ancient wisdom. He knew war, and his focus on its end became his sole obsession. Anything less than total conquest would be a loss. Everything else in his life fell away. Drummond was Saladin. Drummond was Drake. Drummond was Cromwell. When you knew the rules better than anyone, you knew which ones to break when necessary. He never lost the part of him that was inclined to be a revolutionary. He channelled his army's energy and created an efficient, professional, unparalleled fighting machine. Drummond was Washington. Drummond was Wellington. A patriot and a figurehead, heaving with purpose and with the dignity of his office. Drummond was MacArthur. Drummond was Yamamoto. Drummond was Yamashita. Resourceful and ingenious. Just when his enemies thought they knew him, he would surprise them. Only Drummond could have manufactured such unambiguous victories from uncertain odds in a messy war. Drummond was Churchill. He did not relent until he knew his enemies better than they knew themselves, and he manipulated the victories he wanted out of them. When it came to strategy, he was without equal. Drummond was Drummond.

To adapt to this new aggressive, asymmetric guerrilla warfare, the intelligence community, the armed forces and police were disbanded and reassembled into three bodies: Intelligence Command, Police Command and Field Command. Police Command oversaw the domestic rule of law at national and state levels. Field Command consisted of the former army, navy and air force, though at a fraction of the size. Intelligence Command assessed and dealt with international threats and comprised the operatives who went into war zones first. Designed to determine specifics that could only be obtained by specialists on the ground, they would neutralise threats or remove hindrances that would cause more causalities than were deemed necessary. They gathered precise information and fed it back to Field Command, whose agents would then take appropriate action. This could range from boots on the ground to airstrikes, drone attacks to strategically manipulating or blockading terrorist-controlled territories. When the instruments of war no longer did their job, Drummond changed the instruments.

By placing a greater emphasis on good intelligence and integrating it with the conventional army, Drummond manoeuvred the war to an end. Unlike some of his counterparts, he was uncompromising when it came to cutting out more than the infection. Enemy combatants fleeing their heartlands either accepted Intelligence Command's propaganda or were never seen again by their families. An aggressive regime of indoctrination was inflicted on the populations that had harboured terror cells, knowingly or not. Though it took time, Drummond forged a peaceful world, and he would defend all those who had helped him shape this prosperous but paranoid nation—and that included Sandy.

CHAPTER TWELVE

Sandy wrapped her hands around a mug of hot chocolate. It was unlike any of the hot chocolate she had ever tried before. It was thick and spiced. Cardamom maybe? She could not quite pinpoint the taste. For some reason, it reminded her of the Middle East. A specialty of Hamilton's chef.

"It was an elaborate test of some sort," Sandy said, sighing.

"A test?" Hamilton queried from his spot behind Sandy, on a large chair in the computer lab.

"Something about making sure I was still combat-fit."

"Did you pass?"

"I don't think it was as simple as a pass/fail test, but I think by any definition, I surpassed expectations," said Sandy, nodding.

"Excellent. Excellent. Do you think they suspect anything?"

"Muro doesn't know—or think—the power cut was me. She must know it was me who beat up those hoaxers, but she would never say so. Not without hard evidence."

"You're certain?" asked Hamilton.

"She could never prove it. Black-ops suits have no tracking devices of any kind. Any sort of signal could be traced or intercepted, compromising the safety of the agent."

"How did IC make sure agents got back after missions during the Long War?"

"They didn't," said Sandy, her voice devoid of emotion.

"Ah."

"If we got the job done, that was all IC cared about. If we came back, that was a bonus." Sandy looked down. "Toward the end, IC was getting desperate. Things that used to matter suddenly just didn't matter."

Hamilton changed the subject. "I would like you to add another dimension to the model."

"Oh, yes?"

"Instead of just making a map of all the researchers and their professional networks, could you add their immediate families, as well?"

"Their families?" Sandy was quizzical.

"Yes. Those entries don't have to be in as much detail, of course, but I think they're necessary."

"Okay." Sandy nodded in acknowledgment. Her disconcertion at this request was not evident on her face, because she was not surprised by it.

"Are you testing it? Does it work as it should?" Hamilton hovered over her.

Sandy approached the map.

"For the networks that have been mapped so far, it works. I've programmed the algorithms so that it's a living database. It knows what to look for now. It scans the Web for information and attaches it to the person it belongs to. If an academic announces they're working on a new project, the model will pick up the press release and add it to that academic's entry. If you touch here," Sandy said and pointed to a digital marker on the map, "you can see that this researcher has recently moved universities. You can see where they moved to, who they worked with, who they're working with at the new university and who's doing their old job now."

The digital marker expanded under Sandy's finger to show a profile, including the name and a picture of the bespectacled man to whom it belonged. The profile expanded when Sandy double-tapped it. As she swiped her finger across, it listed everything he had ever worked on, which was instantly available to be read at leisure. It also listed his address, his immediate family connections, his telephone number, some emails from his landlord and his bank account details.

Hamilton looked impressed, his mouth rounding upwards. "Hmm," he muttered, "he was almost late paying his rent this month."

Sandy looked on grimly. It was almost as if she could see Hamilton's thought process. He was assessing this man's vulnerabilities. She closed the profile, and it shrank. Sandy thought the data markers looked like little green clouds bobbing around an overwhelming Earth.

###

Bribing the accountant of the local Sun Circle Group chapter had been unexpectedly cheap. Muro would have needed a warrant to get the information she needed during peacetime, but bureaucracy was slow. The truth, though, was that she did not have sufficient grounds to get a warrant even if she had tried. Regardless, she was now mulling over a copy of the group's bank account statements. It was as Commander Nichols had told her: several companies partially owned by Hamilton, had made small but frequent donations to the Sun Circle Group. Those donations had then trailed off, and larger donations had started to come from other companies in Hamilton's sector. Muro realised she would need more information than this. If she were to question the donations, all of them would be explained away with reasons that did not implicate Hamilton. What IC really needed was evidence that Hamilton was giving money to these companies with explicit instructions to donate it to the Sun Circle Group. Muro slumped down in her chair. This would not be easy. The folks over at Hamilton InfoSec would not be so easily bribed. Hamilton was said to inspire a great deal of loyalty in his staff, and he paid them well for their loyalty. Muro thought for a moment, then leant forward to push a button on her phone.

"Amos Harling," she said, and the phone began to connect.

"Commander Muro?" a voice answered in a broad West Coast accent.

"Hello, Amos. I would like to speak with you, but best not to chat over the phone. How quickly can you be in my office?"

"Two hours, ma'am."

"See you then."

"Yes, ma'am."

She leant back down in her chair and smiled to herself.

###

Amos Harling's height always surprised Muro. He walked into her office using half the number of strides anyone else would have. Muro loved how he wore his hair: sun-kissed, wavy, blond and chin length. Even his gait showed off his pleasant disposition. He was the only man who made her wish she were thirty years younger.

"How long was the flight from California?" Muro asked.

"Half an hour. Sorry for the delay. I was in the middle of…something when you called," he said with a cheeky intonation.

"Sorry for interrupting," said Muro.

"That's quite all right," Amos replied courteously. "What can I do for you?"

"You're not going to like me."

"That could never be." He flashed his broad, bleach-white grin.

"I have a task that I don't feel I can trust with any of my own officers and requires your specialist expertise."

His eyes lit up. "This is getting more exciting with every word."

"I need you to look into Hamilton InfoSec's financial records."

The grin fell from Harling's face.

"Amos, I also need you to look for financial misconduct in Lyndon Hamilton's personal accounts," Muro continued.

"Lyndon Hamilton's on the Ruling Council, isn't he?" he asked in alarm.

"No, he's never put himself forward for election. I'm sure if he did, he would be voted in straightaway."

"Am I allowed to know why you need me to investigate Hamilton? This is a big ask."

"No, that's classified, I'm afraid," said Muro.

"I'm good at what I do, Commander, but I'm not omnipotent. He makes good systems. They're very secure. I imagine his own is the most advanced on the planet."

"You have carte blanche on this particular mission."

"Carte blanche? What do you want me to do? Burn the building down?" asked Harling.

"No, but I need you to find something for me," said Muro.

"What are you looking for?"

Muro paused. "I don't know."

"Then what am I supposed to be looking for?"

"Something that doesn't add up. When I say you have carte blanche for this mission, I mean financially, as well."

"I would never do this for the money." He paused. "But how much are you talking?"

After class ended, Massi darted from his seat so quickly that Natalia could not tell in which direction he had headed. Massi had been less talkative ever since the enormous bruise on the left side of his face had appeared. Still, she thought she had not done a good enough job distancing herself from him. Her plans remained unchanged.

She headed to the computer lab as always. When she turned the lights on, she nearly screamed in fright. Massi was sitting in the corner, reading by the light of a small torch he kept on his keychain.

"You can't hide forever, you know," she said, her alarm receding.

"I wasn't hiding. I was just resting."

"With the lights off?" asked Nat.

"My eyes hurt," said Massi, protesting.

"You were reading."

"Yeah…"

"Why don't you go back to the boys' barracks?"

"We always hang out here."

"False. We do not hang out. I do extra work, while you do the work you're behind on."

Her words stung, but the hurt only showed on his face for a second. "I'm not leaving. I've as much right to be here after hours as you do."

"Fine," she replied calmly. "Don't disturb me."

She sat down and turned on her computer. Massi watched her. She typed away for a few minutes before letting out a faintly audible gasp of displeasure.

"What's up?" Massi asked.

"Nothing."

"It's never nothing."

"Corio didn't leave anything for me today." She was more disappointed than she let on. "He said he would."

"Oh, dear." Massi hoped he had sounded sympathetic, though he was secretly pleased.

"That's that, then," she said, beginning to close down her computer and standing up.

"Wait!" Massi said. Natalia turned towards him. "Can you do something?"

"What?"

"If you can hack into IC's system, then you can hack into the Academy's system, too—right?"

"Nope."

"You can't?"

"Of course, I can. But not for you," she said unsympathetically.

"Why not?"

"I won't."

"Come on, Nat!" He stood up. "What's happened to you? You used to like me. We're not even friends now. Why do you treat me like this now? I know the other girls aren't your friends. We used to get on."

She hid her eyes from him. She enjoyed his company more than anyone else's.

"You know something," Massi continued, but his tone had changed. It had become more aggressive. "Why they're letting them bully me. You know why. You know, because you go into the system all the time. What do you do when you're poking around in there? Do you steal the answers and cheat?"

"I don't ever, ever cheat. And I've never been into your records." Her cheeks flushed red in anger.

"But you know why they're doing it, don't you?"

"I can't say for certain." She looked at him with the eyes of a guilty child, hoping her voice had not given her away.

"Then will you look in the system for me?"

"You're asking too much of me," she said and turned back to her screen, preparing to leave the room.

"Come on. Do it. You've treated me so badly lately."

"Stop this," she said firmly.

"Do it. You owe me," he said.

"Fine."

She sat back down at her machine. Massi stood behind her in a way that he knew would make her squirm with discomfort. She felt intimidated by his presence, but she also felt an urge to placate him at all costs. She did not want him to stop coming to the computer lab. Natalia liked that he sat behind her, watching her, desiring her.

Within a few minutes, she was inside the Academy's system.

###

Harling knew there was a weak spot. *There's always a weak spot.* Hamilton built his own systems to be completely hack-proof, but he still had to engage with other entities—be they companies or individuals. It was within these entities that Harling would find the weak spot. First, Harling acquired the bank statements of smaller companies only partially owned by Hamilton's main holding company. From these statements a pattern emerged. There were several unidentifiable offshore entities that had made investments in all these smaller companies on a regular basis. These companies then gave huge sums to businesses that were dependent on Hamilton's custom. It was these companies, Hamilton's suppliers, that then transferred funds to the Sun Circle Group.

Most companies across the globe had agreed to be a part of an international registry designed to prevent financial crime. When Harling cross-referenced the account numbers of the unidentified entities with the company registry, their names did not appear. Harling felt despondent. He had assumed he would have found the smoking gun already. Maybe he was losing his touch. Perhaps Hamilton just wanted to support his causes privately. If a super-rich client had asked Harling how to fund a cause without the media finding out, this arrangement is exactly what Harling would have suggested: opening bank accounts in countries that did not make all companies put their accounts on the registry and having them donate by proxy.

Before he moved on, he decided to check one last thing. He would create a program that would do a reverse search. He could not find the owners of the ghost accounts, but he could find the accounts the ghost accounts had made transfers to.

It took Harling three weeks to create the software he needed. It took the software fifteen hours to do the search. When the search was complete, Harling was left with a spreadsheet of the hundreds of thousands of domestic accounts the ghost entities had made deposits to. Harling scoured the data but nothing looked remiss. These entities could be perfectly legitimate foreign investors or clients of Hamilton's smaller companies. *There must be something*, he thought. There must be a small kink in the pattern. After playing with the filters on the spreadsheet for twenty minutes, that kink presented itself to him.

The ghost accounts had made their deposits exclusively in corporate accounts with the exception of two individuals: a three-year-old girl named Connie D'Souza and a certain Alisande Attiyeh.

"Are you in yet?" Massi demanded.

"Don't rush me," said Natalia.

"Not as good as you thought you were."

"Shut up." Natalia paused. "Okay, I'm in."

"And?"

"I need two minutes," she sighed, exasperated. "Records are not straightforward. They're made up of tutor shorthand and codes."

"So what?"

"So, you're failing. I think you know that." She looked at Massi.

"Yes, but why, exactly? I perform well."

"The record acknowledges that, but it's not all about performance; it's about unit cohesion."

"Unit cohesion? What does that even mean?"

"You're so stupid. You're such a fool. Don't you see? They've been telling us to distance ourselves from you. They want you isolated." She stood up from the computer and tried to pick up her things. Massi took hold of her by her upper arm and pulled her into him.

"Why? Tell me why!"

"I don't know. I genuinely don't know. They're testing you; I can see it in your file, but I can't decipher why."

He then took hold of her with both his hands clasping her arms with a force that surprised her.

"Are you lying to me?" he asked.

"I don't lie."

"You'd lie to me," he accused.

"I don't lie to anybody."

"You know how I feel about you."

She remained silent. His grip around her arms was so strong it almost hurt. She became aware of how much of him was muscle. He could overpower her if he wanted to. Her body was now fully against his, and she could feel the heartbeat inside his firm chest. She turned her face away from him. She did not want to acknowledge or admit to the way contact with him made her feel. His grip remained constant. She moved her face back towards him.

"I know," she said as her parted lips met his, kissing him.

They embraced each other for a moment, but Natalia interrupted it, breaking away too early.

"In half a year, when we're both eighteen and graduated, perhaps we could pursue this. I can't do that now. You have to understand. You have to respect that I don't want to do this now."

"I could wait."

"If you want to. You can wait," she said.

"Do you want me or not?"

She closed her eyes and softly exhaled the words, "Yes, I want you."

She picked up her books and left the lab as fast as her legs could carry her. Massi stood still for a moment. He would live off her words as though they were manna from heaven, and he were lost in the desert. For her part, though her words had been true in the moment, Natalia had only uttered them because she wanted to calm him. Having now seen his records, she did not think he would make it to graduation.

CHAPTER THIRTEEN

Sandy had designed the operation to breach I-WISE's facilities meticulously. She had been especially looking forward to it, as the venture was more in line with Intelligence Command's typical information-gathering missions. For Sandy, this would be a return to the fieldwork of her youth: breaking and entering, picking locks, grabbing documents, eavesdropping and borrowing data just long enough to transmit it back to ICHQ. The thought of the action thrilled Sandy so much that she had had a permanent grin plastered on her face as she worked out the plan while sitting on her living room floor. She had used Hamilton's projection to find the schematics of I-WISE's vast warehouse complex. I-WISE was not inept, but as with every corporation, Sandy knew there was a weak spot. *There was always a weak spot.* The weak spot in this case was the architect who designed the buildings: the floor plans were accessible by remotely hacking into his email account.

Unfortunately, Sandy's strategy entailed a heavy reliance on the features of her black-ops suit. Now that Muro had confiscated her old suit, Sandy would need a replacement. She combed the black market and found a respectable knock-off but recoiled in horror when the seller told her the price.

###

"I won't pay," said Lyndon Hamilton, indignant.

He and Sandy were sitting together, alone in the lab. This was not the reaction Sandy had hoped for.

"I need it," said Sandy.

"Why?" asked Hamilton.

"I designed the operation knowing I would have the suit. It's necessary now."

"Can't you redesign it?" Hamilton pressed.

"No. Well, I can, but that would take me more time, and you're the one who wants this done."

"How long?"

"It also makes the operation much more risky. You're putting me in a more compromising position. If you want this, you'll get the suit for me." Sandy put on her most authoritative voice and hoped that Hamilton would not react badly to being deliberately ignored.

"How long would it take to redesign the operation?" Hamilton asked again.

"Long. A long time. Six weeks," Sandy said, stumbling over her words.

"Let me see. Maybe I could wait…" Hamilton rubbed his hands together as he thought.

"Losing my old suit was unfortunate, but I can live without it, especially now that IC no longer sends me on missions. I don't need a suit for myself. I'm doing this for you."

"I didn't get where I am today by spending my money on frivolities," Hamilton began.

"I can't do it without a suit, Lyndon. I won't," Sandy finally admitted.

Hamilton met her gaze.

"I see," said Hamilton. "It's expensive for a security blanket."

"That's not how it is. All my training. All the operations I've done have been with a suit. I might forget I'm not wearing one. With the suit, you can just walk past CCTV cameras without anyone even knowing. That's priceless."

Hamilton nodded. Sandy breathed in.

"Okay," he relented, "but I expect a return on my investment."

He stood up and exited the room, leaving Sandy feeling anxious but relieved. Perhaps she could have redesigned the manoeuvre without the suit, but carrying out any operation without it was a powerful psychological block she could not overcome.

###

The payment took place through an intermediary. The new suit was delivered by an unregistered drone to a parkland popular among dog walkers on the outside of town. One of the porters in Sandy's building took an elderly neighbour's dachshund for walks every day. Sandy convinced him to let her walk the dog, and that weekend she retrieved the package from its landing spot without hindrance or suspicion.

Considering all the effort and expense, the new suit was not very good. Outside of IC's suits, it was the best that money could buy, but it was still not very good. Sandy could recognise the amateur work of someone who, though not unskilled, did not really know how black-ops suits actually worked, despite having seen one in person. The engineers who specialised in the technology were rare, and almost all of them were employed by IC. There were very few companies that could compete with a military budget, no matter what incentives the black market offered.

In the original suit, when an agent was standing still, the only part of the suit still visible was the narrow visor. The new suit's seams were thicker, and the scales were not as tightly layered. Even worse, the new suit's scales did not change to reflect the environment as quickly as IC's suits did. It was a lag that could cost her vital seconds.

###

The schematics for I-WISE's storage facility showed the DC Metro running under it. After midnight, Sandy donned her suit and took an autocab to the station nearest I-WISE. In the pocket of her suit she had tucked an ElectroFyte, a handheld self-defence device that delivered a non-fatal but incapacitating shock to the target's body. She also carried a small amount of plastic explosive and three transmitters. As always, she had a gun strapped to her right ankle.

Earlier that day, she had dented the rails that allowed the gate to close fully; now, there was a gap between the gate and the ground just wide enough for her to roll under. Sandy walked through the empty station until she reached the platform. She clambered onto the track and entered the tunnel. She walked for twenty minutes through the dark until she reached the service door she was looking for. The door led to a steep set of steps, which she climbed until she reached a manhole cover. The manhole cover was not locked, as Sandy thought it would be. She had brought the explosives to open it, so she was pleased that she would no longer have to risk the small sound they would have made. Earlier, Sandy had skimmed maps of the I-WISE facility to see where the manhole would lead her. When she pulled herself above ground, she was, as she had predicted, behind one of I-WISE's warehouses.

There were seven warehouses in total, each about the size of a football pitch. Sandy walked to the door of the nearest warehouse and pushed on it. It did not move. The door had a glass pane, and inside Sandy saw what she had expected to see: rows and rows of filing cabinets packed tightly together. They struck Sandy as being oddly arranged. If the contents of the cabinets were all paper, a single spark could do a lot of damage. Though she knew I-WISE's unique selling point was that it kept sensitive information safe and off the Web, she had anticipated state-of-the-art facilities. From the information she had stolen from Sheila-Marie, however, Sandy knew that I-WISE did not solely rely on paper documents, despite the company's claims that its physical storage methods made it unhackable. Paper degraded and was vulnerable to the environment. Sandy reasoned that the data must have been electronically scanned and stored somewhere unconnected to the Net. She left the warehouse and walked to the offices housed in the other half of the complex.

A large dog started to bark loudly, startling Sandy. *Who still uses guard dogs these days?* Dealing with a guard dog had not been a part of her plan. She had known there would be guards, but not dogs. *How could I have missed that detail?* She was pinned against a wall, almost at the central office. The Dobermann was about fifty metres away. It thrashed and pulled at the lead as its handler, looking around anxiously, tried to placate it. He momentarily shined his light toward her but then began moving in the opposite direction. Sandy was invisible to the guard, of course, but the dog had picked up her scent. Her plan had hinged on following a guard into the building. She had access codes if she needed them, but if she opened a door by herself, its movement would be caught on CCTV, and I-WISE security would know the building was compromised. There were cameras everywhere. Sandy walked sideways along the wall until she found the door she was looking for. Now she just had to wait.

Another guard appeared from around the corner. Sandy flinched for moment, thinking he, too, had a dog. He did not, but he stopped as though he sensed something. Sandy's heart began to beat more rapidly, and she realised she was holding her breath. She began to breathe slowly and silently, trying to calm herself. Seeing nothing, the guard continued his watch. When he opened the door to the I-WISE offices, Sandy slipped inside before the door shut, then waited patiently as he walked ahead.

Inside, I-WISE's offices were open and friendly compared to the stark, fortified outside space. Sandy had already looked up the I-WISE staff on social media but had found no pictures of them in the office. There must have been stringent policy in place forbidding it. That would not have been an unusual policy for a security company to have. With the guard gone, Sandy found that she could move through the building freely. There was one room in particular that she needed to get to: the data bank, where I-WISE employees scanned and housed copies of all the precious data. She reasoned that the data bank must be one of the large rooms she had seen on the floor plans. She moved toward it.

She found what she was looking for in the very centre of the complex. Her jaw dropped in amazement. The room hummed and glowed. Stacks upon stacks of memory boards were gathered together in cubes stretching from floor to ceiling. It was eerily beautiful, like a mountainous landscape made of silicon and wire. Sandy had been underwhelmed by the company's warehouses but was awed by the sheer size of its electronic data bank. It was little wonder that Hamilton considered I-WISE his biggest competitor. Enormous fans pumped cool air through the room, preventing the buzzing nests of computers and wires from overheating.

Sandy walked deeper into the room. She wanted to be in a position where her activities could not be seen by the cameras. She crouched down and carefully slid open a panel on one of the data banks. She tinkered with it until one of her small transmitters was firmly in place. From the moment she turned the transmitter on, Hamilton would know everything I-WISE knew. She repeated this elsewhere with the other two transmitters, just in case the first was found.

She waited until she saw the guard on his patrol. He looked bored and was walking restlessly back to the door through which he had unknowingly let Sandy in. Treading carefully, she walked a few steps behind him. He opened the door, and Sandy followed him out. Still directly in front of her, he stopped to take a long stretch and yawned loudly. Sandy was almost crushed in the doorway, but she silently slid out of harm's way, nearly collapsing just behind the guard's feet. Luckily the man failed to hear the small scuffle of her feet over his extended yawn. The guard began to walk away from the manhole, which Sandy now needed to get back to. She hurried across the courtyard.

The flicker of a flashlight stopped her in her tracks: it was the guard with the dog. Sandy dashed behind one of the warehouses. She could hear the dog becoming agitated again, pulling at its chain leash. Sandy thought about reaching for her gun but stopped herself when it occurred to her that shooting the dog would be the stupidest thing she could do, even if it ensured her escape. Instead she reached for her ElectroFyte. She walked in the direction opposite the guard, who was now on the other side of the warehouse. She was also walking farther from the manhole. It was now a slow game between her, the guard and the dog. A game they did not even know they were playing. The sun would be rising soon, and she had to get back to the tunnel. Creeping around the warehouse, she watched the guard and the Dobermann move away from her, disappearing around a corner. The tunnel was so close.

A flurry of padded footsteps, a fierce growl and a man's voice broke the night's silence. The dog had wrested himself away from the guard's grip, and before Sandy could move, the dog was racing toward her. She held her arm out as stiff as she could and zapped the dog just as it was about to launch itself upon her. It whimpered and cried out. Sandy was knocked back to the ground. Both guards ran toward the commotion. Sandy scrambled. She needed to be on her feet as quickly as possible. She backed away from the yelping animal. Both guards were now running toward her position. She stood still. As the two men began to fuss over the dog, Sandy tiptoed around the corner of the warehouse, never taking her eyes off them. She then lifted the manhole cover, slid into the tunnel and lowered the metal disc gently back into place.

She had been victorious.

CHAPTER FOURTEEN

Harling presented his findings to Commander Muro as tactfully as he could manage. She flicked through the documents briefly and was now staring at the wall behind him. It was inevitable but not surprising, Muro thought, that Sandy had somehow been sucked into Lyndon Hamilton's alluring orbit.

"We can't prove that those ghost accounts belong to Hamilton?" she asked.

"Not yet," said Harling, not meeting Muro's gaze.

"Can you find out?"

"I can get anything you want, but it'll take more time. Trawling the international banks requires a little more sophisticated work. It's also technically illegal," he said, his mouth becoming tense.

"Oh, that doesn't matter." Muro dismissed his concern with a shake of her head. "Will you go back to California?"

"I can stay here if you want," he said.

"I would prefer that for the immediate future," she said with a nod, still not looking at him, "but it's not an order."

"Fantastic," he said congenially.

"You'll need to make up a reason for being here."

"I'll think of something," he said, his blue eyes lighting up.

"Thank you for staying at short notice. Please send in Gerald on your way out."

Harling smiled and left. Gerald entered with some trepidation. His boss had been in a foul mood lately.

"I need Lieutenant Attiyeh tailed," Muro said. "Please organise this. Use someone good."

"She'll smell a rat," said Gerald.

"Then work harder!" Muro had not meant to shout. "You're an intelligence officer. Why do I not seem to be able to rely on my own spooks anymore?"

"Yes, ma'am. Sorry, ma'am."

Gerald scuttled out of her presence. Something was happening. Muro felt her iron grip on the small piece of the world she governed—the one she had once held so securely—slowly weakening.

Sandy was alone in Hamilton's super lab, and she loved it. It was like something out of a science-fiction novel. The room was perfectly designed for exactly what she needed. There was even a separate entrance and lift up to the lab so she could come and go as she pleased without being noticed or questioned. She was never disturbed by any of the other InfoSec staff, other than Hamilton and his quiet manservant. She reflected on how frequently she found herself in situations that required improvisation. But this time was different. Ironically, despite having been trained at the most well-equipped military academy in the world, when it came to the nitty-gritty of wartime, she had been forced to make do with very little. Long gone were the days of bragging to her colleagues, and even to her superiors, about being able to kill anyone with anything. Once a valued skill, it now struck her as perverse. Embarrassment crept over her as she thought about it. Objects like nail clippers and even sheets of tissue paper had become deadly weapons in her fatal, resourceful hands. Her throat clenched in shame as she vividly remembered shoving wads of tissue down the gullet of a nameless man. She could not remember her motivation for doing so. No doubt she had one at the time. When committing such an act of violence, one really ought to have a reason. All she remembered was that she lacked enough strength in her hands to choke the incapacitated man's thick throat, so she grabbed the nearest thing within reach and perverted it into a weapon.

Sandy shook herself out of the disturbing memory and instead moved her hand across the smooth, shimmering surface adjacent to her workspace. Its perfection soothed her. Hamilton's facilities were flawless. Every eventuality had been prepared for. It was as though Hamilton was constantly testing himself to see just how good he could get. He was clearly the type of man who enjoyed pushing boundaries, just for the sake of pushing boundaries. No wonder Muro could not get enough of him. "Those two deserve each other," she chuckled to herself.

"Something amusing?" Hamilton asked, startling Sandy. He was standing a few feet behind her. She had thought she was alone.

"Speak of the devil," Sandy replied.

"Were you speaking about me?"

"No, I was thinking..." Sandy hesitated. "Never mind."

"How's our pet project looking?"

"Very healthy. Very healthy, indeed," said Sandy, grinning proudly. "The I-WISE mission went so well. I can see the projection pulling in their data now."

"So, it should be done?"

"Very soon," said Sandy.

"How soon?"

"Imminently," she said, suddenly unsure of herself under Hamilton's stern, judgmental eyes.

Hamilton remained silent, so Sandy turned back to the keyboard and continued working. She had thought he would be thrilled with what she had accomplished just a few nights before, but Sandy had not gotten the praise from Hamilton that she thought her heroics would incur. Instead, he was only mildly appreciative. He had purchased something from her. She had delivered it. The transaction was over as far as he was concerned. She wondered why she needed his approval so badly.

Now Hamilton stood behind Sandy, unmoving, making her feel self-conscious. She was dressed in civilian clothes, and peeking out from beneath her tank top, he could clearly see an inky stain.

"You have a tattoo." It was not a question; rather, he said it faintly as though he were thinking out loud.

"Yeah," she said, not looking up from her work. "It's my regimental tat. We all got them done together." Sandy smiled, remembering a happy, youthful day when she and her comrades had gone to a tattoo parlour, laughing all the while.

"I see," he said grimly.

Sandy's reminiscence turned sour as the happy memory faded into a vision of her friends' tattooed flesh rotting to dust in their graves.

Sandy tried to change the subject. "Do you have any? Tattoos, I mean."

"Absolutely not," Hamilton asserted.

Sandy looked up. She had not thought her question offensive, but Hamilton's tone suggested he had taken umbrage. Sandy's white phone rang, a welcome reprieve from the awkward silence.

To Hamilton's further annoyance, she excused herself. Even though she had turned her back to him, he kept his eyes fixed on her.

After ending the call, she turned back towards him and said, "I have to go. That was the hospital. Sorry. It's an emergency." She signed out of the computer projection's interface and departed without a moment's hesitation, leaving Hamilton quietly seething in the lab.

###

Massi stood with his back against the wall in one of the Academy's large courtyards. By his side was Jared Fletcher, one of the few cadets who was still speaking to him. Jared had no friends either. He had a round, flat face speckled with acne and, despite all the physical exercise required of the cadets, still appeared stocky. It was just his build. He even moved in a lumbering, clumsy way. Massi thought Jared was the most unappealing teenager he had ever seen, but he was also the only teenager still willing to talk to him, so there they were. Massi was looking out into the courtyard when a gaggle of excited girls entered from the opposite side and moved in their direction. They were squealing and chattering with delight.

"What's going on with them?" Massi said.

"Amos Harling is giving a surprise lecture at the Academy," replied Jared.

"Who's Amos Harling?" asked Massi.

"A sex god," said Rebecca Andrews as she and the other girls fluttered past them on their way to the main lecture hall.

"He's a financial systems expert," said Jared. "He's employed by Intelligence Command on the West Coast, but he does consulting, too, I believe." Jared was good for something after all.

"How does everyone know except me?"

"It was in an email just now; don't you check?" asked Jared.

"I swear I checked just earlier."

"You'd best check again. They'll be furious if you don't know your stats."

Massi walked back to the computer lab. He'd thought his emails had seemed delayed during the past week. Now he knew he was not dreaming. When he reached the lab, he found Natalia there at her usual station.

"Have you heard?" asked Natalia, turning to him and grinning brightly. "Amos Harling is giving a lecture. This is the best thing that's ever happened to me. He's almost never on the East Coast. He's either in California or surfing somewhere exotic." She was swooning.

"No, I haven't heard," said Massi begrudgingly. "I checked my email this morning, but mine don't seem to be getting through as fast as everyone else's."

Natalia looked away.

"It's like I'm being frozen out!"

"Have you thought about why that might be?" Natalia nudged.

"It's just unfair. They're just doing it to spite me."

"Perhaps whoever doing it is doing it to test you rather than to spite you."

"It can't be the Academy; they're not allowed to treat some students different from others. It's against the guidelines."

"If you say so." Natalia rolled her eyes.

Sandy raced down the hospital corridor and stopped in the open doorway of the private, quiet room. Her excitement evaporated. Luca was in his usual comatose state. She felt like a burst balloon. *I'm such a fool!* Why had she expected anything to be different? She sat beside the bed, feeling numb and impotent. The colour drained from her cheeks as she attempted to extinguish her hopes of him waking up. She felt under the covers for Luca's hand and gripped it tenderly, willing him to react. In the semi-darkness of the hospital room, she allowed herself to feel all the emotions she usually kept beneath an airtight seal. Tears streamed down her cheeks, but she made no noise; she simply let herself be in the moment.

Dr Reuben strode purposefully into the room, disturbing Sandy's solace. Startled by her presence, the young doctor let out a little yelp.

"Oh, hello. You got here very fast," Dr Reuben said, regaining her pleasant composure.

"Yes, I was working nearby." Sandy turned away and wiped her tears.

"Okay." The doctor could sense Sandy's disappointment. "Lieutenant Scott may look the same, but actually there has been some progress."

"Oh yes?" Sandy perked up.

"We've put him through the first stage of nano treatment, and his body has responded well. There was some damaged tissue in the brain and nervous system that we missed, and the nano bots have repaired it. We're now going into the final stages, and the bots are going over his body again to check that there is no more damaged tissue that we missed the first time or in any of our scans."

"Do you think you'll find anything?"

"I couldn't possibly say. When I say we found damaged tissue, we're not talking great swathes. We're tinkering around the edges, but the damaged tissue was in the brain."

"He's healthy, basically," Sandy said.

"Yes, very healthy in fact." The doctor hesitated before adding, "Physically."

"Then why is he still in a vegetative state?" asked Sandy.

"Humans are not like machines, Sandy. You can treat them in a perfect way, but sometimes they still won't do what you want them to."

Sandy nodded.

"I have to leave you now, but before you go, there are some forms you need to sign. We need your consent to continue treatment."

Sandy nodded again, and Dr Reuben backed out of the room without making another sound.

After leaving the computer lab, Massi went straight to the canteen. He grabbed a tray and some cutlery and helped himself to the Academy's usual offerings of lean meats, nutritious stews, and sautéed and roasted vegetables, all of which were served by a surly kitchen staffer. The food was neither Spartan nor rich, and there was never any dessert other than fresh fruit and Greek yoghurt. Sitting down with his tray, Massi tucked into his meal without looking up. Out of the blue he smelt something foul. He sniffed and looked around. The canteen had gone quiet. He realised that the room was predominantly full of male cadets, as most of the girls had gone to the Amos Harling lecture. The boys were looking at him, some of them smiling. Massi took the knife and jabbed at his stew. He hit something firm and uncooked. He flicked it over and saw the beheaded, furry, rotting carcass of a rat. Heaving, Massi sprung to his feet. He had already swallowed three full spoonfuls of the stuff. He tried to grab the tray and leave the canteen with dignity, but as he walked to the waste bins, he dropped his tray and vomited forcefully. The boys let out a roaring laugh as he slipped in his own sick and fell to the floor. Massi was so nauseated he thought he was going to pass out. A teacher whose name he did not know pulled him by his upper arm and escorted him to the medical centre. He managed to walk despite being doubled over in pain and feeling as though all fluids had evaporated from his body. He collapsed onto a bed, and before the matron could attach a saline drip to his arm, he emptied his stomach two more times.

As he lay back on the pillow, he remembered his childhood dreams. He had longed to be a soldier. Being accepted to the Academy had been the happiest moment of his life thus far. Even his father had wept with pride. His childhood dreams were now something terrible. Something he had to survive.

###

At the hospital, Sandy signed papers agreeing to proceed with the final rounds of Luca's current treatment. After leaving, however, she could not bring herself to go back to the InfoSec lab straight away. She walked through a nearby public park and sat on a bench, trying to process and compose her emotions. Hamilton's project had distracted her from her reality. A reality she did not like. She was usually so good at banishing Luca from her thoughts, but when he did enter them, he lingered. She meandered through the park's paths and then made her way to the shops adjacent to the park. She ate by herself at a nearby Italian restaurant, where she chose a piping hot dish of carbonara that offered her the comfort she needed, until she lost her appetite halfway through.

When she finally returned to the lab, Farlow was waiting for her.
"Mr Hamilton wants a word," he said colourlessly.
"I imagine he does," she replied. Her tone was insolent.

As she made her way to Hamilton's office, Farlow paced behind her. When she slowed, Farlow prodded the small of her back ever so slightly with an open palm, pressuring her to her pick up the pace. Soon enough, Sandy found herself standing in front of Hamilton. He was writing at his desk and made no effort to look up at her.

Growing impatient, Sandy said, rather insincerely, "I'm sorry I was away from the project for so long this afternoon."

Hamilton stopped writing and folded the piece of paper he had been working on.

"I really had hopes for a higher level of professionalism, Lieutenant."

"I said I was sorry, but it couldn't be helped."

"I think it could have been. You left the hospital three hours before you returned to this building."

"Are you having me followed?" she asked in alarm.

"I called the hospital and asked."

"Ah, my mistake." She flushed with embarrassment.

"I don't appreciate that you abandon the work I pay you to do in order to see to personal affairs and emotional issues," he said.

"My apologies." Her eyes were still red, and her face was pale. "It won't happen again."

"Good. I would hate for us to fall out. I have enjoyed working with you. I thought you were a professional; that's all."

"The model is almost done," she said, looking vulnerable.

"But it's not complete, is it?"

"We're nearly there."

"But we're not there," said Hamilton.

"I'll put in some extra hours tomorrow."

"Wonderful. That should do it. Off you go now."

Sandy did not welcome being spoken to as if she were a naughty child, but she held her tongue.

CHAPTER FIFTEEN

Sandy had just turned seven years old the first time she was shot. The bullet had grazed her left arm as she ran with the others, clinging to her mother's hand. The pain must have been why she let go. After that, she stumbled but did not fall; her body was kept upright and moving by the flurry of terrified people in the shopping mall. When her feet hit the floor again, instinct took over. She knew she had to keep running, though she could not see where she was going. The crowd lurched in another direction. The exit they had been aiming for was blocked.

PUK! PUK! PUK!

The noises were steady and rhythmic. An adult fell to the ground in front of Sandy. There was glass everywhere; it even seemed to be suspended in the air.

PUK! PUK! PUK!

They were not trying to kill every adult. They were aimlessly firing into the crowd. They were laughing and smiling. They were enjoying it. They wanted the crowd to run, to scream, to writhe and to bleed without dying. They wanted fear.

Sandy could no longer see her mother or father. She felt nauseated from the smell of blood, and her legs were growing weaker. She ducked behind a column, crouching down and making herself as small as possible. The polished, sparkling floor was now a grisly tableau of smears of blood, broken glass, personal items and bodies. From what she had overheard in the news, these types of incidents often ended with an explosion.

She remembered where the entrance to the shopping mall was but did not know how to get there without being spotted. She wondered if the men with guns had moved to a different part of the shopping mall. Their voices were less audible than they had been earlier. Nearby, a man lifted a chair and thumped it against an outside window, willing it to shatter. The commotion lured the gunmen back towards Sandy, and they picked off the distracted man with a single bullet.

Most of the people had now moved towards the main entrance of the mall, but given the amount of noise they were making, Sandy could tell that they were still inside the building. They must be trapped. If the gunmen had blocked the exits, there was no point in going to the entrance.

The small group of masked men walked away from Sandy. She had held her breath, but she could tell they had not seen her. They were preoccupied. The tone of their voices had changed. Something was wrong. They bickered with each other, and Sandy could hear their angry, muffled words.

The light streaming through the arching glass roof became interspersed with rapid, choppy shadows. Sandy looked up. Outside, a helicopter slowed to a halt. A hand emerged from the airborne vehicle and casually flicked an item onto the glass roof below. There was a loud crack, like a firework. Nothing happened. And then, everything happened all at once. The ceiling shattered, and the glass seemed to linger, suspended in mid-air for a second before crashing to the tiled floor below. Sandy instinctively protected her head with her arms. Without hesitation, three figures wearing blurred combat suits and masks leapt from the chopper and landed on the splintered floor. It took mere seconds for the suited figures to immobilise the distracted gunmen.

PUK! PUK! PUK! PUK! PUK!

The gunmen fell to the floor like skittles at a bowling alley. Before running to the gunmen's bodies, the suited figures detached the thick, black cables that had lowered them into the mall. Sandy watched in absolute silence. They fiddled with what looked like a solid, dark cube about the size of a footstool. After a few intense moments, they relaxed. One of the figures spoke muffled words, possibly talking into a mic. He then instructed the other two to grab the bodies of the gunmen and drag them to the cables still hanging from the chopper. The bloody assailants were lifted into the sky and pulled into the vehicle as it flew off.

A different helicopter moved into position, and more suited figures, these wearing white uniforms, dropped into the cavity. They ran to the dark cube and erected a triangular metal structure around it. They moved away from it, and soon after, a dull, hollow bang came from within the structure as it puffed up like an exploding kernel of corn. The white suits casually walked back towards it, chatting and gesturing as they went. The bomb had been defused.

A gust of fresh, cool air coming from the direction of the main entrance stroked Sandy's cheek. The doors were open. Sandy crawled out from her hiding place, keeping her eyes on the suited figures. She could tell by their relaxed postures that all threats were now gone. She had the urge to approach the suited figures. She liked the way the fabric of the combat suits shimmered and, at some angles, appeared almost translucent. She tried to stand, but her legs failed her. Slumping back down, her thoughts turned to her mother and father. Soon, however, she found herself scooped into the warm arms of a man in a blue uniform, who carried her towards the wide, open entrance of the mall. The building was filling up with aid workers searching for survivors. They scurried in and leant over bodies, checking pulses and moving the groaning, injured victims into more comfortable positions. Sandy looked up at the man carrying her and studied his face. She could still remember every curve of his chin, every blade of dark stubble. He did not look down at her until he placed her in the back of a waiting ambulance. Their eyes met. She would never forget their light-blue shade. He then walked back inside the building, as if he had not just rescued a little girl. He was just doing his job.

Emergency services workers were already removing bodies, some in black bags and others on stretchers, from the building. A lady with a kind face checked Sandy over and cleaned her cuts, all of which were superficial—even the graze on her left arm. A handful of other survivors were asked to sit in the ambulance for a short while until those with minor injuries could be taken to the hospital for further checks. Before they closed the ambulance doors, Sandy scanned the faces of the injured and weeping. Her parents were not among them.

###

Along with three other frightened children, Sandy waited in a hospital room until late into the evening. The room was quiet except for a smattering of snuffles and gentle sobs. A familiar face burst through the doors, disturbing the silence. Sandy was swept up into Cora's large, warm arms, and the stunned little girl gripped her tightly. Grateful to have privacy at last, Sandy buried her face in her aunt's oversized coat before being whisked to a rental car waiting outside.

Cora buckled Sandy into the front seat. After strapping herself into the driver's seat, she stared into the distance for a moment and then began to sob. Sandy said nothing and watched as her aunt broke down, her hands gripping the steering wheel tightly. After a few minutes, she composed herself and started the car.

Without looking at Sandy she said, "I've just seen your parents." She paused. "They won't be coming home with us today. We're going to get your sister. I'll be sleeping at your house tonight. Tomorrow, you'll both come home with me."

###

Years later, Sandy believed she had forgotten the exact moment she was told her parents were dead. She could not remember who had broken the news to her. The truth was that no one had ever explicitly sat her down and told her. Life would go on, but differently, and she was expected to accept a new reality. She would live with her mother's elder sister rather than either of her grandparents, a decision she assumed was made because Cora was the only one with room enough to take in both Sandy and her only sibling. Neither Sandy nor her sister had been present for that conversation.

The first explicit acknowledgement that her parents were dead was at the funeral itself. Sandy had been told to put on a black dress selected for her by her aunt. Her sister had been crying all morning. Her cousins, William and Caroline, were wearing black too. They looked sad, but they were not crying. Sandy was not crying either; she preferred to cry alone. Especially at night. She missed her mother's stories at bedtime and her father's soft kisses on the top of her head in the mornings before he left for work.

It had rained the night before, and the air smelt like wet grass. The ceremony was brief. The caskets had been lowered into the earth before the funeral service and were now buried in fresh, thick, wet clods.

The tombstone read:

IN LOVING MEMORY OF
AARON & PHOEBE ATTIYEH

AN AFFECTIONATE SON, HUSBAND AND FATHER
A DEVOTED DAUGHTER, WIFE AND MOTHER

BELOVED BY ALL WHO KNEW THEM
TAKEN BEFORE THEIR TIME

Sandy had been too young to recall what the priest had said, but she did remember that for almost the entire day, someone had been holding her hand. At first it was Cora, then her grandmother, then her other grandmother; her hand was passed from relative to relative throughout the day as if she were an emotional parcel. The adults at the funeral looked at the little girl sympathetically, but nobody really spoke to her. Instead they talked *at* her. Sometimes they answered their own questions. "You'll be just fine, won't you? Yes, you will. Brave girl." And other such platitudes. They seemed to be more tactile with her elder sister, who was more visibly in distress. Sandy continued to wander around the funeral until it ended. The expression fixed on her face was one of stunned grief, which did not ease until she was tucked into bed by her aunt at the end of a very long, sad day.

Two months later, Cora sat at her bureau writing in her journal and reflecting on the sorrow-filled length of time since her sister and brother-in-law had died. Her reading glasses had slid a little way down her nose. Her study was filled with warm, yellow afternoon sunlight; it was her favourite place in the whole house. A house now filled with twice as many children. Cora was overwhelmed, but she was managing. She was just not the type of person who went to pieces under strain. Not for very long, anyway.

She felt two dark eyes looking at her. She turned to see Sandy standing in the doorway. After a pause, Cora spoke first.

"Sweetie? Is something wrong?" Cora always involuntarily adopted a warm, calm voice when speaking to children.

"It's about school," Sandy began.

"School?"

"I don't want to go to South Street Elementary."

"Sandy, please—don't be difficult. This has been hard to arrange at the last minute. They didn't have any spaces; they took account that you were a special case."

Cora's exasperation was lost on young Sandy. "I'm not going."

"Why aren't you going? It's a nice school, and it's close. Caroline goes there, and she loves it. They have a good theatre programme. You'll like that."

"I want to go somewhere else."

"What somewhere else?" Cora held up her hands in vexation.

"I want to go to the Magnus Ryde Academy."

"Sandy, that's a military school." Her aunt looked perplexed.

"I know. I want to go there." Sandy's voice was serious and firm. Too self-assured for a child her age. Years later, Cora would look back at this moment and realise it was the first time the adult Sandy began to appear.

"No," Cora said emphatically. "It's in the opposite direction of South Street and Billy's middle school. I don't think they allow boarding for your age. I'd have to drop you there every morning."

"I'll walk, then. I'm not going to middle school like Billy."

"What are you going to do then?"

"I'm going to the National Academy. I read about it online."

"You're seven, sweetie. You don't have to make decisions like that yet."

"That's where I want to go." The look in Sandy's eyes was cold and unfeeling. Something about the little girl's lack of emotion alarmed Cora.

"You can go if you really want. But you know there won't be as many girls for you to play with."

"I don't care about that. I've made up my mind."

"But it will be hard. It's not all running around outdoors."

"If you don't let me go, I'll never forgive you."

Cora understood this was not an idle threat. "Okay, I'll call Magnus Ryde tomorrow, and I'll see if they have any places. If they don't, please don't blame me."

"They will have places. They don't get enough girls. I looked it up already."

"Why don't you go play outside, Sandy? Don't spend so much time at the computer. It's a lovely day."

Sandy did not reply; instead, she left the room as silently as she had entered it, leaving Cora with a lingering feeling of unease.

CHAPTER SIXTEEN

Hamilton entered his pristine lab and was greeted by an unwelcome sight. Sandy Attiyeh was not working; instead, she was playing with her black phone and reclining in her chair with her feet propped on a desk. The model was switched off. Since it dominated the lab, its absence was conspicuous.

"May I enquire as to why you are not working?" Hamilton demanded.

"There's no more work left to do." Sandy spoke without looking up at him.

"So, the model is complete?" he inquired.

"Yes. The model is done."

"This has taken longer than I had hoped."

"Yes, I thought it would be finished sooner too." She put her phone down and met his gaze. "As I was working I noticed that the entire model was riddled with bugs. They were left there by someone before me."

"Ah, well, the person who was working on this before you...wasn't very good." He paused. "That's why I fired her, of course."

Sandy stood up so suddenly, so furiously, that her chair tipped over backwards.

"Don't you dare say that. Don't you dare. She was very good; she was excellent, in fact." She and Hamilton stared at each other intensely. Sandy was livid. Her anger had gone from zero to sixty in a second. "Those bugs were left there deliberately. They were hard for me to untangle. They were put there to sabotage the project, weren't they?" A rhetorical question.

"What did you do? What did you do to the model?" Hamilton said, panicking, his usual stoic countenance disintegrating.

"Relax, I just switched it off."

He limbered to the console and fiddled with the panel until the model sprang back to life. A look of relief swept over his face. For a few seconds, he looked euphoric. He jabbed his hands at the projection, trying to use it as Sandy had showed him. However, the neon-green digital planet Earth was unresponsive to his touch. The screen read:

INVALID COMMAND
INVALID COMMAND
INVALID COMMAND
INVALID COMMAND
INVALID COMMAND
INVALID COMMAND

"What have you done? Where has it gone?" His panic rose again.

"Chill out. I just locked it."

"Locked it?" he asked, turning and looking at her intensely.

"Encrypted key-code." She shrugged. "Fairly standard, but with my personal touch."

He loomed over her. Despite being about five metres away, Hamilton's height now felt intimidating to Sandy. She was apprehensive, though still confident she could best him in any physical tussle. Hamilton was tall, but he was definitely not a fighter. Nothing about his body suggested he was a brute. Considering his measured way of moving and talking, Sandy guessed he did not like getting his hands dirty. That was not his way.

"I paid you. The work is done. Give me the code, then leave."

"What type of colossal idiot do you take me for? Even if I were going to hand the key-code to you, it's worth ten times what you paid me," she sniggered.

"I'll give you more money."

"It's not happening," said Sandy shaking her head.

"You're being dishonourable. I paid you. Give me what you owe me."

"I'm the dishonourable one, am I?" Sandy chuckled.

"You owe me," He repeated. Hamilton was fuming. "I saved you. I know what you were doing on that balcony the first night we met. I saved your life. I saved you from yourself."

Sandy flinched.

Hamilton continued. "With this model, I could save everyone else on this festering planet, just like I saved you."

"You want me to believe that saving people and the planet is the real purpose of this? You want control; that's it. That's all this is. Why don't you run for the Ruling Council instead of this shit?" She gesticulated at the projection.

"You know nothing of my intentions."

"Oh? Pure as the driven snow, are they?"

"My intentions are pure," he announced sincerely.

"You want to pump the world with your own personal propaganda. You want to manipulate the news and the climate of opinion until the only rational way for people to act is the way you would have them act."

"Don't you see? I will make the world perfect. I will change this world. Without the shot of a single gun. Without leaving my office." Hamilton did not deny Sandy's accusations. "I will diminish human suffering and eradicate the last of the squalor left on Earth. I will teach them discipline. I will teach them how to delay gratification. I will teach them how to forgo the transient pleasures of the flesh. When humanity reaches its true potential, when everyone is happy, living cleanly, rich and healthy – then I will be vindicated. I will be a hero. Right now, you are standing in my way."

"How can you be so stupid? How much control do you really think you'd have? Life is messy. It was always messy, and it always will be. And you know what? I like it that way." She softened her tone. "Enjoy it. Don't fight it."

Her words fell on deaf ears, and Hamilton refused to yield. Behind Sandy, Farlow entered the dark lab. By his side were half a dozen members of Hamilton's security team. Sandy looked over her shoulder and nodded. So, this was how it was going to be. She calculated if she could take them out as well.

"You don't leave until I get what I'm owed," Hamilton said.

Sandy smiled disingenuously then dipped down retrieving the pistol strapped to her right ankle in one lightning quick, fluid motion.

"Touch me and he dies," she said to the men behind her holding the gun pointed at Hamilton. Hamilton's security team stood still. While everyone froze, Sandy's eyes looked for options. Hamilton was standing between her and the private entrance she had been using to get to the lab unseen. Farlow and the security team were standing at the only other door.

"Move," she said to Hamilton.

He did not budge or even react to her words.

"Move," she repeated.

Still, Hamilton did not shift. He looked relaxed.

"Move or I will kill you," said Sandy brandishing her weapon more aggressively at Hamilton. Hamilton's security team flinched as if they were eager to pounce on her but had to stop themselves.

Then Hamilton laughed to himself.

"Don't worry, boys, it's not loaded," said Hamilton.

The smirk dropped from Sandy's face.

"I looked you up on the model." Hamilton chuckled to himself. "At first I thought it was rather odd that you put yourself in, but then I realised you were using yourself to beta-test it, and you'd filled your files with fiction. I had someone else do some real research on you while you were preoccupied. I've always found it fascinating: what people want the world to know about them versus everything there is to know about someone. People usually don't lie. They just don't tell everyone everything. Anyway...that gun isn't military issue. You bought it fairly recently because of the protestors. They scare you more than you like to admit. We do the security for that arms shop. Only took a few minutes with a facial recognition program to find that on the day you bought that gun you never bothered buying bullets. Aside from the legality and dangers of carrying a loaded gun around everywhere, someone like you would know that statistically, in most cases, just brandishing a gun is enough to get you out of imperilling situations. The threat of violence is a powerful thing."

Sandy exhaled, subliminally acknowledging that she had been bested. She lowered her pistol, dropping it on the floor, and raised her arms in surrender.

Hamilton grinned triumphantly. "And you think you're not just like me."

She was then robbed of the rest of her personal belongings and manhandled down to a cell in the basement of the InfoSec building.

###

Sandy's cell was not uncomfortable, though it was very small. The walls were an off-white colour. A simple bed was opposite a lidless steel latrine. The door was heavily bolted on the outside but became a seamless part of the room when closed. It was inlaid with a large Perspex window with small holes in it. Sandy had now spent a full day in the cell and had passed the time reclining on the bed, considering her strategy. Hamilton would not kill her before he had the key-code. But after? She had no idea. Regardless, someone would notice her absence eventually. But how would anyone know where she was? She felt a pang of regret for not letting at least one person know she had been spending time with Hamilton. Maybe it would have been a better strategy to lock the model and disappear. She knew why she had not done so, however: she had wanted to confront Hamilton and experience the thrill of an adversary once more. Her wish had been granted.

Two men in InfoSec security uniforms unbolted the door to her cell, causing a loud <u>clunk</u>. Sandy sprang up from her resting place, and, for a moment, the men only stared. Then one of them stepped forward and grabbed Sandy, pulling her upwards. She was wearing a black tank top with a lightweight, hooded black long-sleeved jacket and a pair of jeans. (After Hamilton's reaction to her tattoo, Sandy had begun dressing more conservatively.) The two men pinned Sandy to the wall and deprived her of her jeans and jacket. She was left in her underwear and tank top, hastily trying to recall her physical assault training. Until now, she had not needed it. Until now, she had never been caught. The two men kicked her clothes aside and dragged her out of the cell and into a long corridor. Once at the end of the corridor, they pushed her into what initially appeared to be a large kitchen.

Across the room, Hamilton and Farlow leant against the counters, looking suspiciously casual. Now that Sandy could see better, she realised the room was more like a chemistry lab than a kitchen. Lining the walls were dozens of shelves full of clean bottles, racks of test tubes and complex glass flasks. Sandy closed her eyes for a moment and contemplated just how badly she had misread Hamilton. She did not think Hamilton would kill her. He would never get the key-code if he did. But it was more than just that, she reasoned: he did not want to kill her. He wanted her to agree with him and with his plans. He wanted her to tell him how clever and wonderful he was. *Tough*, she thought. She would not lie. Not even to save herself.

The two men holding her arms pushed her forward. Hamilton gestured at the counter next to him, and they then forced Sandy to place her left arm on it. It was then that she saw the Bunsen burner, lit and hissing furiously. Farlow turned, and Sandy saw the knife. Farlow held it over the flame until it glowed an ominous red.

Farlow then turned to Hamilton and said, "The chip first?"

Hamilton nodded.

Farlow removed the blade from the flame and took two steps towards Sandy before deftly dragging the sharp knife into her left wrist. Sandy gasped and looked at Hamilton, disbelieving. Farlow halted momentarily, leaving the blade buried in Sandy's wrist. He turned towards his boss and said, "She's not even screaming. This one is going to be no fun."

Hamilton sniggered and said, "Continue."

Within a few seconds, Farlow had removed Sandy's chip. He flicked it onto the counter, where it lay covered in blood. Clutching her left arm, Sandy slid away from the counter and fell to the floor. The two uniformed InfoSec men picked her up and pulled her onto the counter so that she was lying on her back. Hamilton looked over her lean body in disgust.

"So many scars. Hideous," he said to himself.

Farlow returned to the Bunsen burner, where he paused, waiting for Hamilton's instructions.

"Top of the thighs first, I think, Farlow," said Hamilton, as if he were reciting a recipe.

Farlow pressed the side of the red-hot blade onto Sandy's upper right thigh for several seconds. This time she did scream. She squealed and writhed in agony. Farlow, seeming pleased with himself, reheated the knife and repeated the torturous act on her left thigh. Two matching red welts quickly formed on her legs.

"Hmm," mused Hamilton, "top of the chest and her upper arms on the sides."

Exactly as instructed, Farlow proceeded to press the side of the burning blade onto Sandy's body. Four new shark-fin–shaped welts appeared on her skin. The two security guards holding her down were sweating and panting, as they had to use all their weight to keep her on the counter.

"Flip her over." Hamilton sounded bored, as though he were giving instructions on setting up furniture.

The men flipped Sandy onto her belly. Her energy for fighting was running out. The counter felt cool against her wounds at first, but then the pain increased. Sandy felt her mind go blank. She could no longer tolerate the pain. She felt as if she were watching the sorry scene from outside her body, hovering above it all. Farlow made eight more triangular burns: two on the sides of her thighs, two on the backs of her thighs, two above her buttocks and two on her upper back.

"Ah, I nearly forgot," Hamilton added. "Soles of the feet."

It was the burn on her left heel that shocked Sandy awake before she slipped back into darkness.

Her body was cool, but her mouth was dry. Her black-ops suit had a hydropack in it with a tube feeding water to her mouth, but she was drawing from it sparingly. She saw the tents lit up in the distance. Each one had a slightly different hue. How beautiful they looked. Her target was in one of those tents. The desert was so dark and the night was so clear that she could see any star that wanted to be seen. She could also approach the tents without being noticed, her mechanical second skin making her invisible at night. She felt apprehensive but not scared. The worst-case scenario was that he was not here, that the intelligence was wrong—that the intelligence another officer had died for was wrong.

Her dream was interrupted by ice-cold water on her back. It felt like pure bliss. It washed away the oppressive, searing heat of her wounds. But only for a moment. She gasped. Hamilton lumbered over to her.

"I'm not giving you the key-code," she rasped. She was only semi-lucid.

"I didn't ask for it," he replied obtusely. "We knew you'd be a...slow burner." He almost laughed at his own joke. "But I'll get what I want—what I paid for—eventually."

The two security guards were no longer holding Sandy down. They did not need to. Hamilton turned to Farlow.

"Finished?"

"Yes, sir," said Farlow. "Unless..."

"Unless?"

"Just one more? On her face this time?"

"Not today."

Farlow let out a disappointed sigh.

"Let's keep our powder dry for now," Hamilton shot back.

Farlow turned off the flame, and the room fell oddly silent. Sandy, still face down on the counter, saw Hamilton's shoes move into her line of sight.

"I honestly didn't think you'd be difficult, Sandy. I like you. I really do. I've gathered that not many people feel the same way these days."

Sandy closed her eyes. Her voice was hoarse and faint. "I knew you were a bad thing from the start."

"That makes me sad." His tone was sarcastic. "Why did you agree to help me, then? Ah, that's right, nothing else to do. Wasting away. Waiting for your lover to rise from the dead and carry you off into the sunset."

"Shut up," Sandy whispered.

Hamilton seemed irked. "What's his name? Lucian. Luca."

"Shut up," she repeated.

"That's what you call him, isn't it?"

"Shut up." Her voice was getting fainter.

"Wasn't it you who caused his little mishap? That's what I heard."

She did not reply.

He continued. "You tried to save him from that ambush, didn't you? The one that wiped out the rest of your regiment. But you failed, and now they're all dead, and he's broken beyond repair. Your sorry behind had to be saved as well."

Drawing from a deep well of rage, Sandy mustered all her remaining strength to turn her neck and spit right in his face. Hamilton reeled backwards in disgust. Farlow lunged forward and punched Sandy firmly in the jaw.

"Hand me the knife," Hamilton angrily commanded Farlow, who did as he was ordered.

Grabbing a fistful of Sandy's hair, Hamilton pushed her face into the counter. He leant in close, lowering himself to her level, and spoke in a slow, aggressive whisper. "I want nothing more than to press this knife into your flesh and cut that filthy tattoo out of your skin. But I won't." He shook his head and lowered the knife. "I'm not an animal.

I can control my baser instincts. I could teach the whole world to rise above the parts of them that are still animal."

All that she could manage was to softly utter, "Is that so?"

"Why can't you see that I'm doing this for the greater good?" Hamilton asked quickly and angrily, pulling her hair even harder.

Sandy spat a wad of bloody saliva onto the floor before turning to Hamilton. "Because you're the one holding the knife."

CHAPTER SEVENTEEN

Several members of Muro's team stood in front of her desk, all of them looking sheepish. Among them were Manning, Hackett and Gerald.

"You can't find her?" Muro's screech was so loud they all flinched. "Useless. Useless! Sometimes I wonder how we won the damn war." She stood up and paced around her office to calm herself down. "Okay, tell me what we know so far."

Hackett and Manning looked at each other, willing the other to speak first.

It was Gerald who finally delivered the bad news. "Sandy left her apartment at zero nine thirty the day before yesterday, according to the porter of her building. She didn't return that evening and hasn't been back to the building since. We've checked the surveillance footage in the places she usually eats and shops. There's no sign of her. We've called her known relatives and acquaintances—though there are very few of them—with the exception of Lyndon Hamilton, who's under investigation in another missing-persons case, as per your instructions. Her aunt confirmed that Sandy isn't at her childhood home and hasn't been in contact recently, though that isn't thought to be atypical behaviour."

"Thank you, Gerald. Does anybody have anything else to add?"

"I tried calling her yesterday," said Phillip Manning, "but the call was intentionally rejected. She doesn't usually do that. Not to me. I tried calling later in the evening, and the phone had been switched off. We couldn't trace it."

"Maybe she knows we intended to tail her?" Hackett added, eyeing Manning suspiciously.

"Not unless you told her," barked Manning, angry at the insinuation.

"Okay, that's enough of this. I need to think," Muro said, anguished.

Her team shuffled out of the room. Once they were gone, Muro called Sandy. The phone was unreachable, as Manning had said. Muro cursed herself. She had ignored and rebuffed Sandy's calls all year, and now that she needed to speak to her, she was nowhere to be found. Typical. Muro gripped the phone so tightly it almost cracked. She had intended to throw it, but she stopped herself and instead sat down. She inhaled deeply. There was now only one stone left unturned—the one that had been deliberately avoided.

Muro closed her eyes and rubbed her temples. She did not want Sandy to be in trouble. She wanted Sandy out of her life, yes, but she also genuinely wanted Sandy to be happy. Though Sandy had aced the test in the vertical farm complex, her recent behaviour was not consistent with that of a sound military operative. Consequently, Muro did not feel an ounce of guilt for sidelining her. While it was not what Sandy wanted, Muro could not jeopardise the lives of other agents and compromise missions by using a combatant whom she did not entirely trust. She could not discharge Sandy without reason, though she had done everything in her power to find one, and the girl would not resign. Muro sincerely hoped that Sandy would move on from her military days, take up a hobby and find someone to settle down with.

Neither did Muro like the fact that Sandy was keeping Lucian Scott alive or that she had been subjecting him to further treatments. Still, Muro had never seen Scott as her personal responsibility. She chided herself for not keeping a closer eye on that situation. But how could she have? She had an international security agency to run—sure, the job was easier in peacetime, but it was still a huge responsibility. If Scott were to die, news of his death would make headlines because of his valiant service in the Long War. It would also draw attention to two operations, Surabaya and Locket Vault, which Muro preferred not to think about.

In Surabaya, IC had lost more operatives in a single night than it had in the preceding eighteen months. Her son had been maimed during Locket Vault. She pushed the images out of her head. All her tears had already been shed. Since the end of the war, Sandy had hung around ICHQ like a bad smell; her sudden disappearance was so out of character it made Muro fretful for her safety. Sandy's premature death would also be a PR disaster. Commander Nichols already liked to mock Muro for her personnel's high fatality rate during the war. Losing control and, subsequently, the life of a high-profile operative like Sandy in peacetime might prompt her own resignation. Muro knew what she had to do. She arranged a meeting with Drummond for early the following morning.

###

Five senior officers, including Colonel Mathers, were seated at a long table in front of Massi. His shoulders straight and tense, Massi sat facing them but not at the table itself. His hands were clasped and nestled in his lap. He felt exposed and vulnerable. One of the panelists, a woman with glasses and a neat bun on the top of her head, used a transcription device to record the hearing. As soon as she had acknowledged that the machine was up and running, the hearing began.

The woman leading the hearing spoke first. She was in her mid-forties and had short, bobbed hair. "Cadet, we understand you've filed a formal complaint. Could you please elaborate for the panel?"

Massi cleared his throat. "I feel that I'm being bullied. I'm being deliberately targeted. I don't know why."

"What makes you believe this?" she asked, looking at him innocently.

"Before, it was just teasing." Massi said soberly. "Now my locker and the stuff in the barracks are regularly tampered with. My food was contaminated. I was hung up on the flagpole."

"Who are the individuals doing this, the tampering and so forth?"

"Well, the flagpole thing, I didn't see their faces. I don't know. I'm not there in the barracks when they touch my stuff. I don't know how they have a key to my locker. I still don't know how they snuck the rat into my food."

"So, you can't name any names?"

"Not exactly, but it's like they're all in on it. So many of them have just stopped talking to me. It's like they're organised."

Another member of the panel, a balding man, said, "Organised? Could you elaborate on that, please?"

"It's like there's a group of them doing it, and they plan these sneak attacks."

The man continued, "Are you sure this isn't friendly roughhousing?"

"Friendly?! There's nothing friendly about this. I'm not friends with these guys."

The first woman responded instantly: "Cadet, these guys are your fellow soldiers and trainees. We expect you to have cordial relationships within your unit. You are a part of a team."

"Then why are they bullying me? They don't seem to care about having a good relationship with me."

Colonel Mathers interjected, "You don't think you're like them?"

Massi hesitated and reluctantly asked, "In what ways?"

"You tell us," said the balding man sitting to the left of the colonel.

"I don't think I'm different. We're all cadets, right?"

The panel did not respond for several minutes, making Massi think that perhaps he had finally given them an answer they wanted.

Breaking the silence, Colonel Mathers said, "You need to deal with this, cadet. If I have to tell you again, I will have to begin formal proceedings against you, and that would give me no pleasure."

"Against me?" Massi objected.

"We feel that if you were removed from the equation, there would be no more discord among your year of male cadets."

The woman with the bobbed hair added, "Do you want to stay in the Academy or not?"

"I want to stay," he said, the hurt he was feeling now evident in his voice.

"Are you sure?" she asked.

"Yes. I want to be here. It's all I've ever wanted."

"Then I'm afraid you'll have to try harder to be a part of the team," said the first woman, "I'm bringing this panel to a close. You don't have specific complaints about any individual in particular, so I don't see what action we can take, anyway. The people in your year will soon be your fellow comrades in arms. Perhaps you should consider what you must do to fix the broken dynamic between you and your unit. You may leave."

Massi left the meeting feeling more confused and frustrated than ever. He knew he should head back to the barracks. He should spend more time with the other male cadets, but he did not want to. He wanted the sweet succour he found only in Natalia. The scent of her hair. He wanted to look at the way her uniform clung to her body. If only she would let him touch her just a little bit more. He needed to stay at the

Academy and graduate; then he would get to touch her. He knew it. He still wanted to succeed at the Academy, but he wanted her, too. Those two goals had become inextricably entwined. Whenever one appeared within his grasp, the other seemed a dream. It was as though the two could not exist together.

He entered the computer lab and found her sitting in her usual spot. He strolled in and leant against the wall but did not sit down.

"I've just been to the panel to discuss my complaint. That was a waste of time."

Natalia did not respond, so he moved around the room to try and catch her eye.

"Nat, you know why they're treating this like it's my fault. Don't you?"

She said nothing.

"Nat?"

She blanked him completely. He was hurt by her silence. It was the cruellest thing she could do, far worse than her being angry at him. He moved behind her chair and leant down. He needed her to engage with him.

"Nat, please," he whispered in her ear. She pushed him away. "Nat!" He tried to grab her as she stood up.

"Don't touch me," she said firmly.

"I'm sorry. I just want you to tell me what you saw that time you hacked into the Academy's system."

"I already told you." She sounded angry but also hurt. "You can't just come to me when you need something."

"Can you show me again?" His tone became pleading.

"No," she said, reaching into her pocket. She pulled out an ElectroFyte. All the girls in the Academy were equipped with one as a part of their standard kit. "If you make me do anything that I don't want to do ever again, I'll use this. I'm not joking."

"You can't be serious, Nat. I would never hurt you. I would never make you do anything you didn't want to do."

"You already have." She switched off her computer, and without taking her eyes off Massi, she backed out of the room. Massi felt his heart sink in his chest. He had had no idea she would react that way. His mind almost physically hurt trying to understand it. He wondered if he should just leave the Academy. He could not take much more.

Muro stepped out of the elevator and made her way into the swanky rooftop bar. The evening was clear, and the stars sparkled through the giant floor-to-ceiling windows. She scanned the room.

"Reservation under Harling," she said to the hostess without looking at the woman. Muro was dressed in a smart, pale-pink suit jacket with a matching short skirt and high-heeled court shoes.

Harling had already spotted her and was trying to catch her attention. He was also admiring how well preserved she was. She looked good for her age without ever seeming to try too hard.

"There you are, Amos." She kissed him on both cheeks. "I need a strong one this evening."

"Manhattan?" He flagged down a waiter.

"Yes, please. What are you drinking?"

"Cosmopolitan." In his oversized hand, the glass looked almost miniature.

Muro raised an eyebrow.

"What?" he said, laughing. "Surprised I'm not a beer drinker?"

"You don't seem like the type who loves a Cosmo either."

"I'm not. I usually prefer White Russians." He grinned. "I thought since I'm on the East Coast, I should drink a Cosmo, and I'm not afraid to be seen with a pink drink." He winked at her, and she laughed.

"How are things back your way?" she asked.

"The usual. We're not too taxed, to be perfectly honest."

"Yes, I'm having the same problem, really," she lamented. "Things are so dull now, in many ways."

"If there's one thing to be said for war, it's got a sort of excitement." Harling took a swig of his cocktail.

"The trouble is when the real problems go away, smaller, less serious but more annoying ones pop up to replace them," said Muro, musing wistfully.

"How's Martin these days?" he said, changing the subject.

"Amos!" Muro said, deeply offended. "He was killed eight years ago. I thought you knew."

Harling looked up in shock and embarrassment before realising her mistake. "Oh, Claudette, I didn't mean Martin Sr. I meant Martin Jr." He emphasised the last word. "How's your son?"

"Ah, I see." She blushed. "He's well. As well as can be expected."

The waiter returned with her drink. She took hold of it clumsily, only narrowly avoiding spilling it.

"Are you okay?" he inquired. "You seem preoccupied."

"It's this thing with Lyndon Hamilton." She waved her free hand as if to brush away the thought.

"Am I allowed to ask what's the deal with that yet?"

"Oh, it's just a missing-persons case. Some scientist. If we bring Hamilton in about it and he's got nothing to do with it, IC could lose funding. I know that the missing person knew Hamilton, but the connection could be genuinely professional. Now this thing with Sandy..." Muro stopped herself. She should not be discussing this here; still, she longed to confide in someone.

"What's up with Sandy these days, anyway? I've been hearing rumours that she's been giving you trouble for a while now," said Harling almost inaudibly.

"I've done everything I can to get rid of her, but she just won't go. She won't retire. Drummond won't let me fire a perfectly healthy, able soldier with experience. But she's not his problem, is she?"

"I used to be friends with Lucian Scott, you know," Amos said, his voice becoming solemn.

"Ah, Luca." Muro's face softened at the thought of him. "He was friends with everyone. He was the most competent of all my officers. Quiet but so capable. It's always the ones you think are invincible that go in the blink of an eye, and the ones you think won't last a moment who live forever."

Harling paused. Then, in a subdued tone, he said, "What happened to him? What really happened?"

"He was injured in the Surabaya gas attack with the others, from what I recall. It was an ambush. Sandy tried to save him, of course. I would have to look up the details. It's been so long now."

"I was thinking of visiting him at the hospital. Do you know if he'd recognise me?"

"No. He's not able to respond," she said. "I don't think he's coming back, Amos. If you two were close, then his...current state might upset you."

"I think I'll still pay him a visit before I go back to Cali."

"If you go, let me know. I think I need to see him again too. I have to see Drummond tomorrow morning, but we should go together in the afternoon."

###

The next day, Muro regretted the libations of the night before. She could feel her head throb as she stood in front of Drummond's desk, waiting as he looked through the folder she had given him.

"Have you found Sandy yet?" Drummond asked.

"No, but we do think we've found something else."

"The husband?"

"Maria D'Souza's husband is not being cooperative. He still maintains that his wife left him, but there's no trace of her. It seems unusual that she would abandon her child in the manner in which she did."

"Do you think enhanced interrogation would do the trick?"

"Er...no, sir. I don't think that would be necessary in this case."

He continued to read the file. Muro recited its contents in her head, trying to allay her doubts. Maria D'Souza and Hamilton both sympathised with a cult called the Sun Circle Group. That could be a coincidence. Ghost entities gave money to companies in Hamilton's sphere of influence, which then gave huge sums to businesses that relied on Hamilton's custom. Those businesses, in turn, gave money to the Sun Circle Group...though there was no proof Hamilton coerced those businesses into making the donations. Those same ghost entities gave money to Sandy and to Maria D'Souza's daughter. Maybe Sandy gave some speeches or lectures for Hamilton, and maybe Hamilton just felt sorry for the little girl whose mother abandoned her. Maria D'Souza had a professional relationship with Hamilton and may have known him personally, though this was unconfirmed. Sandy had recently become friendly with Hamilton, and Muro had even seen her leaving an event with him. Still, he may have only wanted a quick chat. For a little over seventy-two hours, Sandy's whereabouts had been unaccounted for. This was not, in itself, uncharacteristic. Muro felt she was right to pursue this, though she did need to reassure herself. She knew the facts, and she was good at her job.

Drummond finished reading and closed the file. Exhaling loudly, he turned his head to look up at Muro. "I trust your judgment, Claudette. It's going to take a ridiculous amount of paperwork to justify, but you have my permission to engage Field Command. Do what you feel needs to be done."

CHAPTER EIGHTEEN

Sandy had lost track of time in the windowless cell. She had been unable to sleep since Farlow had repeatedly pressed a smouldering knife into her flesh. It must have been the fourth day of her incarceration. Or was it the fifth? Or third? When she had first tried to lie down after being dragged back to her cell, she realised that her wounds were both precise and purposeful. She could not stand or walk because of the burns on the soles of her feet. She could not lie down comfortably because of the ones on her legs, back, arms and chest. She managed to find respite only when she knelt in front of her bed in a praying position.

Despite the coolness of her cage, she was sweating profusely. The first symptoms of narcotics withdrawal were rising from within her. Engaging with Hamilton's project had meant that her consumption and reliance on drugs had lessened; still, her hands were now shaking, and her head pounded so aggressively that she could hear every thump.

The sound of footsteps disturbed her strained and painful silence. Then Hamilton's long, solemn face appeared in the cell door's window.

"We swiped your chip against the model's console. It didn't unlock."

"Did you think it would be as easy as that?" Sandy did not turn to look at Hamilton and his men.

"What is it?" Hamilton asked bluntly.

"What's what?"

"What is that thing you put on the model? When we swipe your chip, another program comes up. What is it?"

"It's a game," she said in his direction, still kneeling as though she were praying.

"A game? This is a not a game. Come on!" Hamilton thumped his hands on the cell door aggressively. "Do you think I enjoy hurting you? The sooner you give me the code, the sooner this will end."

"Oh, you'll let me walk right out of here, will you?"

Hamilton said nothing, so Sandy continued staring at the mattress while she spoke. "What did you do to the woman who was working on this before me?" she said, her tone derisive. She managed to rise by balancing her weight on the balls of her feet. She walked to the door of the cell. Hamilton turned up his nose at the wretched sight of her. "Did you kill her? You killed her because she wouldn't give you what you wanted? Poor little rich boy. Can't get his way."

Sandy moved to the window. Hamilton now had his back turned to her completely.

"You're the sad one," he said. "A sad, spoilt, lonely little girl."

"Yes, I'm the spoilt one. You have your own dungeon for people who won't let you have what you want." Sandy knew mockery was the thing that irked him the most.

As Hamilton looked back at her, his facial expression changed, as did his tone. "A sad, little girl who has no friends left. All of them are dead. Dead because of the choices you made."

Sandy rolled her eyes but did not reply.

"Too bad you have one less friend today," he said smugly.

Sandy's face sank as she wondered what he meant.

A cruel smile widened on Hamilton's face. "Lucian Scott is dead," he whispered.

"Oh please, try something else." Her face contorted into a cynical sneer.

Farlow handed him a tablet. Hamilton cleared his throat theatrically and began to read from it. "Lucian Scott, a hero of the Long War, was disconnected from life support today. This loss makes him the most recent official casualty of the Long War."

"Liar," spat Sandy, her eyes wild with rage.

He continued. "If a serving officer is no longer able to make medical decisions on his or her own behalf, his or her legal guardian becomes the commanding officer in the absence of any immediate family." He sucked his teeth. "Ah, so you and Lucian were never married. It says Muro was the one to flick the switch. Hmm. Never mind."

"Liar...liar," she said.

Hamilton pressed the tablet against the glass. Sandy's heart pounded frantically as she scanned the news story. He pulled the tablet away from the Perspex before she had finished reading. She wailed in pain and dropped back to the floor, folding herself back into the semi-recumbent position she had held all night. She continued to sob frenetically.

"Good for Commander Muro, I say," he spoke triumphantly. "Life that's too weak to survive without assistance shouldn't be allowed to waste all of our time and resources."

"He wasn't weak," Sandy spluttered. "He was the strongest of us all."

"Ah, true love till the end." Hamilton leaned in and softened his voice. "That's how I know you were really planning to jump that day we met. He was never really going to come back, and you knew it. You knew it, and you didn't want to be alive without him."

Sandy buried her face in the mattress.

"Give me the code, Sandy, and I'll give you a knife. I'll leave you in peace and quiet so you can do it. So you can end your sorry life and be reunited with your beloved."

She looked up, her expression hateful and angry. "Not before I've taken care of you."

"I don't think so. You've lost this one, soldier. I have the resources to keep you alive indefinitely no matter how much pain I inflict on you. Just give me what I want."

Sandy gradually stopped sobbing and became still. Hamilton's eyes were hopeful. He thought this was it—she was going to capitulate. But then she lifted her head and turned to face him.

"I know why you want to do it. To try and control them. I hate them too, Lyndon," she slurred. "Joe Public. The plebs. The great unwashed. They don't know what it's like. What war is like. They're ungrateful. They waste their days on the most inane activities. They eat too much, then complain they're fat. They drink too much, then cry because they have a hangover. Even the most average of them have the riches and comforts the kings of old could only dream of. Everything's great. But they're still unhappy. And whining. Always whining."

"Yes." Hamilton's eyes lit up. "You understand."

"I do. They don't know the meaning of sacrifice. So much of this world is still broken. If only they could get their shit together, so much misery and waste could be avoided."

"Yes, I know. I know. Give me the code," Hamilton pleaded hopefully, "and I will fix them. I will make the world a more perfect place."

"No," she answered in resolution.

"No?" he asked tersely.

"I have made peace with what people do with the privilege and prosperity I gave them. So must you."

He battered the door loudly and then roared, "Then you will die in this cell!" He then turned and stormed away.

"Luca," Sandy whispered before her head lolled forward and she closed her eyes in pain and exhaustion, too weak to stay upright a moment longer.

###

The Field Command uniforms were much like Intelligence Command's black-ops suits but without the advanced technology that made the black suits almost invisible. They were patterned with whatever camouflage was most appropriate for the mission. Since today's mission would be infiltrating a residential home and a commercial office block, Commander Muro had instructed her counterpart in Field Command to have his combatants wear the standard urban camouflage.

At a small base outside of town, Muro addressed several officers. She wore her white uniform with a bullet-proof vest.

"Do you all feel adequately briefed?" Her voice was filled with authority.

The Field Command personnel nodded in agreement.

"Excellent. Then I formally give the order for the breach of the Hamilton InfoSec Building. Lyndon Hamilton is to be treated as a dangerous suspect and is to be apprehended alive if possible."

###

The cadets were told to meet in the canteen for an announcement. As they trundled in, they were surprised to find a large screen. The tables and chairs had been pushed aside, and the cadets stood watching the screen in unknowing anticipation. Massi entered with the other boys. He had neither seen Natalia nor entered any of the Academy's labs since she had threatened him. The lab was her territory. Her sanctum. And he was no longer a welcome guest. Although he had not endured any bullying since the hearing, none of the boys were talking to him—at least not without being prompted and not unless they absolutely had to. Massi wondered if they had been given instructions.

Without notice, the screen sprang to life. After a few seconds, it became apparent that the video feed on display was from a camera mounted on an operative's armoured balaclava. This first-person view reminded Massi of the mysterious day he and Natalia had been hauled to ICHQ to report on the performance of an unknown soldier who had deftly shot his or her way up a vertical farm. The soldiers in the video were sitting in a moving vehicle. Each held an advanced rifle with a serrated bayonet. Massi felt his palms clench in excitement. He could not tell whether the cadets were witnessing a training exercise or not, but it looked like the real thing. Light burst into the vehicle, and the soldiers exited with rapid precision. There was a sharp, collective inhale among the cadets. The soldiers moved towards a large set of doors to what looked like an office block.

"That's the InfoSec building," Massi heard Natalia say in a hushed tone. She was behind him, somewhere within earshot. He did not dare to look her way.

The soldiers hustled to the sides of the doors and crouched down. Another soldier yelled, "One, two, three, fire!" The cadets watched in silence as InfoSec's revolving doors were blown to dust. The soldiers ran into the building like a swarm of hornets. Receptionists and office workers were made to lie on the floor. One man was tackled for continuing to shred documents after being ordered to stop. The unfortunate individual had not even had a moment to register the command before being pushed back into a wall. The soldier with the body cam continued upwards, then ran down a corridor. Old piles of files exhaled dust as they were disturbed from their places of rest. The soldier approached a closed door. Several other soldiers immediately crouched down outside it. They used their hands to signal to each other; it was a code that Massi and the other cadets had also been taught. They were going in. One of the soldiers kicked down the office door, and the operatives darted through it. Inside were two men. They had obviously heard the commotion but had decided to take no action. A man Massi recognised but could not name sat behind a large desk.

"Hamilton," a bewildered Natalia whispered behind him.

Lyndon Hamilton put his arms up and courteously cooperated with the soldiers' every order. Some of the operatives stayed in the office, but the soldier with the camera moved back into the blasted remains of the lobby. As the soldier exited the building, Massi caught a glimpse of Commander Muro walking over the broken glass. Many of the soldiers had left the building, and the InfoSec staff were being led outside. Some were in handcuffs. Massive piles of documents were put into large plastic boxes and towed out of the building on trolleys. The raid was over. Investigators and police officers with dogs entered the building. With that, the transmission cut off. Massi felt exhilarated. The other cadets were not so easily impressed.

"Is that it?" Rebecca Andrews asked.

"That was a bit OTT," another cadet snarked.

Massi agreed in a way. No one had been shot; everyone had surrendered themselves and their documents to IC immediately. Still, IC was looking for something serious enough to merit an armed raid on a civilian office building. After the screen had been switched off, most of the cadets had begun to chatter loudly. Massi, however, was silent; he could not understand why the Academy thought it important for the cadets to see the footage. There were no teachers or even canteen staff around for him to question. Massi assumed the footage had been presented without comment to acclimatise the cadets with a taste of what their lives would be like beyond the Academy. Raiding civilian office buildings was not what he thought he had signed up for.

Muro sat in the InfoSec computer lab with Amos Harling. Despite being riddled with anxiety, her body was still. Harling inspected the lab, making occasional involuntary sounds of awe as he discovered its impressive features. Hamilton and Farlow had been apprehended, cuffed and placed under armed guard in Hamilton's office. Muro's team had found nothing but horrified InfoSec staff. The offices were mostly flawless, with not a single document out of order. No sign of Sandy.

No sign of the missing scientist. Harling could see that Muro was lost in thought.

She was already practising the apology she thought she would soon have to deliver to Hamilton in her mind. Ah, yes…Lyndon Hamilton. Outstanding in his field of expertise, he was a widely-revered entrepreneur, philanthropist and clean-living patriot. And she had humiliated him. At the upcoming press conference, she would announce her resignation and retire from public life. She pondered where she would settle down and grow old. Somewhere alpine and mountainous, perhaps? Aspen, maybe, where she could ski in the winter and, in the summer, take long walks with the puppy she did not yet own. Her thoughts were jarred when Peter Hackett stuck his head into the room.

"Ma'am, we finished our first sweep. We haven't found anything yet, but when all the staff are entirely out of the building, we'll do another sweep with the dogs."

"Thank you, Hackett." Muro then turned to look at Amos Harling, a perverse sort of grin creeping across her face, "Well," she announced sprightly, "that's the end of my career!"

CHAPTER NINETEEN

It was late afternoon when Claudette Muro made peace with her mistake and decided to admit defeat. War had been easier. In war, the enemy was obvious. But now, she did not know if the enemy was outside her organisation or within it. Her team had now had time to question the evacuated staff, and none of them reported seeing either Maria D'Souza or Sandy at InfoSec in recent months. One of the company's managers said he recognised D'Souza and confirmed that she had consulted on the firm's security system as well as on Hamilton's personal security system, but he had not seen her since the completion of those projects.

Muro gathered her senior team for the final debrief. Hackett, Manning and several others assembled in the computer lab, awaiting further orders. Harling was there for moral support. Hackett had been responsible for searching the building and had commandeered Police Command's canine unit for the task. The dogs, however, had found nothing. Muro needed to debrief those officers, as well. She was not looking forward to them reporting her failure to Commander Nichols. He had instigated this entire humiliating spectacle, but it was she who would have to take the blame.

"All right," Muro sighed. "Manning, please bring Hamilton up to see me."

Phillip Manning nodded dutifully and went to fetch Hamilton.

Muro turned to Harling. "Glad you overstayed your visit?"

"I am, actually; this was exciting." His voice was deep and earnest.

"Sorry about the anticlimax."

"Was it an anticlimax? This lab is like nothing I've seen. I'm not even sure what this is." He pointed to the circular projector. It was turned off, and there were no switches on the console. Muro had seen Harling playing with it earlier, but he had not managed to awaken it. It made a slight noise when he swiped his wrist across it, so Muro assumed it could be switched on only by InfoSec staff.

Hamilton entered the lab, startling Muro. Farlow followed behind him. They were both still in handcuffs but did not seem bothered by them.

"Hello, Claudette."

"Lyndon." She mustered a slight, insincere smile.

"I would say it's good to see you, but I'm afraid I'm very confused about all this."

"All will be explained," she assured him.

"I assume you have a warrant for this disruption to my business?"

"We do." Muro looked down guiltily. "Lyndon, we'll have to take you in for an interview."

"Of course—whatever's best for you." He sounded as though he had been told his dinner reservations were to be rescheduled. His genuine calmness unnerved Muro, making her even more embarrassed about her decision to raid the InfoSec building. She reminded herself that there was still the matter of why Hamilton had given money to both Maria D'Souza's child and Sandy. Without any evidence of foul play involving either woman, however, that connection could be explained away. Nevertheless, Muro needed to know exactly what that explanation was.

One of the cadaver dogs began to paw at Farlow's leg. Farlow tried to nudge the dog away with his foot, but the dog's handler objected. Amos, thinking quickly, grabbed Farlow from behind.

"Let's check those pockets, shall we?" said Amos, assertively.

Farlow instinctively tried to struggle before remembering that he was surrounded by officers who equalled him in size and strength.

Harling reached into Farlow's trouser pocket and pulled out a small leather-bound book. The book looked ancient but otherwise perfectly ordinary to Harling. The dog, however, continued to paw and bark at it. Harling ran his large hands carefully over its cover and found two unusual lumps that interrupted its smoothness. He tore the book apart, separating the pages from their cover. He then peeled the book's leather skin away from its cardboard structure to reveal two wrist chips that had been disunited from their owners. Substantial speckles of dried blood were still caked onto both. One was small and oval. The other was larger and square: a military version.

Hamilton's eyes closed as Muro's widened in fury.

Muro's voice had gone hoarse from shouting orders during the chaos that followed the discovery of the microchips. The canine unit was now conducting yet another sweep of the building. Hamilton and Farlow had been taken into custody. A chip reader had been brought to the lab from ICHQ. Amos winced and turned away as it announced Sandy's full name when the larger chip was scanned. He had only known her superficially. Sandy had been three years below him at the Academy and was a friend of his good friend, Lucian Scott. But for Amos, everyone who wore the uniform was a part of the family, united by shared experiences, an ethos and a creed. The list of his still-living former academy classmates was growing painfully short. He sorely missed the company of Lucian, who had been in his same year at the Academy. Sandy and Lucian had been on the field-agent track, while he had been on the tech track. Amos did not realise that Lucian had been romantically involved with Sandy until after reading reports that she had tried to save him during an operation. He had watched news reports of Sandy, her eyes etched with pain, as she returned Luca to his home country. He found it strange that Lucian had never mentioned he had a girlfriend, but during the war a lot of things had gone unsaid.

Muro had left the room soon after the chips had been read. She had taken herself somewhere to be alone. Before she left, Harling had struggled to read her expression. She had seemed simultaneously relieved and pained. Harling thought she would have been happier—her investigation had been vindicated, after all—until it occurred to him that she was grieving.

The last of Muro's officers had either gone home or joined the search teams, leaving Amos alone in the lab. Deciding to take a few liberties, he removed the chips from the evidence bag they had been placed in. One by one, he swiped the chips over the console in the centre of the computer lab. Maria D'Souza's chip had no effect. When he swiped Sandy's chip, however, the projection turned on and lit up. A green globe spun slowly on its axis. Amos reached out to touch it, but when he did, it morphed into another program. His lips parted in awe. The projection was now an incandescent, digital, moving waterfall. As beautiful as it was, he still had no idea what it did. Perhaps it was for decoration? No, he corrected himself, a chip would not be required if the display were merely decorative. He prodded the projection. It responded to his touch as if it were made of real water, but after he moved his hand away, it returned to its original form. Harling was not used to not knowing how technology worked, so he stood there in silence, hoping the waterfall would yield its secrets.

"Amos." Muro entered the room behind him. Her eyes looked tired. She and her team had now been in the building for over twelve hours. "What is that?"

Harling shrugged his shoulders.

"It's beautiful," said Muro.

"It came up when I swiped Sandy's chip," said Amos.

"Extraordinary. My tech team. They need to come back."

Several grumpy engineers stood around the translucent, shimmering waterfall. They had been recalled to the building after an unusually long day. Some of them had even been pulled out of their beds. One by one they examined the console, but every attempt to access it pulled up the words:

INVALID COMMAND
INVALID COMMAND
INVALID COMMAND

The words would swirl around the globe for five minutes until they morphed back into the waterfall. Each member of the tech team drew a blank. Muro threw her arms into the air in frustration.

"None of you know what this is?"

They looked down at their feet.

"No one has anything to add?" she pressed.

They remained silent and looked at each other hopefully. Muro was disappointed, but she was also getting tired. She made a mental note to send her entire team for extra training. The technical team had been standing for twenty minutes. They were now shuffling their feet awkwardly, none of them daring to leave or sit down before Muro gave them permission. The lab was silent; the search teams were still in the building, but they had moved to lower floors. The day had turned to night, though everything looked the same inside the windowless lab. Muro surveyed the men and women in front of her. It crossed her mind that she should fire each and every one of them, but then her eyes lit up, and she turned to Gerald.

"The female cadet. With the long braid. The one we brought in for the vertical farm simulation. Bring her here. Immediately."

Massi was reading in bed. All the other cadets were also settling in for the night. They were still ignoring him, but Massi found that tolerable. The relative quiet was interrupted by Jared Fletcher's flat, round face bursting into the barracks.

"Massi," he said, puffing and panting as he attempted to catch his breath. "It's Nat—she's being taken away."

Massi threw his tablet to the side and leapt from his bed. He ran out of the barracks and down the corridor to the front of the Academy. He looked down through the glass windows and saw three military police officers escorting Nat to a waiting car. How could Nat possibly be in trouble? She was the most competent cadet he knew and was definitely not a natural rule-breaker. Then it hit him: Corio! The hacking. All the other clandestine activities in the computer lab. He spent so much time with her in that lab but understood little of what she was actually doing. No! Nat was not a traitor. He could not believe that of her—not without everything else he knew about the world being a lie. Shaken, he walked back to the barracks, all manner of conspiracies running through his mind.

"Massi, what happened?" one of the cadets asked as he entered the barracks.

"Military police. They took her. I don't know why." It was all he could muster.

The young men were stunned. Natalia's reputation as an unwaveringly loyal and rule-abiding cadet was widely acknowledged.

"She's just not the type who would be in trouble," said Jared. The cadets nodded, confused by the development.

Massi turned away. He did not want to look guilty for knowing about Nat's extracurricular activities in the lab.

"Are you crying, man?" asked Harry Macey.

"No!" said Massi turning around.

"You've got the hots for her though, don't you?" another cadet chimed in.

"Course he has. Look at the way he leapt out of the bed," Harry said, miming how Massi had exited the barracks only minutes ago.

Massi shook his head and lay back down on his bunk.

"Come on, Massi, give us something." said Harry.

Massi shook his head again.

"We know you two sneak off together," Jared said.

"Yeah, what do you two do?" said the third cadet.

"We go to the lab; we do homework," said Massi, trying to return to his reading.

"Oh, come on. You must have thought about trying it on?" said Harry.

"Everyone's thought about it," said Massi.

"Yeah, we have," said the third cadet, nodding. "Her body is so damn hot."

"Come on, Massi, absolutely nothing?" said Jared. "All that time doing homework? Your grades aren't that good." The other cadets laughed.

Massi smiled to himself, remembering the kiss. Remembering her body pressed up against his.

"It's true; look at his face," Harry said, pointing excitedly. "Nice."

"Lucky bastard," said the third cadet. "How far did you go?"

Massi shook his head, fighting the urge to brag about his closeness with Nat.

"Don't be shy. Give us details," said Jared.

Massi remained silent.

"I don't blame you," Harry continued. "If I could get away with it, I'd pin her down; I'd give it to her."

The cadets' conversation continued to get more graphic and vulgar until the boys lost energy and fell asleep. Massi did not particularly like the way they spoke about Nat, but he enjoyed having something they wanted. If Nat had done something wrong, however, it would be wise to downplay their friendship. Maybe this is what Nat had meant when she said they spent too much time together. He entertained the thought that she was trying to protect him all this time; it was easier than thinking that she just did not want him around.

Sandy crawled to the latrine in her cell. Her perspiration had accelerated her dehydration. Her mouth was dry. So dry that she was now looking down at the small measure of chemical blue water in the bottom of the steel bowl and contemplating whether it was drinkable. Something was not right. It had been too long since she had last seen Hamilton. He was not going to let her die of thirst or hunger so soon. She saw her reflection in the water and decided not to drink. She also decided not to go back to the bed and wait. Instead, she started to tap the knuckle of her right index finger on the rounded steel of the latrine; it was as much noise as she could muster.

Natalia had been shaking with fear for the entire journey. The car's windows were blacked out, and the IC officers who were escorting her had barely said a word. They were even unresponsive to her questions. She felt a momentary twinge of regret and began to rue the day she had decided to enroll at the Academy. At first, she had loved the stimulation the Academy had provided her, but this was serious. Up until this point, she had been enjoying herself. She remembered once telling her anxious parents that the Academy was just a different type of school. It was not just a school, though. The Academy prepared cadets like an entrée and fed them into the jaws of Intelligence Command. But what type of organisation was IC, really? An organisation with the highest attrition rate of all branches of the armed forces during the Long War. Of course, it could just be that IC had fewer officers than Police Command and Field Command had, which skewed the percentages. Natalia tried to comfort herself, hoping that her current excursion was merely a routine procedure. Maybe it had something to do with the last time she had been called to ICHQ. IC never told anyone more than they needed to know. There may be a perfectly innocent explanation for her trip. She prayed it had nothing to do with her hacking. If she was to be questioned, she decided that she would confess. She would not prolong any interrogation. She would fess up and accept her punishment. Maybe it would be better if she was expelled from the Academy. Her feelings for Massi had become complicated, and if she were expelled, she would not have to make a decision about him.

The car came to a halt. In the darkness, she felt her eyes strain to adjust to the unfamiliar setting. The building in front of her seemed eerily familiar. It was the Hamilton InfoSec building. Her heart began to beat rapidly. The building was surrounded by uniformed officers, police dogs and vans with their headlights running. The raid. What could this possibly have to do with her? She stood motionless until a firm arm guided her inside, through the lobby and into the elevator.

She was led into a round room at the top of the building. She saw two individuals, their backs to her, as she entered the lab. She could not see what they were looking at, but whatever it was, it glowed ominously. They turned towards her, and she realised she knew them: the lissom Claudette Muro and the beautiful, hulking Amos Harling. Natalia instinctively saluted, though she did not know if that was the correct protocol in this situation—whatever this situation was. They saluted back, much to Nat's relief.

Muro spoke first. "Good evening, cadet. Since you exceeded expectations during your last performance, we were hoping you might be of some assistance again."

Nat stood in silence, her body frozen in anxiety. Muro gestured to the strange projection in the centre of the room. Natalia took it as a sign to move closer.

"Can you tell us what this is?" asked Muro.

Natalia's body relaxed. At least she was not in trouble. She looked at the waterfall, distracted by its beauty.

"Oh," she exhaled.

"Look familiar?" Harling pointed at the projection.

"It looks like a modified version of an obscure Internet game called 'Sapeeco'," said Natalia. "The original version is designed to teach kids maths and coding, but this looks different." She paused. "This looks like it's almost real. The original version is only an eight-bit game. It was designed to look vintage."

"I think I've heard of it." The deepness of Harling's voice made the hair on the back of Natalia's neck stand up.

"Okay, how do you work it?" Muro said, losing patience.

"In the game, the character walks upwards and then enters behind the waterfall." There were no avatars, so Natalia traced her finger along a path that started at the very bottom of the waterfall. As her finger hit the centre of the waterfall, the projection shifted.

"See, it's like we're looking at the waterfall from a cave behind it. Now we have to solve the puzzle to get to the next level."

"I see!" exclaimed Harling.

"You know this, Amos?" said Muro.

"Yeah, I know what it is now."

Natalia continued, "You put in the right combinations of letters and symbols, and you go up a level." An equation appeared in front them, and Natalia tapped in the right answer. A new equation appeared. "This version of the game presupposes that you know the math. It doesn't contain the teaching element."

"That's because it's a digital padlock," said Amos with a knowing look. "How many times do you have to do this to get to the end?"

"I don't know." Natalia shrugged. "There could be hundreds of levels."

"I'll bet I can unlock this in, like, twenty minutes," said Amos, completing a few levels himself.

"Guess again, Amos," said a voice behind him.

Natalia turned around, letting out a little yelp of shock before slapping her hand across her mouth. Sandy, having been dragged into the lab by Phillip Manning, stood before them. She was dishevelled, half-dressed and was clutching her left forearm with her right hand. Her burnt skin was angry with jagged crimson welts.

Muro, her mouth agape, looked Sandy up and down in horrified silence.

CHAPTER TWENTY

Sandy Attiyeh had been taken to hospital by several armed guards. Muro was too furious with her to even attempt a conversation. Sandy had been severely dehydrated, still bleeding and losing the ability to speak coherently. Muro knew Sandy too well to assume that she was wholly innocent in the events leading up to her own confinement. Once Sandy had left, however, it occurred to Muro that they should have asked Sandy what the projection was. Amos Harling and Natalia Sanghera were left alone in the lab under strict orders to play the game until they got to whatever was on the other side. Muro had gone home as soon as she had realised they would not be finished any time soon.

Harling was glad to see her leave, as she had become unintelligible from rage and exhaustion. Hamilton InfoSec was now deathly quiet. The search parties had left for the night, but they would be back tomorrow, picking the space clean as if devouring the flesh of a cooked bird, leaving only the skeletal remains behind.

Harling observed Natalia's lovely face and form. The cadet paid him no attention; she was so absorbed in the game. Her fingers darted steadily over the projection as she moved up the levels.

"I'm impressed," said Harling not looking at the projection.

"Sorry?" said Nat, disrupted by his words.

"Where did you learn this? This is way beyond the level you should be at, even in the final year of the Academy."

"Oh." She paused, thinking. "My dad is a university professor. He specialises in computer science, and he gives me puzzles like this to solve all the time."

Harling could tell that she was lying. The way her eyes dipped down just after speaking. The way her mouth tightened ever so slightly. He thought about challenging this act of dishonesty but then decided against it. He did, however, make a mental note to probe this little piece of information later.

Stepping back from the projection, he watched as she resumed plugging away at the strange, cryptic waterfall. Her braid swung to the centre of her back. All the male cadets had to have short hair. Girls were encouraged to wear their hair neatly, which usually meant keeping it just long enough to braid tightly. Natalia's hair seemed unnecessarily long, however. It was like a piece of herself and her heritage that she did not allow the Academy to have. She was not Harling's type, but her intensity was attractive.

"Are you eighteen yet?" he asked.

"Not for another few months," she said.

"That's a shame," he said. "I was going to ask you if you wanted me to get you a drink. It'll have to be juice rather than vodka."

Natalia blushed, realising that he was flirting with her.

"I could use some water," she said, feeling the need to put a little distance between herself and Harling. "I'll go get it; you take over."

"All right," he said, assuming her place.

In total, it took them about ten hours to unlock the projection. They took turns, painstakingly completing each level until there were none left. At that point, the waterfall froze for several seconds until it morphed into an animated drop of water, which then swirled into a spinning globe that rotated on a vertical axis. Raised tags hovered above cities. Natalia cocked her head to the side, trying to figure out what they meant.

When Amos jabbed at one of the tags, the profile of a young female journalist popped up. "Does she look familiar?" he asked Natalia.

"She's a newsreader, I think."

"Yeah, and there are her bank details. Hmm," he murmured to himself.

Natalia tapped at more of the tags, and more personnel reports appeared, each of them complete with intimate information: letters, journals, articles, numbers of bank accounts and credit cards, employers and relationships.

"I don't think this is normal, is it?" asked Natalia.

"Nope," said Amos. "It's illegal."

Muro looked at Amos and Natalia wearily. Her sleep that night had not been peaceful.

"Tell me it's just a fancy video game. If it's not, lie," said Muro, flummoxed.

"It's a living database," said Amos. "It looks like this whole lab is geared towards powering it."

"What's it for?" asked Muro.

"Have you interviewed Hamilton yet?" replied Harling.

"Not yet," Muro said. She turned to Natalia and said coolly, "I think it's time you went back to school."

Natalia gave an obedient nod and left the room.

Amos's eyes followed her as she walked. "You need to keep an eye on that girl, Commander," he said, his face tired and grave.

"She's already in custody. There are guards at the hospital. I'm seeing her straight after we're done." Muro was looking at the projection, but her mind was miles away.

"Not Sandy. Natalia."

"The cadet?"

"Yeah, she could be dangerous."

"Dangerous?" His choice of words startled Muro.

"That program was way beyond what we teach them in the Academy. I would be interested to know where she really got those skills."

Sandy lay in hospital, staring at the ceiling, feeling happier than she had ever been in her life. A clicker in the palm of her right hand allowed her to send morphine rushing through her veins. It was not her usual drug of choice, but, boy, was she glad to have it. She had slept late into the morning, feeling clean, cosy and high enough to ignore the shark-fin welts that were now beginning to scab over. She had awoken with the unsettling sensation of not knowing where she was, and it had taken a few minutes to register that she was in a hospital bed. Her withdrawal symptoms had abated, and her mind felt pleasant and numb. Sitting up in bed, she became aware of her body and had the strange feeling of being temporarily excused from it. Her left arm was still heavily bandaged; she felt the dressing but not her arm within it. She unclipped the morphine IV drip, leaving the cannula protruding from her right arm. Lightly testing her feet on the floor, she wondered if she would be able to walk. She gingerly shifted her weight onto the burned soles of her feet. Her wounds had been treated with a sticky, pale-white substance that had left her skin feeling cold. Carefully pulling herself up to a standing position, she was able to shuffle to the door, though she had to make an effort not to slip. It was then she noticed the two figures standing outside the door—soldiers she did not recognise. She opened the door, and they jumped in surprise before turning to face her, instinctively clutching their weapons.

"Take me to Lucian Scott," Sandy said urgently, her voice authoritative. The soldiers looked at each other, seeming to temporarily forget whatever other commands they had been given. Despite their reluctance to leave their post, they acquiesced once they saw how slow and painfully Sandy was moving. She was definitely not a flight risk. They led her to a corridor in another part of the hospital, remembering their orders were to never leave her unattended.

Sandy soon found herself standing outside Luca's room. She pressed both her hands against the glass window. Unsettled by her reflection, she had unconsciously stopped herself from entering, not wanting Luca to see her gaunt and damaged. Her muscular physique had been given more definition by the starvation and dehydration to which she had been subjected. Every ripple and sinew showed beneath her skin, the little extraneous fat she had possessed having been starved away. Captivity had dulled her eyes and sunken her cheeks. All she wore was a light slip of a hospital gown.

Sandy heard footsteps marching towards her, and without having to look she knew they belonged to Muro. Her light, swift, catlike stride was unmistakable.

"You didn't switch him off, then?" asked Sandy.

"Who? Lucian?" Muro looked puzzled.

"Yes," said Sandy

"Why on earth would I do that?" Muro's eyes narrowed.

"Hamilton told me you'd switched him off," said Sandy. "To taunt me."

"Forgive me if I don't feel sorry for you," said Muro flatly.

"You wouldn't switch him off, would you? Without me knowing?"

Muro frowned. "He's not mine to switch off."

Sandy smiled, her worst fear fading away.

"Sandy, I would like a very full explanation of the events that have led up to this point."

"Right now?" Sandy turned to Muro.

"No, not necessarily now," said Muro, losing patience.

"All right, then." Sandy turned back towards Luca.

"Sandy, you do realise you're under arrest?"

"Oh, yeah." She nodded.

"After you leave the hospital, you'll be taken to ICHQ for questioning, then placed under house arrest."

"Fair enough," she replied.

"Preferably with your ass no longer hanging out of a hospital gown. Oh, God, he burnt your legs too," Muro said in disgust as she recoiled at the sight.

Sandy gathered her gown around her legs and fixed her robe to preserve her modesty.

Muro shook her head. "I'm disappointed, Sandy," she said. "I am so disappointed in you. That thing in Hamilton's lab. The map."

"Oh, of course. I'll tell you everything." She paused. "But I want a full, complete pardon, or I don't say a thing."

###

Natalia had been given the morning to catch up on her sleep. A rare permission slip for missing classes had been prepared especially for her. As she lay her head on her pillow, she struggled to process the excitement and seriousness of all she had witnessed the night before. After waking at about noon, still several hours short of sleep, she dressed and hurried to the computer lab while everyone else was still eating. She did not want to join the others and be bombarded with questions about her sudden disappearance. Not yet. In the silence of her sanctuary, she revelled in her victory. A real victory. Whatever that thing was, she had defeated it. Muro had asked for her specifically. Nothing had made sense for the others until she had turned up.

Massi's sudden appearance disturbed her thoughts. She immediately noticed the look of relief on his face. Seeing him, she felt a wave of happiness wash over her, even though he seemed so short and slight compared to the strapping Amos Harling.

"You're not meant to be in here with me, remember?" she scolded him, only semi-sincerely. Her bright smile was still wide.

"What happened? Are you in trouble?"

"No, I was at the Hamilton InfoSec building. You know, the raid we just saw yesterday. They arrested Lyndon Hamilton."

"No way!"

"I know, right? I couldn't believe it," she said, exhilarated.

"Why did they make you go there? Was it to do with the soldier in the vertical farm?"

"No, there was this puzzle, and she wanted me to solve it. Commander Muro, she asked for me especially. Amos Harling was there too."

Massi's face contorted with unease for a second, and his voice became deep and sullen. "Why was _he_ there?"

"There was a puzzle, and I can't say too much, but in order to get to this…database, we had to solve the puzzle. We were left there all night."

"You and Harling? Alone?"

"Yeah." Natalia was too joyous to register his change in tone.

"So, you did it together?"

"Yes, he couldn't unlock the puzzle at first, which is why they called me, but once we were inside he knew exactly what to do. He's a great coder, actually. So bright."

"Natalia, don't you think that's suspicious?"

The look of excitement dropped away from her face.

"What do you mean?"

"They have this puzzle that only you can solve. Do you think they suspect something?"

"What? What do you mean?"

"Natalia, this sounds like a trap. They know you hack into the Academy and ICHQ's systems." He pointed his finger at her belligerently.

"Massi, that's ridiculous. It wasn't about that." She shook her head and looked away from him.

"How do you know?"

"If you'd been there, you'd know it wasn't about that. It was something to do with Sandy Attiyeh. She was there too, but..."

Massi cut her off. "So you spent the night with Amos Harling, and you don't think that's suspicious? His job is to catch people who hack into systems they're not supposed to hack into."

"That's not right, Massi. If you'd been there, you wouldn't think that. This whole thing wasn't about me."

"What did you talk with him about, then?" Massi said.

Natalia grinned. "Oh, just a lot of nothing. It was late." She giggled to herself, then added, "He asked if I was eighteen yet."

Massi's face hardened. "What a total sleaze," he scoffed.

"He's not a sleaze," Natalia lied. Truth be told, she had found Harling a little inappropriate.

"Did you tell him you were seventeen? Or are you leading him on, too?"

The hurt that initially registered on her face was soon overcome by anger. "I don't lead anyone on." Her voice crackled with offense.

Massi rolled his eyes, and his lips twisted into a bitter sneer.

"Massi, I don't lead you on. I told you I liked you. But I'm just not..." Her brows furrowed. "I'm just not ready for what you want."

Massi shook his head in disbelief.

"Romantic relationships aren't even allowed." Her eyes started to tear. "Do you think no one has noticed how much time we spend together? Do you think it reflects well on either of us? Do you think the way you're behaving is even attractive?"

Massi covered his face with his hand. "You're right," he said, rubbing his eyes. "I'm sorry. I'm sorry I upset you. I was just worried."

She relaxed. "And this is how you show your concern?"

Glaring at her intensely, he stepped towards her. "I see you being taken away by military police. What am I meant to think?"

She put her hand on his forearm to comfort him. He leaned in. He knew the concern, the love and the lust must be evident all over his face. To his surprise, she kissed him. Not like the other time. She kissed him warmly, eagerly, passionately. Like she needed him too. Like she wanted his approval. This time she did not break away. He ran his hand up her back, then moved his palm downward. Natalia let out a moan of pleasure. She ran her hand up his firm chest and bit his lip just firmly enough not to hurt him.

Just as all the tension and strife began to drop away from their bodies, a female teacher walked into the lab.

CHAPTER TWENTY-ONE

Every member of the Ruling Council had agreed to an emergency meeting. They sat together in silence. At the round table, the chief treasurer, chief custodian and chief of civilian affairs nervously looked at Christopher Drummond, all of them hoping he would make sense of everything, but the high commander looked far away in thought. Everyone was still reeling from the news that Lyndon Hamilton, a man they all knew, had been arrested on data violation, conspiracy to commit domestic terror acts, unlawful detention and suspected murder charges. To add insult to injury, Sandy Attiyeh, one of Drummond's own soldiers, appeared to have been aiding and abetting him.

Never at a loss for words, it was High Ambassador Clement McCawley who finally broke the pensive, anxious silence. "Lyndon Hamilton made good systems," McCawley said. "If he's convicted, we'll be able to confiscate his facilities. Can you imagine what else he's got in there? At least that could be good for us—even if we just sell it."

"We can always rely on you to see a bright side, Clement," said Drummond soberly.

"That's just as well," McCawley added nastily, "because thanks to Lieutenant Attiyeh, I've been spending a lot of my time with the ambassador of the Central Arabian Republic lately. They have, somewhat unsurprisingly, taken the fact that Attiyeh was helping Lyndon Hamilton as a sign of her bad character."

Drummond looked down at the tablet in front of him as McCawley continued speaking. "They want an inquiry into the Hazirat incident, Chris. I've been trying to talk them out of it for months, but thanks to

Sandy Attiyeh's arrest, they're emboldened. I don't want an inquiry into Hazirat, and I don't think you want one, either."

Drummond shook his head. "I think the high ambassador and I have matters solely of foreign policy to discuss. Would you please excuse us?" Drummond said, signalling with his eyes for the others to leave. They gathered their things and scuttled out of the room obediently. As he turned back to McCawley, Drummond's face hardened. "An inquiry into Hazirat doesn't concern me," he lied. "Sandy, like all my officers, received a blanket pardon for her actions during the Long War as part of the armistice agreement. The findings of any inquiry are redundant. What could they possibly hope to achieve?"

"They want to know the truth about what happened to that refugee camp, Chris. If one of your soldiers even set a single foot in that camp, we violated international law. The Europeans will still give us hell for it." McCawley gave Drummond a lingering, knowing look. "If you tell me the truth for once, maybe I can figure something out. But I need the truth."

"Do you know what he was called?"

"Who?" asked McCawley.

"The terrorist. The mastermind behind the Soft Terror. Do you know what he was called?"

"Al Shahidi?" offered McCawley, scratching his chin.

"No, not his name. Not his real name. What they called him. His nickname."

McCawley blinked and looked at Drummond blankly.

"Al Thubaba. The fly. Because every time you try to catch a fly, it flitters away beyond your reach. They named him that to mock me. And if I hadn't given the orders that I did, we might still be at war."

McCawley shuffled his feet.

"It's against international law for military personnel to step within even a five-kilometre radius of a refugee camp. But terrorists don't care about international law." Drummond paused, then continued. "The terrorists were playing the game on a different level, and I had to debase myself to that level to win. He hid in that refugee camp, because he knew that if we went looking for him there, we were exactly the monsters he said we were. So, I sent in my finest little monster."

###

Massi was facing a panel of teachers once again. This time he was not sitting. He was standing like a prisoner in a dock, only without the shackles. Accused. This time Natalia was there, too. She was visibly shaking, having had little experience of being cross-examined by authority figures. Massi fought the urge to make any sort of comforting gesture or reveal any emotion.

"Cadet Moretti, we're sorry to see you at a disciplinary hearing again so soon," said the woman with the glasses. "We thought we'd seen a change in your behaviour." Massi recognised her from the previous panel. "Cadet Sanghera, this is unexpected and very disappointing. I think you need to explain yourself."

"I shouldn't be here," Natalia blurted thoughtlessly.

"Oh? You allowed yourself to be seen—by a teacher, no less—in an embrace that was described to me as 'passionate'."

Massi cringed.

"It wasn't like that," Natalia said, flustered. "I didn't want that to happen. I didn't want to kiss him. He made it happen, and I..."

"Are you saying that this...<u>incident</u> was unwelcome?" the woman with glasses interrupted.

"It was unwelcome," said Natalia. "Very unwelcome."

Massi's mouth tightened.

"Unwelcome sexual touching is something we take very seriously, no matter how small. This is an expellable offence." The woman picked up her pen.

"No!" Natalia exclaimed. "It wasn't sexual. It was just a friend comforting a friend. I would just have preferred if my friends didn't need comforting."

"Oh!" said the teacher. "I see what you mean, though your phrasing was a little confusing."

No shit, thought Massi.

"As the victim of this unwelcome behaviour, whatever it may have been," the woman continued, "do you feel that Cadet Moretti should be reprimanded? If so, what type of punishment do you think fits the discomfort he caused you?"

"Definitely more drills," said Natalia without hesitating. "He should be banned from the labs outside classroom times too."

"That sounds reasonable. Moretti, you're on double drills until I'm satisfied you've learnt your lesson. If you exhibit any other aggressive or <u>unwelcome</u> behaviour towards any other female cadet, you will be expelled instantly."

Massi shook his head.

"Do you disagree with my decision?" the woman asked.

"Yes," he said, though he was losing the will to fight them. "I don't think I should be treated like some sort of predator. Though I do understand if Natalia's upset."

"Then you accept your punishment?" The woman looked at him over her glasses.

Massi swallowed his feelings of fear and confusion. "Yes," he said stoically.

As he left the room, he thought about Natalia and hoped that she had heard the pain and betrayal in his voice. It was evident on his face, but he had not once glanced back at her or met her gaze. Sprinting back to the barracks, away from the hurt and the threat of expulsion, he began to pinpoint the exact moment everything had started to unravel for him. The moment he realised he did not want to touch any other woman's body but hers. The moment the other attractive girls at the Academy had faded into the background. The moment everything clear and lucid in his world had become clouded and blurry. The moment he had realised he was in deep, inconvenient, all-consuming love with Natalia.

He knew what he had to do. There and then, he made up his mind never to look at or speak to Natalia ever again.

Claudette Muro made her way to the table in front of the press pack. Cameras clicked furiously as she took her seat behind a multiplicity of microphones. The cacophony soon died down, however, as Muro always made the press wait before she would begin speaking. This was her little trick to remind them that these conferences always proceeded with her concurrence and at her pace. Like a horde of tame dogs willing their owner to throw them a juicy steak, the journalists hushed themselves. Muro dulled her senses to the onslaught of blinking camera lights and then decided to give anyone watching a master class in how to hold a press conference.

"Good afternoon." Her voice was clear and firm as she read a prepared statement from the autocue in front of her. "This is a press conference to address the Intelligence Command operation that took place at the Hamilton InfoSec company premises earlier this week. Before I begin, I would just like to remind the press that the subject of this conference is still part of a live investigation. Incidents of irresponsible reporting or alarmist, speculative articles will not be tolerated."

Before a strand of glossy hair had the opportunity to stray onto her face, she flicked it away with her right index finger.

"Four days ago, a large-scale search of Hamilton InfoSec took place under a warrant mandated by High Commander Drummond himself. During the course of that raid, we found sufficient evidence to arrest Lyndon Hamilton and some of his employees on suspicion of violating several data security acts. He is also suspected of committing other offenses that I cannot discuss at this time." She paused. "The same day the search took place, IC officers also arrested Lieutenant Alisande Attiyeh, who was being held in a concealed part of the building against her will."

It was not difficult to hear the sharp, collective intake of breath.

"Lieutenant Attiyeh has been placed under house arrest while we investigate this unusual finding. We're uncertain at this point what Lieutenant Attiyeh's relationship with Lyndon Hamilton was, or if she was involved in any criminal activity. It would be inappropriate for me to comment on that while the investigation is still ongoing. Lieutenant Attiyeh is due to be interviewed by Intelligence Command military police as part of this investigation. Thank you for your time."

Muro collected herself and rose to leave.

A journalist thrust himself forward and said, "Some questions, please, ma'am."

Muro leant down towards the microphones and said, "I will not be taking any questions at this time. Another press conference will be scheduled when the investigation has been completed."

With that, she left the room.

###

INTELLIGENCE COMMAND MILITARY POLICE

CLASSIFICATION: TOP SECRET AND CONFIDENTIAL
UNAUTHORISED ACCESS MAY RESULT IN PROSECUTION

SUBJECT: LIEUTENANT FIRST CLASS ALISANDE ATTIYEH [9021787] POST-OPERATION INTERVIEW RE: HAMILTON INFOSEC CONFINEMENT WITHOUT PRIOR CONSENT OR WARNING

Military Police 1: Please state your full name for the record.

Sandy: Alisande Layla Attiyeh.

Military Police 1: What is your age, profession and rank?

Sandy: I am thirty-one years old, I am an officer of Intelligence Command, and I have obtained the rank of Lieutenant First Class.

Military Police 2: You have been arrested on suspicion of violating the data security act, on suspicion of conspiracy to commit or aid the committal of acts of domestic terror and of treason. Do you understand what these charges mean?

Sandy: Yes.

Military Police 1: You were arrested after being found at the offices of the Hamilton Information Security company. You were found in a cell, adjacent to a corridor concealed by a false wall. It appeared to the officers who found you that you had been held against your will. Is this correct?

Sandy: Yes.

Military Police 2: Could you please describe the events immediately before your confinement?

Sandy:	I was in the laboratory on the top floor of the InfoSec building. I had just completed work for Hamilton. I locked his systems. I refused to hand the passcode over to him. He then ordered his security team to incarcerate me until I agreed to hand the code over to him.
Military Police 2:	Could you please clarify the nature of the work you did for Hamilton?
Sandy:	Three months ago, Hamilton employed me to finish a living database for him. This database is programmed to harvest personal and sensitive information from the Internet.
Military Police 1:	By database, are you referring to the projection in the laboratory?
Sandy:	Yes.
Military Police 2:	Are you aware that the acquisition of data of this nature is illegal for civilians and non-military entities?
Sandy:	Yes.
Military Police 1:	When did you become aware that this project was illegal?
Sandy:	I knew it was illegal when I first agreed to work for Hamilton.
Military Police 2:	And you still chose to continue building this database?
Sandy:	Yes.
Military Police 1:	You say that Hamilton employed you to finish a living database. Does this mean that you were not the initial creator of the database?
Sandy:	I was not. When I was employed by Hamilton, the database was already in a partially constructed form.
Military Police 1:	Do you know who initially started building the database?

Sandy:	No.
Military Police 2:	Why did you agree to continue building the database even though you knew it was illegal?
Sandy:	I was bored.
Military Police 1:	When you were held against your will by Hamilton, were you subjected to physical or sexual abuse?
Sandy:	I was subjected to physical abuse by Hamilton's employees on Hamilton's orders. I was denied food and water. I was not subjected to sexual abuse.
Military Police 1:	How did you lose your chip?
Sandy:	It was cut out of my skin by Hamilton's employee on Hamilton's orders.
Military Police 2:	Why did Hamilton want your chip?
Sandy:	I programmed the projection so that my chip is the only one that can unlock the database.
Military Police 2:	How did Hamilton intend to use the database?
Sandy:	He told me it was so that he would know the information security industry more thoroughly. I suspected that it was really because he wants to control the news cycle and the policy agenda.
Military Police 2:	Why did you deny Hamilton access to the database after you had agreed to complete it for him?
Sandy:	I had no intention of ever giving him access to the finished database.
Military Police 1:	Have you ever heard of an organisation called the Sun Circle Group?
Sandy:	No.

Military Police 1: Do you believe the current government should be replaced with a different type of government?

Sandy: No.

Military Police 2: Do you still consider yourself a loyal officer of Intelligence Command?

Sandy: Yes.

CHAPTER TWENTY-TWO

It had been three weeks since she had betrayed him. Three weeks since he had spoken to her. Three weeks of painful double drills, which he was only just getting used to. He had vomited during the first day of them and spent hours being rehydrated via an IV drip. He had almost passed out the next day. He had not complained. He had just kept going. Massi's world seemed different. For the entire time he had been at the Academy, Sandy Attiyeh had been recognised as a paradigm of military excellence. Now she existed in a state of dishonourable limbo, somehow involved in a seedy data-theft scheme with an eccentric billionaire.

He had also been deprived of his main source of humour and good company: Natalia. Her warmth and appealing form had soothed him at the end of the day, after the bracing trials of the Academy had been overcome. They had originally formed a bond, because neither of them quite fit in with their respective cohorts. Both of them craved more quiet and solitude than the Academy naturally provided. And since the computer labs were the only parts of the Academy not occupied during meal breaks and after tutorial hours, both Massi and Natalia had gravitated to them in their earlier years at the Academy. In the past two years, something had changed, and they had started seeking each other out. They would check each lab for the other before entering. Massi thought back to when they would laugh together over lunch, not making conversation other than swapping jokes.

It was him. The problem was him. He had ruined their relationship by becoming more suggestive and tactile, then unhappy and sullen when she shirked his touch and refused to flirt back. How he wished he had not begun to think about her in a carnal way, but it always seemed out of his control.

Colonel Mathers blew a whistle, signalling the male cadets to stop their morning drills, which were a complex circuit of mandatory cardio and callisthenic exercises. On the playing field, the male cadets panted in the summer heat. The heat was blistering even though it was only eight in the morning.

"All right, everyone. Back inside. Shower. Not you, Moretti." Mathers shot Massi a dirty look.

Double drills did not mean that the drills were literally doubled, but it still meant doing an extra forty minutes of the circuit.

"Why is Massi still on double drills?" whispered Jared to Harry Macey.

"He's got to use up all his extra energy, or else he can't control his sexual urges," Harry replied. All the boys cackled, even Jared.

"Enough!" Mathers interrupted, almost yelling.

As the other cadets scurried back to the barracks, Massi continued his drills without complaining.

By the time he was finished, the male barracks were empty. An upside of his situation was being able to shower and dress in peace. The downside was the added humiliation of being late to class. It was the Academy's own version of a walk of shame. After a short, un-indulgent shower—the hot water having been used up—he walked briskly back to his locker, pulled out his uniform and hastily threw it on the bed. In his eagerness to minimise his tardiness, he had accidentally knocked a handful of possessions out of his locker. He swept them up, conscious of every second he lost, and stuffed them back in, knowing he would have to repack everything for inspection later. A white rectangle glistening on the dark-grey concrete floor stopped his frantic movements. He picked it up. It was a business card. It was pure white on both sides, and the digits were only visible because of their slight shine against the matte background. The card was designed so that anyone picking it up might assume it was blank. But it was not. The digits were Sandy Attiyeh's number. It was the card she had given him the day she had spoken to the cadets three months ago—before his world had changed.

Like most of the cadets, Massi kept his keys on his dog tags. At the bottom of every standard issue locker there were two small drawers. He unlocked the bottom drawer and retrieved his phone. He checked over his shoulder to make sure no one was around, then dialled the number, his heart racing, the fear of being late to class evaporating from his mind.

"Hello?" The voice was clear and questioning.

"Hello, er, yes, is this Sandy?" said Massi.

"Speaking. Who is this?"

"I don't know if you remember me, but you gave me your card. A white card. Almost all white."

"When did I give you my card?" she asked calmly.

"When you came to speak at the Academy. I'm a cadet. I came up to talk to you after."

"Oh," Sandy said, her tone changing. "Yes, I remember you. You have black hair, right?"

"Yes, yes, that's me. I just wanted to talk to you, to see if these things they're saying on the news, the things..." He trailed off, struggling to articulate his thoughts.

"Yes, you can ask me anything," she said, "but not over the phone. Come to my place tonight. You can leave the Academy, right?"

"Uh, yeah, yes, I can come. After classes."

"Okay, I need you to pick something up for me. When you get it, come straight to my house," she ordered. "There are military police around my building, but you'll be let in. Wear civilian clothes."

###

An authoritative rapping on the door disturbed the quiet of Sandy's penthouse. She had been sitting on her balcony, drinking orange juice and enjoying the summer sun. She knew he would come, but she had not realised it would be quite so soon.

"Good afternoon, Sandy."

"High Commander, good afternoon."

Christopher Drummond wore a deep crimson uniform. It was the colour of the setting sun raging just before nightfall. His many medal bars and ribbons bedecked his broad chest. He walked into Sandy's apartment, hunching as though he were trespassing.

"May I offer you a drink?" asked Sandy.

"I don't drink during working hours."

"I meant orange juice or something." She smiled insincerely. "I'm not that type of girl. Water?"

He raised his eyebrows, then said, "Yes, please."

She ushered him to the balcony. He seemed ill at ease in such a casual setting. She turned towards the kitchen to fetch more orange juice and Drummond's water.

"Busy?" she asked as she poured his beverage for him.

"Yes, more so lately." He sighed. "What were you thinking?"

She sat down opposite him, her face glum. "I have no answer."

"Nichols's forensic team found that scientist, you know. Buried under the cell you were held in. What was left of her, anyway. She had been mostly melted down with lye. I never realised how hard it was to make a body go away."

Sandy sat motionless but her eyes were chaotic. "I didn't know he was a killer. Not in the beginning. I just knew someone else had worked on that projection. At first I assumed he'd paid them off."

"Hamilton's trial starts next week. The human remains are enough to convict him for murder. Not sure about the other charges. His people spoke too."

"Were..." she paused, "enhanced interrogation methods used?"

"Yes," he answered.

"Good," said Sandy.

"The projection," he said thoughtfully. "What is it, and what is it for?"

"I've spent at least eighty-four hours talking to your people about it already."

"Tell me," he commanded.

"It's a database. He wanted to blackmail people into doing what he said, mainly researchers and journalists, so he could influence policy and control the news cycle."

"Domestic terror," said Drummond. "Have you defected, as well?"

"He wasn't going to be violent. What he wanted was to change the world without anyone knowing. By influencing behaviour. Brilliant, when you think about it. But no, I don't want to change the world. I just wanted to be a part of it."

"Do you understand what you've done? The new president of the Central Arabian Republic is pushing hard for an inquiry into Hazirat.

McCawley managed to talk them out of it, saying there'd be no point because of the armistice agreement. You have undone all our hard work." He squeezed the tumbler of water so hard his knuckles turned white. Sandy thought it might break, but the glass was thick and solid in his pale palm.

"Are they refusing to honour the armistice agreement?" she asked. "That's tantamount to declaring war."

"No. But now they look justified in publically asking for an inquiry. Before, they were only asking privately."

"I received a pardon like all our soldiers. If they undo my pardon, they undo everyone's pardon."

"No one else is about to be tried for charges that include domestic terror."

"Muro already promised me a pardon. I cooperated with the investigation. I've told the military police everything I know. I was never actually going to let him have the projection anyway."

"Do you not even think about how this will play out? You still have to be tried. You are still guilty of violating several data security acts. You will still be declared guilty, then pardoned at your sentencing."

"Then we can all get on with our lives," she said, taking a swig of juice.

"Do you have no self-respect? Why did I even bother lobbying for you to be pardoned? After the war, and for this? You don't deserve it. Where's your honour?"

Sandy looked away for a minute. Her body was racked with tension. Her eyes looked hurt. Her glare drifted to her bandaged left arm. She put down the glass and looked Christopher Drummond straight in the eyes. "Do you really want me behind bars? Where anyone can visit me?" Her voice was soft and sinister. "People like journalists?"

"No, you're too good for that," said Drummond stoically, unfazed by her thinly veiled threat. "I have found some other use for you anyway."

###

The air was heavy with humidity and alive with the chirps and whistles of katydids. Massi had feigned illness in order to leave his classes early; that way, he had time to shed his uniform and sneak out of the Academy unnoticed. He had donned a black shirt and blue jeans, messed up his hair, grabbed a backpack and left the barracks through the back entrance. He walked around the outside of the Academy, making his way towards the front gates. Administration did not let underage cadets leave unaccompanied, but Massi had already turned eighteen, so technically he was not breaking any rules by leaving. Still, he would need to think of a good excuse for his departure. For the moment, however, he was more concerned about being seen by his fellow cadets.

As he slunk around the outer rim of the Academy, he saw a familiar figure in the darkness. He stopped. It was her; of course it was her. Would he ever be free of her? He began to back away, but she turned around and gasped, clearly startled. She reached for her ElectroFyte.

"Don't come any closer," said Nat, visibly panicked by Massi's presence.

"Shut up," he hissed malevolently. "I'm not here for you. What are you doing outside, anyway?"

"Just getting some fresh air," she lied.

The air was so hot and uncomfortably sticky, he instantly knew that she was avoiding the other girls.

"Where are you going?" she asked.

"I'm going to see Sandy Attiyeh," he said.

"That's not funny."

"I'm not joking."

"You can't see her; she's under arrest," said Natalia.

"House arrest. She invited me over," he said smugly.

"She invited you?" Her face lit up with incredulity.

"Yeah, she gave me her number." He flashed the card at her. It seemed luminescent in moonlight—so white it had an eerie glow.

Natalia's face went pale. "You have no idea how much trouble she's in. I saw her when I was called to the InfoSec building. She was a mess. She looked like she'd been tortured. She was working with Hamilton."

"I'll ask her myself." He started moving again.

Nat stood in front of him, deliberately blocking his path. "What are you doing? Think this through. You can't leave."

"This isn't a prison, Nat. Tomorrow's Saturday, anyway."

"Okay, then you shouldn't leave. You're in enough trouble. You'll get expelled."

"What does that matter now?" he asked accusingly.

Nat looked at the ground. "I did it for your own good. I could have had you expelled already. You spend too much time with me."

"Well," he said, heaving his backpack back onto his shoulders, "now I spend no time with you."

Pain knotted her guts for a second.

Massi noticed that his words had hurt her. *Good*, he thought. *She deserved it.* He pushed past her and carried on with his journey.

Natalia watched, speechless, as he disappeared into the darkness.

CHAPTER TWENTY-THREE

The Academy's sprawling complex had been deliberately built in an obscure location deep in the North Virginia countryside. Even its entrance was hidden by a wall of tall trees. As Massi made his way towards the bus stop, the night grew blacker, and the streetlights became sparse. He wished he had brought a cap or hat. Feeling vulnerable, he became acutely aware of how secure and comfortable he was in the Academy. He unexpectedly missed a sense of shelter he never realised he took for granted.

The bus was almost empty, and it took an hour and a half to get to the northwest quadrant of Washington, DC. There were no stops for the first twenty minutes after arriving in the city; the first came after the bus had fully passed through a neighbourhood of massive homes, whose affluent occupants slept soundly in their beds. Deep in the Low Streets, Massi exited the bus. He instantly looked out of place. His clothes were a little too norm core for him to fully blend in with the eccentric crowd, but he was disguised by the Friday-night hustle and bustle. Nearby, patrons, chatting and vaping, spilled out of dive bars. The atmosphere of the main street was cheerful and relaxed. The smell of fried food and burnt sugar from street stalls and food trucks filled the air. The young faces around him looked relaxed, unlined and unburdened, unlike the intense, alert ones belonging to his comrades at the Academy. It occurred to Massi that the people here were enjoying a totally different life. He wondered if he would ever be able to walk among them without them knowing he had gone to the Academy. Had the place changed him so much that he was now permanently separated from them in some way? Was his back too straight? Or his walk too forthright? Perhaps he was not as different from them as he felt. This thought was immediately followed by the notion that this was not a good thing. He did not necessarily want to be like them. Looking back on his childhood, it was as though he had been called to the Academy like a priest to Holy Orders. There had been something different about him already, an eccentricity already present that predetermined the unconventional boy would become an exceptional man.

Massi ducked down a side street, and the foot traffic instantly thinned. A few more blocks and turns later, he found himself alone in a dark street. This was it. A shop with an old-fashioned front. The wood had been painted black and then grey. The lacquer was peeling, making it look like scales shedding from murky flesh. Bars and chains hung across the shop's main window. There was no name on the building anywhere, just a small number on the left side of the door frame letting Massi know he was in the right place. He thought the store might be closed, but the doorknob yielded when he twisted it. A small bell rang as he opened the door and stepped inside. The room was empty apart from a long, high counter at the back. When Massi approached it, he saw that it nearly reached his chest. There were no shelves or products behind it.

Hurried, hollow footsteps echoed in a stairway behind the counter, and a young man appeared. He had a shaved head, bolts through his ears and what looked like small devil's horns embedded under the skin on his skull. Panels of black tattoos covered his forearms and continued up underneath his black T-shirt, stopping just below his ears.

"Hey man, can I help you?" he asked.

Massi was taken aback by how friendly and welcoming he was.

"Er, yeah…I need to pick something up." Massi fumbled in his backpack. He took out the white card and placed it on the counter.

The young man took the card and enthusiastically said, "All right!" before traipsing back upstairs and fetching a small brown package the size of a shoebox. It was covered in postage stamps.

"Payment's already taken care of; she called ahead earlier this afternoon." He nodded at Massi and winked.

"Thanks," Massi said, not quite knowing what to make of the perfectly amicable interaction.

It was now time to see Sandy Attiyeh.

###

Massi determined that it was best to take an autocab. Sandy had assured him that it was safe for the guards to see him arrive. She lived in one of the smart buildings overlooking the river on the North Virginia side. All the buildings suggested that they were prime real estate with their slick contemporary exteriors. Sandy's building was not the best of them and probably cost less than she could afford, but Massi could see its appeal. The views were magnificent.

Upon exiting the autocab, Massi was immediately stopped by two guards. Their uniforms were white like Intelligence Command's but with red arm bands, which distinguished them as military police.

"Who are you here to see?" one of the guards asked him.

"I'm here to see Sandy Attiyeh." He paused then added, "I'm her cousin, William."

"Okay." One of the guards withdrew a small tablet from a holder strapped to the top of his thigh and ran a quick search. "We'll need to search your bag."

Massi handed them the backpack, and they led him inside to the lobby, where they ran his bag through a small x-ray machine. The portable machine looked to Massi like its presence in the lobby had preceded Sandy Attiyeh's house arrest. It looked like the ones Massi had seen in Soft Terror-era photos, when they had been at their most prolific. The guard looked at the machine's monitor, then lifted the bag off the belt and gave it back to him.

"Have a good evening, William," the guard said, emphasising the name as he let him pass. They knew he was not who he said he was. Massi, however, did not stop to ask how they knew. He reasoned the pretence was a precaution for his own benefit.

He nodded and walked through the lobby without looking back, trying to get into an elevator as quickly as possible. There were two guards outside the door to Sandy's penthouse, as well. One of them radioed down for permission to let him through. The guards then nodded to each other and allowed him to open the door.

"Good to see you, Billy," said Sandy, smiling as she ushered him inside.

###

Sandy loved it when people were impressed by her home. It was the only domain over which she could truly exercise full control. Being confined to her home was not an arduous punishment. She gave Massi a little tour before leading him to the balcony adjacent to the living room. It was a perfect, clear summer's night. Once outside, she looked at him and laughed.

In response, he changed his slack-jawed expression, attempted to relax and took a seat. Massi thought Sandy's smile made her beautiful. "I love this place," he said in awe.

"Thank you," she said. "It's a small consolation. All the money you make can't buy back your soul. It can, however, buy you somewhere nice to live."

Sandy thought the dark-haired youth was good-looking, but he also seemed boyish, despite being muscular. It was as though the various parts of his body had not quite grown at the same rate. He would even out in the next three years or so. She imagined she would find him quite attractive in ten years' time, though she did not find him appealing now.

"So, what's your name, again?" she asked, pouring herself some more wine.

"Massi."

"Is that short for something?"

"No, my name's Matthew, but when I was little, people would call me Matty. I couldn't pronounce that properly, so I said my name was Massi, and it stuck."

"That's adorable." She smiled warmly. "You want a drink?" She pointed to the crystal decanter on the table.

"No, thank you." He fidgeted in the chair.

"Do you have the stuff?" she asked.

"Excuse me?" he said.

"From the shop," she clarified, twitching.

"Oh yeah." He pulled his backpack open and handed her the brown package.

"Perfect." She ripped the brown paper off the carefully wrapped box. Its contents appeared to be make-up, several lipstick cases, small white boxes about the size of a man's palm and powder compacts. Sandy then disappeared inside her apartment, taking the lipstick cases with her but not the compacts or the boxes. She came back with a handful of small glass containers. To Massi's surprise, she then took the compacts one by one, cracked their casings and emptied the broken chunks of powder into the glass containers.

"You into any of this?" she asked.

"What is that?"

"A blend of natural opioids and other synthetic and semi-synthetic compounds."

"You made me get you drugs," he said, his mouth agape in horror.

She felt a pang of guilt for using him. "Yes," she said, "and no one is or will ever be more grateful to you in this life than I am right now."

"I can't believe you made me get you drugs. That's an expellable offense." He stood up and turned away to hide the violation on his face.

"Well, I couldn't get them myself," she said, half laughing. "Don't worry. It's not illegal to possess any of this. But, yes, obviously IC doesn't like their officers doing drugs."

"No shit."

"Sit back down," she said.

He obeyed.

She put lids on the containers and stacked them neatly at the edge of the table. She then opened one of the white boxes, removed a cigarette from it, took a lighter out of her pocket and lit it.

"You're smoking?" he said with mild disgust.

"Oh, sorry." She took another cigarette from the pack and offered it to Massi without hesitation. "You want one?"

"They're not allowed."

"I didn't ask you if they were allowed; I asked you if you wanted one." She flashed him a knowing smile.

"I didn't even know they made those anymore." He sounded incredulous.

"They still make them in Russia, China…lots of countries. You've lived a very sheltered life, haven't you?"

"I've just been at the Academy."

He suddenly seemed younger than he was, and Sandy felt sorry for mocking him.

"So, how is the old Academy these days?" she asked.

"Not great." He looked down.

"Not great? I thought you were desperate to graduate and get out there to do whatever they do now that there's no war." She flicked away some ash from her cigarette.

"I was, but I don't think I'm going to graduate."

"What's the matter—someone put a rat in your stew?" A sly, lopsided smile crept over her face.

"How...how did you know?" he asked, his eyes widening.

"Because it's an old tradition. Because you're the type. It's a little friendly hazing."

"Friendly?" he exclaimed. "So the Academy is behind the bullying! I knew it. How can they even do that?" His voice quivered, and he sounded as if he were about to cry.

"Look, they do this every once in a while to any cadet who starts glory-hogging, who doesn't blend seamlessly into their army of lemmings. That's why I like you, son."

"How are they allowed to do that?"

"It's a process. You either throw a tantrum and complain, or you conform. That way they know whether you consider yourself a part of the unit or not. From their point of view, the strength of the unit is what matters. Not whether you fancy yourself a war hero." She put the cigarette in her mouth.

"But you're considered a war hero."

"Yes, and look at my life," she said, exhaling. The smoke was a frosty blue. "On missions, you'll work in small, discreet teams. It requires a huge amount of trust. I...neglected my regiment in favour of things I thought were more important. Now I don't have a regiment to work with."

"The Academy is meant to be teaching me this?" he asked.

"You think the Academy is some nice, paternal organisation that just wants you to be the best you can be?" She sat back in her chair. "You are cannon fodder, sunshine. They don't want an individual. They want a malleable, disposable toy they can play their little games with."

"But we're the good guys," he protested.

"Just because we're the good guys doesn't mean we're the nice guys. You need to see IC as they are, not how you wish them to be."

"Why did you sign up, then?" he asked.

"There was a real enemy when I signed up. We were at war. Do you remember having to go through security checkpoints and metal detectors everywhere you went? Not in the last seven years or so, and that's because of me. I won the war for you. So you could move freely through your life without being mutilated at a moment's notice." She looked at him, her expression a mixture of curiosity and pity. "I don't know why anyone would sign up now," she added.

Massi thought for a moment. "What else would I do with myself?"

Sandy smiled and nodded; she knew that feeling. They sat together in silence for a minute until Sandy sensed his desire to ask more questions. "Ask me anything," she said. "You want to ask me something. Ask it."

"What were you doing with Lyndon Hamilton?"

Sandy laughed, stubbing out her cigarette on the brown paper packaging that was still on the table. "I was helping him with a little project."

"I saw him on TV. He looks insane."

"Yes, his whole empire and the future he had planned for humanity have crumbled before him." She smiled.

"What was his problem in the first place?" Massi asked.

"Hamilton's problem is a type of perfectionism. Freedom scares men like him. When people have freedom, they make choices that Hamilton would never have made on their behalf. Choices he perceives as wrong. Unnecessary. Wasteful. He sees humanity as messy. He wanted to be the person who cleaned it up. He wanted to line humanity up like toy soldiers. The world isn't pretty. Life is meant to be messy. In a world where free speech and expression exist, people will always say and do things that are ugly and offensive. We think that just because we're told that free speech is a positive thing, it's also going to be a pretty thing, and then we're surprised when it comes out hideous and offensive. A thing can still be a positive thing even though it's as ugly as sin."

"They say you made something for him."

"I made a database. He wanted to use it to create information blind spots. It's a way of manipulating people by omission. Depriving them of certain information. Bribe a scientist here, blackmail a journalist there. The messages you want flood media outlets. You under-report some things, overemphasise others. It changes behaviour eventually. He was trying to ensure that people would voluntarily choose what he perceives as the best choices for them. It's subtle, brilliant, and some may even call it noble. It also presupposes that human beings are rational actors. Sadly, they're not. They're emotional actors. They'd still make decisions that he didn't like, and then he'd have to use force to subdue them, and we're ablaze once more. There's no sanitising the world."

"You still helped him, though," said Massi emphatically.

"Yes, but I was never going to hand it over to him. I knew his reasons for building that database weren't innocent. Hamilton made it seem like standard corporate espionage, but then he gradually made me map more and more small, independent research institutes and universities that didn't have any need for mass information storage. I saw that he had no interest in other types of companies that used mass information storage, like most banks. The inclusion of his competition was either to nullify his main competitors as a happy side effect, or it was a deliberate red herring."

Massi was becoming frustrated. He was not interested in the how.

"Why?" he said. "I want to know why you did it. I don't care about why Hamilton did it. Why did you do it? You gave us a lecture on how precious information is. Why would an officer of Intelligence Command do something so illegal that it's almost treason?"

Sandy straightened up in her seat. "Because I was bored. That's the truth. I was so bored I could have died."

Massi looked away and thought carefully about his next question. "Did they torture you? One of my friends says she saw you at the InfoSec building."

"Ah, yes, the little lady who got through my modified Sapeeco." Her expression became contemplative.

"Her name's Natalia," Massi said, then wished he had not.

"Natalia," repeated Sandy. "What's her surname?"

Massi stayed silent. Sandy smiled. She did not blame him if he no longer trusted her.

"Where did she learn how to do what she did?"

"I dunno." Massi did not need to lie. "She spends all her free time in the computer labs."

"Hmm...I used to do that." Sandy took a swig of wine.

"I think she taught herself. She's very clever."

"She's very attractive, isn't she?" Sandy teased, sensing his protectiveness over her.

"Yeah, she is," he admitted, nodding his head.

"You in love with her?" asked Sandy.

"No." Massi blushed as he lied.

"Good," said Sandy. "Being in love is the difference between being alive and merely existing, but it is... inconvenient. Don't ever fall in love. If you do, remember that all love should be conditional. Be in control of love. Love selfishly. Or it will torture you."

Massi remembered reading about Sandy Attiyeh's heroics in the war. There had been a name he had often seen associated with her but mostly as an afterthought. Lucian Scott. Where was Scott today? He could not recall what happened to him, but now he remembered his face from newsreels. He had seen that face again and again in Sandy's apartment when she first took him round it. Scott was ever present in Sandy's framed photographs, mostly formal ones of them as cadets but in a few casual ones, too. Scott had been more than just a footnote in Sandy's life.

"It is torturing me," he said.

"Ah, now we have the truth." Sandy grinned. She was enjoying the gossip as well as feeling jolly from the drink. Massi thought he could detect a slight southern drawl creeping into her accent as she got more inebriated. "Love triangle?"

"No, there's no one else." Massi's face turned downward. "There's no one else, and she still doesn't want me."

"Yes, that is worse," said Sandy. "Much worse."

"We were making out. It was nothing really, but we got caught and had to go up in front of a panel." Massi shook his head. "She didn't even hesitate to get me in trouble to save herself. She kissed <u>me</u>, and then she made me out to be some sort of pervert." His brows furrowed at the mere thought of it.

"Women—don't trust 'em. Don't trust a single one of 'em."

"I'm on double drills because of that." He rubbed his hands together.

"Double drills will help when it comes to your finals," said Sandy. "Especially the Combis."

Combis were field combat tests. To graduate, the cadets had to pass the final two Combis with a sixty-five percent or more. To get a distinction, they needed to pass with eighty percent. Getting into a decent regiment was impossible without a distinction.

"I know. I already feel fitter, but...she made it seem like after the Academy we'd be together."

"Forget it. After you graduate, it's unlikely you'll be in the same regiment. You could be stationed on the other side of the world."

"She's on the tech track, so it probably won't happen anyway."

"That's why she promised you she'd be with you after." Sandy jabbed a finger in his direction. "She knew she'd never have to honour that promise."

"I know. Deep down, I always knew. But how do I survive the Academy until then?"

"Listen, the Academy wouldn't be bothering to hammer you into shape if they didn't think you had potential. The part of you that's you—you need to lock that up. Put it in a box and hide it. Don't let them have all of you, like I did. Just be what they want you to be. You need to pass the final two Combis with more than eighty percent."

"I know. I know." He nodded.

"When it comes to the team Combi, all of you need to get over the finish line. Understand? That's the point of the team Combi." Sandy looked very serious.

"Okay," said Massi.

"I can't stress this enough. Your whole unit needs to get over the line."

"I understand."

"Listen, kid, it's almost three a.m. Sleep on my couch. I'll get you an extra pillow. Don't think about the girl."

"I'll try, but I can make no guarantees."

"Try harder. You have to pass those Combis," Sandy said her tone becoming serious.

"I will. I've been distracted, but deep down, I still want this."

"That's my boy, all right," she said, standing up. Her eyes were now glazed over from the alcohol and a lack of sleep. "You need to be back at school by midday tomorrow. And on Monday I have to testify against Hamilton."

CHAPTER TWENTY-FOUR

Early the following morning, Massi disembarked from the bus and began walking towards the Academy. He had slept only a few hours and had thought it best to leave Sandy Attiyeh's apartment sooner rather than later. Sandy seemed more human to him now—and less like a hero. She was more like a tragic princess in a tower, not needing to be rescued, or even wanting to be. Massi felt a powerful sensation of relief as the Academy's buildings came into view. He craved the familiar faces and environments of the school and vowed never to take the place for granted again.

When he reached the barracks, he was surprised to find that his disappearance had not been conspicuous. His excuse the day before, that he had been unwell, had been accepted without question. He settled back into his bunk and enjoyed the day of rest with the other male cadets. The cadets spent their days off reading, watching TV in the common rooms, catching up on lost sleep and playing light sports like table tennis. Their bodies were desperate for relaxation after the gruelling physical challenges of the week.

Massi's meeting with Sandy Attiyeh had left him feeling less like some detached, lonesome outlaw. He did not have as much in common with her as he had once thought, and he now found her position and status undesirable. Instead, he felt as if he belonged with the other cadets.

He did not see Natalia until lunch. In the canteen, he saw her glance his way as he entered, and he made an effort to sit nowhere near her. That day, the canteen was lively and rich with gossip. The students who had been sponsored by Hamilton InfoSec had now been told that their places at the Academy were fully funded and secure. Their dour mood of recent days seemed like ancient history. There was no shortage of companies offering to pay their full tuition in exchange for the option to employ them first after their military service was over. Instead, everyone was talking about whether the cadets would get to watch Lyndon Hamilton's trial next week.

###

On Monday morning, the military police stationed outside Sandy's apartment knocked on her door.

"Just come in," she shouted. "I'm not quite ready yet."

They entered and stood on the cold marble of the apartment's lobby. After a few moments, Sandy walked into the living room, zipping up her uniform and straightening her medal bars. It was turning into a sweltering summer, but she did not want to wear anything sleeveless in court, and her civilian wardrobe consisted mostly of tank tops. The uniform, she figured, would make her seem more respectable and sympathetic. Everyone loved a veteran.

"Okay, let's go," she said.

"You need to wear these." One of her guards held up a pair of Intelligence Command handcuffs. The cuffs were made of a thick wire that went around the wrists and attached to a small metal square. The design forced the wearer to hold his or her hands close together and made it painful to manoeuvre once inside them.

"Are you serious?" said Sandy, shocked.

"You're still in custody, Sandy."

"I'm getting a pardon!"

"That's not public knowledge yet."

Sandy nodded reluctantly, trying not to reveal that her temper was simmering inside her. She held out her hands and allowed herself to be cuffed, wishing she had not worn her uniform after all.

Sandy was led to a waiting car flanked by two military police officers. The part she was most dreading was entering the courthouse. Photos of her in handcuffs were now inevitable.

The ensuing press attention exceeded Sandy's expectations. The autocar often had to halt unexpectedly to avoid hitting paparazzi. After a while, it began moving slowly to allow the crowd that had formed around it to part. Security guards had been stationed outside the courthouse, but the crowd was overwhelming them.

Sandy got out of the autocar, which had parked only a few metres from the main entrance, and was guided up the stairs towards a large wooden door. Her eyes were almost fully closed due to the sheer ferocity of the camera flashes. Sandy turned her neck to avoid the worst of the blinding light. It was then that she saw something that upset her more than an entire sea of photographers. Something that made her guts churn inside her. In the crowd, just before she walked into the courthouse, she saw the woman's face. The protestor. Only for an instant. She did not know the woman's name, but she had seen her before. At the talk show and several times before that. The woman looked at Sandy as though she could see right through her. This woman was someone committed enough to be present at all Sandy's public appearances. Someone who knew the black marks on her soul. It was as though all of Sandy's sins were exposed to her. This woman but no one else. Perhaps she was someone who knew that Sandy suffered from nightmares. Perhaps she was someone who thought Sandy deserved those nightmares. But did the woman really know? Or was she just a protestor very certain of her own guesses? Sandy's heart beat more fervently now. The woman had been nodding, a small smile on her face. She was pleased to see Sandy in handcuffs.

###

Lyndon Hamilton wore a crisp white shirt with a pristine grey suit and a pale blue tie. He sat still, looking down at his polished leather shoes. Like Sandy's, his hands were cuffed. He occupied the dock, which was positioned on a raised, fenced-off platform in the centre of the room. Sandy had been led into the courtroom and sat cuffed in the gallery. Her arms had become heavy and uncomfortable. The cuffs especially hurt her left arm, which was still healing from Hamilton's assault. She was sitting a few metres behind Hamilton. She could not see his face, but she guessed that if he turned to the left, he would be able to see her from the corner of his eye. On the right side of the courtroom and behind a screen of one-way glass, the jury sat facing Hamilton. Sandy found this unusual and did not know whether it was common practice to disguise the jury in such a way. She had not been in a courtroom since the signing of the armistice agreement. Back then, of course, she had not participated in a trial; she had merely given evidence so that the peace negotiators could establish facts.

Directly in front of Hamilton was the unoccupied judge's bench. It was raised, as if it were looming over the defendant. Sandy leaned forward to get a look at one of Hamilton's lawyers, who was sitting in front and to the right of the raised dock. Her view was partially obscured. No doubt Hamilton would have employed the best lawyers in town, but Sandy did not think any lawyer could do much to sway this case. From what Drummond had told her, the discovery of Maria D'Souza's remains meant that Hamilton would not get off scot-free. If the lawyer did manage to make an impact, it would be merely to tweak the lengths of Hamilton's sentences.

Emerging from a door near the jury, a neatly dressed clerk walked into the room and announced, "Please rise for the Honourable Justice Dwight Braddock. The court is now in session."

A middle-aged man dressed in black robes entered the room, passed in front of Sandy and took his place on the bench directly opposite Hamilton.

"Please be seated," said the clerk.

"Lyndon Hamilton, you stand accused of first-degree murder; the violation of Data Security Act 2.11, Data Handling Act 3.21 and the Information Privacy Act 2.49; unlawful imprisonment; assault; conspiracy to commit acts of domestic terror; and treason," Justice Braddock read aloud in a loud, husky voice. "Do you comprehend the charges that have been made against you?"

"Yes," said Hamilton.

Sandy was taken aback that Hamilton had been charged with treason. If Lyndon Hamilton was found guilty of treason, he could be given the death penalty. Before the Long War, the death penalty had been widely phased out both nationally and internationally. When it was resuscitated during the war, it was used predominantly by the military and not in civilian trials. Being guilty of treason was the only time an exception to this rule was made.

The clerk spoke next. "Please state how you plead to the following accusations." She took a breath. "The murder of Maria D'Souza?"

"Guilty," said Hamilton, his voice loud, firm and clear.

A soft gasp rippled throughout the courtroom.

"Violating Data Security Act 2.11, Data Handling Act 3.21 and Information Privacy Act 2.49? You may plead separately to each act."

"Guilty. Of all."

"The unlawful imprisonment and assault of Alisande Attiyeh?"

"Guilty."

Sandy felt all eyes in the courtroom turn in her direction.

The clerk continued, "Conspiracy to commit acts of domestic terror?"

"Not guilty."

"Treason."

"Not guilty." Hamilton's voice rose. "Everything I did was for this country. For humanity."

Sandy was surprised by this outburst from Hamilton. One of Hamilton's lawyers turned to face him and shot him an expression uniquely designed to shut him up.

Since Hamilton had already pled guilty to all charges except domestic terror and treason, the court had to prosecute only those two. As Sandy watched the trial, she contemplated how things would play out when she herself was tried. She intended to plead guilty to the charges of violating the data and information acts, as Hamilton had. If Hamilton was found not guilty of conspiracy to commit domestic terror or treason, then Sandy would not have to be tried for those charges at all.

To win, the prosecution had to prove Hamilton intended to use his database to exert an unnatural level of control over the population. They also had to convince the jury that Hamilton's behaviour was in fact terroristic in nature. Wanting to control the news cycle and influence policy was sinister, but it was not what most people considered terrorism. Memories of the Soft Terror, with all its real, aggressive, ugly violence, were still fresh in many people's minds. Hamilton's fetish for societal control was not intuitively akin to that. Sandy wondered what the demographic of the jury was. A jury composed of older people might be unsympathetic to the suggestion that Hamilton's behaviour was terrorism. A younger jury might resent the suggestion that they could be so easily controlled by someone like Hamilton. Sandy clenched her teeth in silent frustration.

Hamilton's lawyer argued that his client merely wanted to exercise more influence over the research he generously funded and to get it on the news. Allegations of domestic terrorism were ludicrous, he said, and the charges of treason even more so. Hamilton testified that he was never going to use the model to cause any loss of life or even to scare anyone. He had no intention of disrupting the government or making himself a ruler. Sandy knew all this to be true. Hamilton probably considered conventional terrorism to be untidy.

To back up their case, the prosecution presented the jury with more evidence of Hamilton's malicious character. This included the sworn testimony of Farlow, who firmly asserted that it was Hamilton alone who had killed Maria D'Souza in order to keep her quiet. Whatever bonds of loyalty Hamilton had previously enjoyed with Farlow had been loosened. Sandy found herself feeling sorry for Farlow, who now appeared to be no more than a poor, lurching creature. She could see small marks on his skin peeking out from under his shirt at the top of his neck. Her feelings of pity for Farlow did not stop her mouth cracking into a wry smile at the thought of him getting a taste of the medicine he had so gleefully inflicted upon her.

Farlow testified that it was he who had wounded Sandy on Hamilton's instruction, and he corroborated that the assault had been initiated because Sandy had refused to give Hamilton access to the database. Sandy winced as hospital pictures of her burnt, tortured and semi-dressed body were displayed to the jury.

The prosecution leveraged Farlow's testimony by citing Hamilton's relationship with the Sun Circle Group. They presented the court evidence of misbehaviour on behalf of other cult members, including a member who set himself on fire, a member who almost drowned her child trying to 'wash away the sin' and several members who had starved themselves to death, believing their sacrifice would rid the world of gluttony. All the individuals the prosecution cited were acquaintances of Hamilton, and though Sandy thought the link was tenuous, even she would admit the prosecution did a good job of displaying the cult's penchant for unhealthy behaviour. And why, the prosecution asked, would Hamilton kill Maria D'Souza if his intentions were so pure?

Sandy was never quite convinced that the charge of domestic terrorism would stick. Hamilton's lawyers were competent and sharp enough to exploit the prosecution's few mistakes. It was not until the very last moment when the clerk read the jury's decision, however, that Sandy would know for certain what Hamilton's fate would be.

The trial lasted just over a month. At its conclusion, Lyndon Hamilton was found guilty of conspiracy to commit domestic terrorism, but not of treason, which meant that Sandy would still have to be tried for both.

CHAPTER TWENTY-FIVE

Sandy was dozing comfortably on her couch. Outside, the summer sun was bright, and the air was warm. An open window let in a gentle breeze. She slipped in and out of a light sleep. Her own trial was set to start the following Monday, but she was untroubled by it. The facts surrounding the incidents of the past few months had already been established in Hamilton's trial. All that remained was to get her trial over and done with.

Sandy now had time to think about what her life would be like after she was pardoned. This business with Hamilton had allowed her to close the door on her military career. Sitting silently in the courthouse gallery had been the impetus she needed to finally let go of the IC. She had used Hamilton's month-long trial to mourn her former vocation. She knew she should just bite the bullet and go to college. After her trial was over, she decided, she would pick a university and sell her apartment. She could ace any computer science course, but the civilian jobs those courses led to might prove too dull to hold her attention or, worse, too similar to their military forms for her to feel that she had made a clean break. Maybe graphic design? Doing something creative with creative people would be a change, at least.

The sharp ring shocked her out of her thoughts and caused her whole body to stir. She grabbed her white phone from the coffee table and groggily answered, "Hello?"

"Hi, Sandy, this is Dr Reuben. Is now a good a time to talk?"

Sandy sat bolt upright. "Yes."

"Good news. Lucian has shown some movement in his right arm. Obviously, we're thrilled, and we thought you'd like to know."

"Yes, yes, there's never been any movement before," said Sandy, her voice brimming with excitement.

"I don't want to make any promises, but we consider this a really positive sign. Perhaps a familiar voice would be beneficial to him."

"Of course…of course. I'm coming now." Sandy hung up the phone, ran to her bedroom and pulled clean clothes from her dresser. She took a brief moment to rub some concealer onto the few blemishes on her face and to tidy her unruly hair. She dashed to the front door and opened it quickly, startling the armed guards still posted outside.

"I need to see Luca again. You guys can take me to the hospital, right?"

The two guards, a man and a woman, stepped inside the lobby of her apartment.

"Sandy, you're under house arrest," said the male military police officer. Both officers shared an unimpressed frown.

"Yeah, but I assumed I could go to the hospital," said Sandy, still hopeful.

"Not without prior approval," he said.

"Okay, how do I get approval?" she asked.

"I'll send you a link to the form." The male officer retrieved a tablet from his pocket.

"What? Come on. You can just ask Muro. Call her; she knows about Lucian."

"That's not a decision for Commander Muro. You have to apply to the chief justice. Since you're military personnel, Drummond has to approve, as well."

"Are you serious? How long will that take?" The optimism drained from her face.

"Usually six weeks," said the officer.

"Six weeks?" said Sandy, enraged.

"Afraid so."

"Okay, forget it." She pouted. "I'll wait until after I'm pardoned. Which will probably be the end of next week anyway."

"Sandy," the male officer said, his tone softening, "it's rare for anyone in custody to be placed under house arrest. You were granted the privilege in light of your years of service and on account of your injuries." He searched her face for any sign of gratitude.

Instead, she just nodded insolently.

###

High Ambassador McCawley did not eat foreign food. He liked steak, medium rare, with mashed potatoes and creamed spinach on the side. Dessert was always cherry cheesecake with a slosh of American bourbon. McCawley could only tolerate one restaurant in the entire city, and it was in the northeast quadrant, two blocks north of the Supreme Court building. He ate there alone almost every day, but today he was joined by a slim, dark-skinned man with short salt-and-pepper hair and a beard. McCawley finished his meal. His guest, having put down his knife and fork ten minutes earlier and having declined dessert, was now patiently picking his teeth.

"How many years did Hamilton get in the end?" asked Kashif Ahmed Khaled, ambassador to the Central Arabian Republic.

"Life for the murder," said McCawley, "twenty years for the data security violations, twenty years for what he did to Attiyeh, another life sentence for the domestic terror charges. Double life plus forty in the end."

"How many years will Attiyeh get?"

"None," McCawley said, dabbing his mouth with a napkin. "Her pardon, for all charges, has been signed by Drummond already, and just needs to be ratified by the other members of the Ruling Council. It's politically difficult for any of us to refuse another member's pardon."

"A little hacking is not what she should be going to jail for, Clement." Khaled shook his head.

McCawley put down his cutlery.

"Khaled, you know I take you out for a meal because I think you enjoy my company, and every time you ask me for the same thing."

"My thirst for justice has not been sated," he said quickly.

"I couldn't possibly comment on a top-secret operation. You don't even have proof she was there." McCawley shrugged.

"We both know she was there. Stop treating me like a fool. When she took part in the fact-finding inquiry during the armistice talks, she condemned herself." Khaled gathered the used toothpicks into a little pile on the table. "She confirmed she was fifty kilometres from the Hazirat refugee camp on a supposedly unrelated operation called 'Jazan', and then almost two thousand of my people die in a mysterious fire. One of them happens to be Al Shahidi, we find out later. How convenient.

She maintains she was fifty kilometres away the whole time. What kind of idiots do you think we are? You expect us to believe there was no movement of IC troops?"

"I don't think you're an idiot, but a smart, wise person picks his battles carefully. After all, it's illegal for military personnel to go within five kilometres of a refugee camp. It's also illegal for combatants like Al Shahidi to be in refugee camps," said McCawley as he gesticulated to a waiter.

"Is she going to go to jail or not?"

McCawley shook his head, "She most certainly is not."

"What she did was a crime against humanity. She should have been locked away years ago."

"All is fair in love and war," said McCawley. "Your people weren't treated very well by Shahidi, if I recall."

"The week after she is officially pardoned, I will call for a public inquiry." His voice and countenance were calm, but his eyes were a raging sea of hatred and anger.

"It would be unwise for a young nation such as yours to <u>offend</u> one of their allies," McCawley said. "Especially one so committed to rebuilding a war-ravaged nation like yours." He paused. "That's not to say that a nation such as mine would be unwilling to use this as an opportunity to provide a small measure of justice."

"I want her to go to jail for life."

"No one goes to jail for life for data-security violations, which, I'll admit, she was definitely guilty of. That's just not reasonable." McCawley shook his head. "The domestic terror charges? The treason? If those two don't stick—and I don't think they will—and if she goes down for life, it will look a lot like the type of political chicanery that you and I are currently indulging in."

Khaled leant back in his chair. His eyes flickered around the room, then focussed back on McCawley.

"Forty years," said Khaled.

"Ten," countered McCawley.

"Twenty."

"Twenty," said McCawley, nodding.

A waiter appeared with two glasses of bourbon. The two men took the glasses off the tray and clinked them together.

"And Christopher Drummond? What will he say of this?" asked Khaled.

"He encouraged me to have this little lunch. Between you and me, he's wanted her out of the picture for years."

###

The cadets had been allowed to watch Lyndon Hamilton's trial outside class hours, but Massi had found very little time to do so. He had needed extra sleep to cope with double drills. He relied on second-hand accounts of the trial from other cadets. The impression he got was that the whole thing was rather dry. The only interesting feature of the trial had been the involvement of Sandy Attiyeh, but her testimony had been short. She told the jury that she had built a database of some sort but had refused to let Hamilton have access to it. Massi watched reruns of her testimony during the weekend, and he could tell that she was telling the truth. His opinion of her softened. If she had colluded with Hamilton to gain insights into his plans, she had still acted in the best interests of the country. Her motivations now seemed more selfless than they previously had. Their meeting had made her seem more human, but it had also made him like her less.

Massi tried not to let his thoughts take him away from his final tests. The cadets' core curriculum in maths, English, the sciences, technology, survival skills, geography and history (with an emphasis on military history) had ended. For cadets on the field track, like Massi, there were no formal assessments for these subjects. What mattered were the Combis. For these combat operation tests, field track cadets were first assessed as individuals and then as units in the greater team Combi. The tech-track cadets had already taken a series of individual technical assessments in the labs, so they only had the minor team Combis left.

Massi and the other cadets had already been briefed on how the Combis were conducted. The individual Combi took place indoors and included a series of fitness and targeting tests. For targeting, the cadets would be using live ammo. The greater team Combi took place in the wilderness. The Academy owned great swathes of land in the Blue Ridge Mountains and had constructed a corridor sixty kilometres long by ten kilometres wide. This corridor was engineered to be an assault course, complete with androids to pose as enemies. The cadets did not have much contact with graduated officers, and Massi had struggled to get a clear picture of what the Combis were really like.

Since its inception, two cadets had died during the greater team Combi. Upon first hearing this, Massi had assumed that the cadets had been accidentally shot. Later he learned that live ammo was used only in the individual Combi. The cadets were given modified paraguns with which to defend themselves in the team Combi. The deaths had been caused by unfortunate accidents. One cadet had fallen awkwardly off a steep ridge and broken his neck. The other, a female cadet, had drowned after wading too deep into fast-moving water.

Massi had dreamed that during the Combis, the cadets would finally get to wear black-op suits, so he was bitterly disappointed to hear that they would be wearing only the inferior Field Command camo suits. When he became anxious about the Combis, he calmed himself with the words Colonel Mathers had spoken during the briefing: "There is no quota. All of you can pass. We have spent years training you. Trust that training. We want you all to pass."

###

Sandy brushed her hair, braided it and pinned it into a neat chignon. Her white uniform was flawless, and her black boots had been polished to a high sheen. The military police guards were waiting in her living room. She stretched her arms outward and once again allowed herself to be cuffed, this time without argument.

The female protestor who had been present at Hamilton's trial was outside the courthouse again. This time, Sandy shot her a filthy look of her own. Sandy was sick of being judged for her actions in the war. Everybody, it seemed, thought they knew exactly how they would act in life-and-death situations, but not until they were truly tested did they even have a clue. It took years of training to be able to override gut instinct.

Sandy sat in the raised dock that Hamilton had occupied just one week earlier. Commander Muro was in the gallery. The neatly dressed clerk from Hamilton's trial entered, giving Sandy a spooky feeling of déjà vu. Even the judge was the same.

"Alisande Attiyeh, you stand accused of the violation of Data Security Act 2.11, Data Handling Act 3.21 and the Information Privacy

Act 2.49; conspiracy to commit acts of domestic terror; and treason," said Justice Braddock. "Do you comprehend the charges that have been made against you?"

Sandy felt irrationally nervous. She did not have her tabs with her. If she had an episode, she would not be able to control it. "I do," she replied.

"Please state how you plead to the following accusations," said the clerk, mirroring her performance in the first trial. "Violating Data Security Act 2.11, Data Handling Act 3.21 and Information Privacy Act 2.49? You may plead separately to each act."

"Guilty. To all." Sandy started to shiver.

"Conspiracy to commit acts of domestic terror?"

"Not guilty."

"Treason?"

"Not guilty."

CHAPTER TWENTY-SIX

At the age of twenty-four, Sandy Attiyeh had been promoted from the rank of corporal to sergeant. Her surprise advancement had been preceded by a six-month leave of absence to recover from a bullet wound to the neck. The injury had left her with no permanent physiological damage, but she had lost a near-fatal amount of blood. The bullet had gone clean through her neck, nicking an artery in the process. Had she not been rescued so quickly, she most certainly would have died. She had been shot while fleeing a gas attack that claimed the lives of most of the officers in her regiment. Afterward, Commander Levy, the head of Intelligence Command, had strongly advised High Commander Drummond not to use Sandy for his next top-secret operation. The operation in Surabaya had gone so inexplicably wrong that Levy was convinced Sandy was cursed. Drummond had insisted that Sandy was the right agent for his new operation, and he cited her survival as proof she was lucky. Still, Levy acquiesced only when Drummond offered him the retirement he had been denied for three years. Though Levy had observed the Surabaya mission only from a distance, delegating the management of the mission to his best senior officers, the loss of life was a major embarrassment for ICHQ. Too many questions were being asked in the press about Surabaya, and the media attention had become unrelenting. Levy's retirement had silenced them all.

Sandy had been summoned to Drummond's office soon after Levy was out of the way. Her face was hard, but her eyes looked forlorn.

"Thanks for coming, Corporal Attiyeh."

Sandy nodded.

"I'm sorry about Operation Surabaya," he said.

"Me too." Sandy's voice was weak.

"What's done is done. I have a new job for you," said Drummond formally. He paused. "Have you ever heard of the name 'Al Thubaba'?"

Sandy nodded in acknowledgment. Of course, she had heard the name. What member of the armed forces had not heard the name? Al Thubaba was the brain, spine and central nervous system of the most vicious terrorist organisation in history. He had so many aliases, his real name did not matter anymore. There was one moniker, however, that drove Christopher Drummond absolutely apoplectic with rage. A name that wounded his pride on a subcutaneous level. Al Thubaba. The Fly. An unusually comical name for a terror chief, the nickname was a direct reference to Drummond's failure to apprehend him.

"We have what I consider to be good intelligence on his whereabouts. Obtained thanks to your efforts in Surabaya."

Sandy's eyes widened. "How good?"

"Very good," said Drummond confidently.

"We've been wrong before."

"Oh yes, many times." Drummond nodded. "But this is different. One of our best agents died for this information. He managed to transmit what we needed before he..." He trailed off. "I want you for this operation."

"The operation?"

"To kill him. To kill the Fly."

"Yes," said Sandy without hesitation.

"Excellent. You're receiving a new rank, effective immediately. You'll be transported to the base camp for this operation within the next three days. We'll be referring to this operation by the code name 'Jazan', but the real name for this operation is 'Damask'. You'll report to Colonel Claudette Muro. I think you'll like her."

"I've met her a couple of times in passing. She was one of the senior officers at Surabaya, but I didn't report directly to her," Sandy said, nodding.

"Yes, I believe she was out of the country on compassionate leave the night of the...incident." He cleared his throat to swallow back his unease, then changed the subject. "Because of the nature of this mission, this is something you'll be doing solo. I'm glad you've said yes. I can't think of anyone better for this than you."

"I'm honoured, sir," said Sandy numbly, overwhelmed by what was happening.

"You'll do me proud, Sergeant."

Sandy saluted. Drummond stood and returned the salute. Sandy then turned and left his office, trying to process the magnitude of what had just happened. She was being sent to kill Al Thubaba alone.

Sandy could barely see a thing during her journey from the airfield to the base of the operation. She was in a car, the second of a convoy of three inconspicuous ancient jeeps, and the vehicles whipped up so much desert dust that her view of her surroundings was almost completely obscured. She could not even see the base until she arrived at it. Exiting the jeep, she noticed a small cluster of three field tents perfectly camouflaged among the sandy landscape, blending in almost seamlessly with the rocky desert terrain. The tents had their flaps open on either side, willing a breeze to reprieve their occupants of the oppressive heat. Nylon fly nets covered their openings to keep the incessant swarms of desert insects at bay.

Back at the airfield, Sandy had been met by a man named Major Melton Parkins, who now led her to the tent in the middle of the base. Inside, Colonel Muro was hunched over a table. She looked older than Sandy remembered.

"Ma'am," said Parkins.

Muro looked up. "Sergeant Attiyeh?"

"Reporting for duty, ma'am," said Sandy.

"Good to meet you, finally."

"Likewise, ma'am. I served with your son. Briefly. Before his accident."

"Ah, best not to think of it." Muro shook away the thought. "You speak Arabic, correct?"

"Yes, ma'am."

"Perfect. Any other reasons Drummond chose you for this?"

"None that I can think of, ma'am."

Muro glanced around the tent. "Everyone except Parkins, please leave."

As ordered, the two other soldiers immediately left the tent. Turning back to Sandy, Muro gestured to the large map in front of them.

"This mass here," she said, showing Sandy, "is the Hazirat refugee camp. This is where he's hiding. We're here, roughly thirty kilometres southeast."

Sandy flinched. "A refugee camp? We'll be breaking international law."

International law expressly forbade military personnel and combatants from moving within five kilometres of refugee camps. The law was enacted after the paramilitary of a rogue state had ransacked a camp, sold the women and girls as sex slaves and absorbed the boys into their army.

"We're already breaking international law by being here. Don't think about that. Think about how many lives we'll be saving. Think about how he's currently using innocent women and children as human shields."

"How well is the camp protected?" asked Sandy.

"It's sprawling. There was a fence, but the camp has now exceeded the fence by two kilometres," said Muro. "They don't have the resources to keep it well guarded. From what we know, Al Thubaba isn't well protected, either. He's hiding in plain sight. Guns are forbidden within the camp. Which also means you won't be getting a gun. Even suppressed, a gunshot will just be too conspicuous."

The look on Sandy's face revealed her displeasure at the thought of being sent on a mission unarmed.

"You'll have a small knife in your suit," said Muro as if reading Sandy's mind. "At the left thigh."

"Okay," said Sandy, nodding, the strained expression still evident on her face. Sandy had killed many adversaries with guns before…but never with a knife.

"If you could be conservative with the wounds you inflict, that would obviously be better, but we still need you to bring something back so we can test his DNA…"

"Okay," said Sandy, interrupting Muro. "How's this going to work?"

"We're going to drive you twenty-five kilometres from here. You'll need to walk the last five kilometres at night. You'll have a black suit. That's the only way we can think you'll be able to get there undetected. It'll be after midnight when you get into the camp. Major Parkins and a car will wait for you exactly where you were dropped off, but if you're not back before zero six hundred, it won't be there. The quicker this gets done, the better."

"How will I know where to find him?"

"All the tents are marked. He's in H-71142."

"Do you trust this intelligence?"

"This intelligence has not been corroborated, but..." Muro paused. "It's good enough."

"Anything else I should know?"

"I know that six months ago my husband died just after transmitting this intelligence to IC. He was ambushed just after he made the transmission. They dropped his left arm at the consulate so we would know who was killed by their chip. We never found anymore of him."

Sandy inhaled at this gruesome story.

Muro continued, "I know that Al Thubaba ordered the massacre that killed your parents."

Sandy nodded, trying not to reveal any emotion. She did not need to be lectured on the seriousness of the situation, but Muro's intense glare never wavered.

"Your new black-ops suit," Muro continued, lifting the garment from beneath the table. "It's specifically engineered for a desert climate. At night you'll be virtually invisible...and cool."

Sandy ran her hands over the shimmering scales of the brand-new suit. She felt the hard, flat raised lump where the blade was concealed. "It's beautiful," said Sandy. "It's not like my one at home."

"It has an expanded hydropack, but I would still advise you to use your water sparingly."

"When do we begin?"

"Tonight at twenty-three hundred. Rest until then. Hydrate."

Sandy nodded and took the suit. Her palms were sweating in the oppressive heat.

Before leaving, Muro said, "Good luck, Sandy. If you pull this off, tomorrow we'll be living in a different world."

The solitary vehicle did not leave the base until after the sun had set completely. In her tent, Claudette Muro held a satellite phone to her lips.

"Has she gone?" Drummond's voice spoke clearly through the line.

"She's gone."

"Excellent. If she doesn't come back, it's not a problem. Don't expend any extra resources or personnel trying to retrieve her."

"Understood, sir."

"Oh, and Muro?"

"Yes, sir?"

"If everything goes to plan, the head job is yours."

"Understood, sir."

The desert sky was a perfect canopy of shining stars. Much to Sandy's relief, Parkins did not attempt to make conversation on the way to the drop-off point. She was busy preparing her mind. She had made sure to empty her bladder before the mission; she did not want to be distracted once she had set off. Her guts churned inside her. This was the worst part. The anticipation. She knew that things would subside once she started walking.

The car began to slow. When it came to a stop, Parkins made a sideways glance at Sandy. "Remember, be back by zero six hundred," he said. "That's more than enough time."

Sandy nodded, pulled the high-tech balaclava over her face and exited the vehicle. Then she began to walk. The balaclava's night-vision technology helped her see in the dark. She could see the desert's perfect detail, insects, plants and even geckos fleeing from the slight sounds of her footsteps. The terrain was uneven, and for the first half of the journey she could not even see the city of tents. The heat of the day had given way to a cool night. Sandy would have been almost chilly had it not been for her suit's ability to maintain a constant temperature. After she climbed a small hill, a blue glow from the camp became visible, luminescent in the dark night. It was a darkness Sandy had only experienced before in the deep wilderness of Indashin. There was not another town or city for hundreds of miles.

As Sandy got closer, she realised that the blue glow was a smattering of LEDs. They emitted just enough light to guide a person through the maze of tents but not enough to do anything productive at night. The camp seemed unusually quiet, but that made sense if electricity was absent and fuel was scarce. The camp's inhabitants had long gone to sleep, as they rose and retired with the natural light to conserve batteries, candles and oil.

The camp seemed darker once she got inside it. A few times she heard nearby voices, so she stood still and light on her feet until they moved away. At one point she thought she heard footsteps, so she crouched behind a tent. She felt something metal beneath her fingers as her hand touched the ground: it was a seven-inch screwdriver, which she tucked into the sleeve of her suit. Her nostrils were assaulted by a rancid scent. The latrines must have been nearby. Sandy's heart ached for these poor people, vulnerable families who had fled their homes and now had nothing in the world. Then she quickly pushed all those inconvenient thoughts and feelings out of her mind. She needed to find the Fly.

At first, the tent markings made no sense. The numbers were not always in sequential order. Only after ten minutes of searching did Sandy find what she was looking for. Tent H-71136. She walked further. Tent H-71139. Tent H-71141. Then finally H-71142.

Sandy lifted the flap of the tent. It was a thick, heavy canvas. The inside was partially lit by the final embers in a brazier and a night lamp that emitted a faint whitish light. The tent seemed more lush than Sandy had been expecting—there was even a large Persian carpet spread across its floor.

Then she saw him. Al Thubaba, unmoving in a deep slumber. He looked older than Sandy had imagined he would. The only photos she had seen of him were grainy and not taken recently. In them he had been youthful, alert and clean shaven. His eyes were always charismatic, but serious and intense. Now his beard was long, thick and white. His face was marked with the deep crevices that years of hard living etched into human skin. He was lying on his side, facing slightly away from her, and he snored lightly. Sandy felt a fervent rage boil within her chest. *How dare he? How dare he sleep so peacefully?* She loomed over him. Kneeling, she unsheathed the screwdriver and drove it cleanly into his temple.

It was done.

He died instantly, with no more than a slight splutter. An unexpected feeling of relief enveloped Sandy. Her eyes welled with joyful tears. Her throat tightened, and she pulled the balaclava off her face, letting it dangle by the cord that secured it to her suit. Gulping in air, she rubbed her eyes. Her fists clenched. She looked at his face again. It had relaxed further into death. He was almost smiling. The rage in her chest erupted once more. Adjacent to the bed, a copper coffee pot shimmered in the dim light. She picked it up, and, reeling her arm as far back as it would stretch, she brought it down on his face in a series of satisfying, muted thuds. She hit him again, and again and again until his features disappeared into a shapeless bloody mass.

Finally satisfied, Sandy stood up and moved two steps away from the body. Her ears pricked as she heard a soft whimper behind her, and she spun around. Two boys, likely no more than seven and five years old, stood staring at her in fearful silence.

They had seen her face.

They had to die.

She lurched towards them and grabbed them both by their necks. The older boy died almost instantly, his neck snapping easily in her stronger right hand. The smaller boy thrashed and kicked as Sandy struggled to kill him. Once the other boy had fallen away, Sandy clamped both her hands down on the small boy's face and neck until he suffocated to death. In the struggle, the brazier had been upturned, and its glowing coals had scattered across the rug. A small flame bit at Sandy's leg, and she stood up, scrambling to pull her balaclava over her face before leaving the tent. Inside it, the flames had begun to grow.

She moved through the canvas city. Commotion was building behind her as people ran to Al Thubaba's tent. Only when she was about a kilometre from the camp did she look back. By then, the flames were already six metres high. Screams pierced the air and echoed across the terrain. Sandy caught her breath, then turned around and ran without looking back again.

It took her thirty-five minutes to get back to the car. She had run most of the way. Parkins stood outside the jeep, watching the flames lick the sky in the distance. His jaw seemed to be stretched to its physical limit.

"What the hell happened?" he asked when Sandy revealed herself before him.

"It's done," she panted, climbing into the passenger's seat.

"God have mercy," said Parkins before getting into the jeep, starting it and accelerating aggressively.

###

The darkness of the night had broken, but the sun had yet to rise by the time Sandy and Parkins got back to base camp. An anxious Claudette Muro was pacing back and forth between the tents. She stopped and watched the jeep speed towards her, thinking for a moment that it was not going to stop. When Sandy and Parkins eventually spilled out of the car, Muro grabbed her by the shoulders. Seeing Sandy's blood-splattered face, dread crept across Muro's eyes.

"Is it done?" Muro asked, practically shaking Sandy.

"Yes. Yes!" said Sandy, struggling to catch her breath.

Muro's face softened, and she let go of Sandy. "Whose blood is that?" she asked, pointing.

"Not mine," said Sandy, shaking her head.

Muro turned to another officer, who had been roused from sleep by the commotion.

"The sample kit. Do you have it?"

A few minutes later, Sandy sat in a chair in the main field tent and allowed the officer to draw a swab over the still drying blood on her cheek. Muro hovered over them irritably. The officer put the sample in a container linked to a small laptop and tapped at the keyboard. He watched the screen intently for exactly eleven minutes. Then he held his hand to his mouth and let out a small gasp. With tears in his eyes, he turned to Muro and said, "It's a confirmed DNA match. We got him. We got him. Finally."

Muro, tears rolling down her face to her chin, closed her eyes. She hugged Sandy forcefully and said, "Thank you. Thank you, you wonderful girl. You brave, smart girl."

The number of terror attacks did not drop immediately in the wake of Al Thubaba's death. It took another eighteen months for the Fly's organisation to unravel entirely, but after the demise of its leader, the end was inevitable. After this psychological wound was inflicted upon them, the insurgents seemed more dangerous for a time, but also more chaotic and less organised. Drummond did not make the same mistakes his predecessors had made. Sandy had won the war. Drummond won the peace.

Sandy had killed the greatest of enemies. Not just for IC, but also for millions of people legions away—strangers who slept peacefully and unknowingly in their beds. But from that night on, whenever Sandy closed her eyes for a moment too long, she would hear the shrieks and cries of those devoured by the flames that night.

CHAPTER TWENTY-SEVEN

Massi's personal Combi began in what looked like a cross between a gym and a high-tech lab. He would first undergo a standard physical exam. Having to strip down to his underwear made him nervous, even though it was a procedure he had experienced many times before. Three technicians then put him through a series of strength, aerobic and endurance tests. For one test, Massi ran on a treadmill while wearing a respirator linked to a machine that measured his lung capacity. He looked for approval from the technicians, hoping for a sign that he was doing well. They remained stone-faced, however, giving no indication of whether he had passed or not.

The next series of tasks assessed how well he could handle weapons. For these assessments, he would use live ammunition. Until this point, the cadets had used paraguns and other weapons that used non-lethal bullets. Endangerment of the cadets' lives was a concern among the administration. It cost the Academy millions of dollars to train a single student for four years: cadets were literally precious. As a result, accidents with live ammunition were rare. The primary consideration, however, was to discourage IC officers from relying on conventional weapons. IC officers were never intended to be infantry. Cadets were expected to be resourceful. They were designed to be intelligence gatherers. The Field Command cadets, who were trained at a different facility, practised drills with live ammo from day one.

The first target test took place at a standard practice range. Massi was given goggles, ear muffs and a Kevlar vest. The targets were not very far away, and Massi hit them easily, nailing a handful of perfect bullseyes. He was then led to another practice range; this time, the targets moved quickly on mechanised belts. Massi struggled at first but then tuned into the rhythm of the targets and began to hit them in a rapid succession. The third and final target assessment took place at a range identical to the second, but for this test, Massi was positioned on a platform that moved unpredictably. The targets moved too. The room was designed to simulate firing at an enemy from an airplane or other vehicle. Massi had to crouch down on one knee to keep from falling off the platform. He struggled and, after the assessment was done, he left the room feeling unsure about his abilities and, more importantly, his score.

There were two more assessments, one to test his survival skills, something he had always excelled at, and one to test his intelligence-gathering skills. He ultimately thought he passed both tests, but still felt a sense of anticlimax once he was released from the assessment centre. He walked back to the barracks sullenly, imagining that he had done well…but perhaps not quite well enough.

Massi spent the two days after his Combis watching Sandy Attiyeh's trial. She seemed to defend herself well against the charge of conspiracy to commit domestic terrorism. Her testimony that she was trying to hinder Hamilton seemed credible, despite the fact that she looked sweaty, uncomfortable and unconfident for the duration of the trial.

Around mid-morning on the third day, Colonel Mathers summoned Massi to the Academy's front entrance. Once he arrived there, Massi saw that he was not alone. Harry Macey, Jared Fletcher and two other cadets, Liam Greenshaw and Zayn Jackson, had been summoned as well. All were uninformed as to the purpose of the gathering. The boys waited alone for twenty minutes in the lobby, until a minibus approached the front of the building. Colonel Mathers appeared as if out of nowhere.

"All right, cadets, get in." Mathers gestured to the vehicle. The boys obeyed.

As the bus drove away, the boys shot each other anxious glances, each one willing the others to ask questions. They all stayed silent. After the bus exited academy grounds and hit full speed on the highway, Colonel Mathers stood and addressed them.

"Congratulations, cadets. This means you've passed the personal Combi with flying colours. I'm proud of you." His face stretched into a smug smile.

The cadets smiled and cheered in elation.

"Unfortunately, the personal Combi doesn't count for diddly," said Colonel Mathers. "It exists to tell us whether you can survive the team Combi or not. You've all had two days to rest, so the team Combi starts today."

The boys' expressions of joy dropped from their faces, and their eyes widened in excitement and fear.

"We're on our way to an airbase, where you'll be equipped with everything you need, including electroshock guns and appropriate combat uniforms. Then you'll travel as a unit to the start point of the corridor by flight pod. You will be presented with a series of obstacles and challenges. But remember, boys, when it comes to your enemies: there is always a weak spot."

Massi's heart raced. This was it. The other cadets were among the strongest of his comrades, and, looking at them, he felt a surge of confidence. He remembered Sandy Attiyeh's words. The whole unit needed to get over the finish line. Graduating was within his reach.

The five cadets were outfitted with packs, uniforms and guns and deposited at the beginning of the corridor. The countryside featured a verdant forest with a small river weaving through it. They would be walking slightly downhill for most of their journey. While in the flight pod, Massi had tried to memorise as much of the landscape as he could, noting the locations of water and sudden dips in the terrain. He could not get Natalia's voice out of his head. *First you lay an ambush to see if the test subject can deal with panic*, Massi remembered what Nat had told Commander Muro when they had been summoned to observe the solider in the vertical farms.

The unit of five began their sixty-kilometre trek. *Any minute now*, thought Massi. As the flight pod soared out of sight, four man-shaped animatronic targets popped up on either side of the corridor. The boys ducked down and fired their weapons. Narrowly missing the electroshock waves shot in their direction, the boys made quick work of the ambush. They calmly but tentatively continued walking.

The cadets began to relax. The first assault had left them on edge, but they soon realised that they had covered ten kilometres without experiencing another attack.

"That can't be it," said Zayn.

"Definitely not," said Massi. "There's still a long way to go."

"I know, but I was expecting to be attacked almost constantly. Sixty kilometres isn't a long distance in the context of field operations."

"Yeah, I have a feeling it's going to get much harder," Massi replied. "They're waiting until we're tired."

It was now late in the afternoon and the cadets had to cross the river. They found a narrow and shallow stretch of water just before the river began to rage into a waterfall. They took a moment to refill their water flasks, and Massi stared out over the falls, gazing towards where the end of the corridor should be. Something seemed odd. He looked at the map. The bend in the river did not match the river on his map.

"Harry," said Massi, beckoning him over. "Do you have another map?"

"Sure." Harry obligingly handed his map to Massi.

The two maps matched neither the landscape nor each other. They had all been given different maps.

"Do you see that?" asked Massi.

"What?"

"Look at the map, Harry."

"What about it?"

"It doesn't match the landscape," said Massi, nodding, realisation dawning over him. "It's not complete fiction, but it is fiction."

Harry snatched the map from Massi and looked across the landscape.

"You're right. Do you have something we could make markings with?"

Massi shook his head. "We just need to remember the landscape from here."

The boys crossed the river with ease. There were enough boulders close together that they did not even have to get into the water to traverse the river. The boys hopped from stone to stone. They continued walking until the sun completely set, and they couldn't see a thing.

"Okay," said Zayn, "we need lamps."

All five boys retrieved LED lamps from their packs and fumbled around in the darkness until one of them successfully managed to turn his lamp on. The lamps were not very bright, but they provided enough light to see a few yards away. The darkness had crept up on them faster than they had anticipated.

They all sat down except Massi. Jared immediately began to unlace his boots, but Massi flashed his lamp at him.

"Jared, keep your boots on," Massi said sternly. "We can't rest for the entire night. We should take a break and then move as soon as there's light."

"Shut up, Massi," said Jared. "We have two more days."

"Massi, we've walked forty-five kilometres. Only fifteen to go. In two days. We don't need to sweat," said Liam.

"I think we should still be prepared. We should rest in our boots."

"Massi, come on, you're making me anxious," said Harry.

"This has been too easy. We've effectively just gone on a hike. Walking briskly for fifteen kilometres is not a test. There'll be a bigger test."

"I think crossing the waterfall was the test," said Liam.

"That was too straightforward," said Massi. "We didn't even have to get on our hands and knees to get across those rocks."

"Massi, we still need to rest," said Zayn. "We should do it in the dark, when we can't walk."

"They're going to wait until we're tired. Jared, put your boots back on."

Jared was reclining against a tree now. "Sit down, Massi!" he said.

Massi crouched and, keeping his gun in one hand, rifled through his bag and pulled out a few rations. He took a swig of water and ate two peanut butter and chocolate energy bars, trying to finish them as quickly as possible.

The forest was noisy at night. Owls hooted, insects buzzed while trying to cling to the LED lamps and squirrels scurried over leaves. Massi felt dread and unease. They were outnumbered, trespassers in a forest that did not belong to them or to any human. He felt insignificant. He could not sleep; he was too on edge. Except for Jared, the other boys had taken his advice to not remove their shoes, and Jared was the only one who looked entirely relaxed.

"As soon as it's dawn, we need to move," said Zayn. Liam, Harry and Massi nodded. Jared wasn't paying attention.

"If I'm honest, I'm creeped out," said Liam.

"They must be keeping an eye on us out here," said Harry. "I've heard that they have monitors everywhere, but I haven't seen anything that looks like a camera or microphones."

"I know that there are patches in our uniforms that monitor our vitals," said Liam.

"Yeah, that's standard," said Massi.

"Zayn, how many hours until light?" asked Harry.

"I would guess four to five hours."

Sitting against a tree, Massi was more relaxed now, but he did not loosen his grasp on his gun.

It was Zayn who leapt to his feet first.

"What's up, man?" asked Harry.

"Shhh!" said Zayn.

Massi rose, now aware of a slight, deep growl.

"See that?" said Zayn.

"No," said Harry. "What's there?"

Then Massi saw it. A flick of bright-red light, conspicuous against the darkness of the forest. It lasted only for a second.

"I see it," said Massi, raising his gun but not sure where to shoot.

The other boys stood with their backs to each other, their guns ready to fire. But at what?

"Light," said Harry. "Someone shine a light."

With his foot, Massi probed a nearby lamp until it shone outward into the woods. There was nothing there. He could still hear the growl. He moved his head, trying to pinpoint where the sound was coming from. Two bright-red, eye-shaped lights met his, so he fired his gun. The light from the electric beam illuminated the beast. The animal let out a high-pitched yelp, and it retreated.

Massi breathed in heavily as the entire forest became aglow with moving red eyes. The other boys followed Massi's lead and fired at the eyes. In the flashing light, Massi could see huge beasts crawling and running in circles around them. Light reflected off their razor-sharp teeth. Their growls gave way to ferocious barks. The five young men kept shooting until the eyes disappeared back into the night. They remained with their backs to each other, their guns pointing outward, for another twenty minutes until they were sure the creatures had gone. Standing and waiting, Massi listened to his team's panicked breaths.

As the night dragged on, the boys sank to the ground, their backs still together, their guns still ready to shoot. Massi's uniform was soaked with sweat. When the sky was finally light enough, Massi observed the ground around them. Large paw prints were everywhere. The beasts had got so close. But no bodies. Too big to be coyotes.

"Wolves?" asked Harry.

"Yes," said Massi, though he knew there were no wolves that size native to the Blue Ridge Mountains. Shooting moving targets in the dark. *A spatial reasoning test,* thought Massi.

"Are we clear to move out?" asked Zayn.

"Clear," said Massi.

"Clear," repeated Harry and Liam.

"Okay, grab your stuff," said Zayn. The boys nodded in agreement.

Jared Fletcher walked forward to pick up his pack and boots and, at that same moment, stepped barefoot onto the spine of an upturned caltrop.

CHAPTER TWENTY-EIGHT

Jared let out a blood-curdling scream and fell to the ground, clutching his knee to his chest. The spike had gone right through his foot. The boys looked at Jared in abject terror as he writhed and wailed. For a moment, too stunned to do anything, none of them moved. Massi then grabbed Jared, pinning him down.

"Stop moving…stop moving," Massi pleaded.

"What do we do?" asked Harry.

"I have the satellite phone," said Liam.

"Okay, you call for medical help," said Harry. Massi nodded in agreement.

Liam fiddled with the device for several minutes. "I can't get through," he said.

Harry swiped the phone from Liam in frustration and tried to make the call himself. Like Liam, he was unsuccessful. Still crying and wriggling on the ground, Jared seemed oblivious to their efforts.

"Forget it," said Massi. "They're doing it on purpose. This is the test. This is the test."

"What should we do?" asked Zayn. "We only have basic first-aid stuff."

"Let's bandage his foot. Then we carry him," said Massi.

"For fifteen kilometres? What if we're attacked again?" asked Harry.

"Harry, take my gun. I'll do it." Massi thrust his gun at Harry, but he refused to accept it.

"No, we should leave him," said Harry. "You told him to keep his boots on, and he didn't. They'll be keeping tabs on us. They won't let him die."

"We can't leave him, Harry," said Massi. "This is the test. We all have to cross that line together."

"I say we leave him, Massi," said Zayn. "We'll definitely lose points, but the rest of us will get over the line."

"I don't have points to lose," said Liam.

"Me neither," said Massi.

"Don't you dare leave me," shrieked Jared. "Please, please, you're supposed to be my friends."

"We can't leave him," said Zayn, changing his mind. "What if those wolf things come back before IC picks him up?"

"Exactly," said Massi. Then, picking up a stick, he recalled the landscape from the top of the waterfall. He etched a map and route into the dirt.

"We carry him to the river and drag him through the water," said Massi. "That'll be easier than carrying him. We can follow the river for twelve kilometres, even though that means a longer route. Then we have to bear left from the river to get to the finish line. That will be the last five kilometres."

The other boys, seeing the sense in his plan, nodded.

Once they had bandaged Jared's foot, they were ready to go. Massi was grateful for his double drills as he lifted Jared's hulking form over his shoulders. Liam carried Jared's pack and gun, and Zayn carried Massi's pack. Harry was in front of them, brandishing two guns. It took ten minutes of running for them to reach the river.

The boys put Jared's foot, the caltrop still embedded in it, into the water. He grimaced. By now he was slipping in and out of consciousness, moaning and grunting whenever the boys moved him too sharply.

"Hey, guys," said Massi, "there's a lot of loose bark here. Do you have rope?"

They nodded.

"Okay, we can build a raft," Massi said.

The boys worked together to connect several pieces of bark until they made a surface large enough to hold Jared. After shifting Jared onto the raft, they then tied Massi's and Jared's packs on top of him for protection. They ran another rope across Jared's chest and under his arms. This allowed Massi to drag Jared in the water from the river bank like a horse towing a barge. Blood from Jared's crudely bandaged foot seeped into the water.

The cadets began walking along the riverbank. Massi looked back at Jared. He seemed to be asleep, cosily tucked beneath the packs as if they were blankets. It had escaped no one's notice that walking along the river left them completely exposed on one side. Liam and Zayn walked behind Massi, and Harry walked in front. They made good time and estimated that they had walked seven kilometres downriver. That meant five more kilometres by the riverside, then five kilometres carrying Jared to the finish line. It was now mid-morning, and the heat was starting to slow them down. They stopped to rehydrate and to check on their invalid.

They pulled Jared onto the bank of the river, where the water was shallow. He was sweating profusely. Massi was grateful the water was cool. While the other boys ate, Massi kept his eyes on the other side of the river. He sensed that the next attack was going to come from the trees or maybe from the water itself.

It was Liam who first noticed the real danger forming behind them. Eagles. Several of them sat on nearby tree branches, cocking their heads from side to side as they observed the cadets below.

"Do eagles have red eyes?" asked Harry.

"No," said Massi.

Like the wolves, the eagles had glimmering red eyes, this time with no pupils. If these were animatronics, they were works of art. Apart from the eyes, they looked like ordinary birds. More and more of them began gathering on the branches until there were about fifty in total. Massi crouched down and gathered the ropes attached to Jared's raft. He knew if he let go of them, the chance of losing Jared was high. The boys waited with their guns ready. The eagles continued watching them.

"Harry, hand me back my gun," said Massi.

Harry passed it back to Massi, not taking his eyes off the trees.

All at once the birds left their branches and flew in circles above the cadets. One eagle swooped down and dropped what looked like a dark grey egg on the ground near Liam.

"Don't touch it," said Harry.

"Do you think it's a bomb?" said Zayn.

"I don't think they'd go as far as actually bombing us," said Liam.

"I do," said Massi.

Liam stepped towards the egg and nudged it with his gun. Nothing happened. When he bent down to get a closer look, it exploded, releasing a cloud of gas into his face and causing him to cry out in pain.

"Mace!" he screamed, grabbing his face. "Mace!"

"Don't touch those eggs!" yelled Massi.

The boys started firing into the sky, but their guns did not have a long enough range to hit the birds. Then the eagles all started to drop eggs. One of them landed near Massi, and he kicked it into the river. The other boys darted for cover in the trees, but Massi could not leave Jared exposed on the bank. Instead, he began picking up the eggs and throwing them far into the water, letting the river carry them away. It was then he realised the darker eggs exploded more quickly than the lighter ones. He tried to throw those ones far away first before grabbing the lighter eggs and chucking them into the river, too. He tried to avoid the noxious patches of gas from the eggs he could not reach in time, until there was a thick smog of gas swirling round him and Jared. He hid his face in his hand while still grasping the rope and shielding the semiconscious Jared with his body. He felt the skin on his hands and the back of his neck swell from the chemical attack. Massi tried to recall the tests Natalia had spoken about. *Timed exploding gas canisters: a mental chronometry test.*

When the gas had completely drifted downwind, the other boys began to emerge from the trees. Liam's face was a painful cherry red and already looked ready to blister. Massi tugged at his uniform, pulling it away from his reddening skin.

"We've got to move," said Massi. "Jared's bleeding badly."

They managed to reach the end of the riverbank in an hour. Following the river any farther would have taken them in the wrong direction. Now was the hard part: Jared would have to be carried again. Massi handed his gun back to Harry and removed Jared from the raft, positioning him in a fireman's lift despite the searing pain on the back of his neck. Liam and Zayn went back to carrying an extra pack each. They resumed a protective formation with Harry in the lead, then Massi and Jared, and then Liam and finally Zayn. Their pace was slow, and Massi tried to forget how tired he was. Instead he thought of Natalia. *There is always an ambush at the end,* she had said. *Another stress test to see if the subject could still function when mentally and physically tired.*

They had travelled four kilometres in three hours. *The ambush should be coming any minute now*, thought Massi. His urge to keep moving was strong. He had told the cadets to expect another ambush earlier, but he was now so concentrated on not dropping Jared that the thought had left his mind. Just when Massi thought he could see the finish line—and three people in the distance beyond the end of the forest—he crashed into Harry, who had come to a dead stop right in front of him. Unbalanced by the weight of Jared's bulk, he fell backwards. Harry then fell backwards on top of Jared and Massi.

An enormous black bear loomed over the cadets, its red eyes glinting in the shade of the trees. Harry shot the bear several times at point-blank range, and it only reeled back half a metre. Zayn and Liam, who had quickly dived for cover, began shooting at the bear from their positions.

"Stop shooting! Get it off us!" Massi screamed, trapped between Harry and Jared. Liam and Zayn looked at each other briefly before aggressively advancing forward and causing the bear to back away. Then, Zayn, Liam and Harry lifted all their guns together and shot at the same time. Only then did the terrifying beast begin to drift back into the trees.

The route to the finish line was now clear. Massi picked up Jared, who was grunting and whimpering loudly, and together the cadets dashed towards the flags that signalled the end of their ordeal.

Colonel Mathers, along with two medics, waited on the other side of the finish line. When Massi finally heaved Jared over the line, the two medics sprang into action and immediately administered emergency first aid to his foot. A few minutes later, they carried him on a stretcher to one of two waiting flight pods. Harry, Liam, Zayn and Massi collapsed in small heaps on the ground.

"Well done!" said Colonel Mathers, looking at his watch. A fatherly smile spread wide across his face. "You finished in less than forty-eight hours. That's very impressive."

When the boys caught their breath, Mathers led them to the second flight pod.

"All right, boys, we're going back home," he said.

They boarded the plane, stunned expressions still plastered over their young faces.

"I swear I saw my life flash before my eyes," gasped Harry.

"Did you guess that the wolves, the eagles and the bear were animatronics?" asked Colonel Mathers.

"I didn't expect the enemies to be animals," said Liam.

"That, my boy, was the point of the test. You never know what your enemies are going to look like until they're your enemies."

"Would you have let Jared bleed to death?" asked Massi in exasperation and disbelief.

"Of course not," said Colonel Mathers, "but as you once said, we're not training ballerinas. How are we supposed to make you hard enough for the world of war without pushing you to your limits?"

It was late afternoon when they touched down at the airfield. Massi saw the bus waiting to take them back to the Academy and let out a huge sigh of relief. As he moved to leave the flight pod, Mathers grabbed him.

"Thank you, Massi," said Colonel Mathers as he hugged him, tears forming in his eyes. "I needed you to be a different sort of man, and you became that man today. I am so proud of you."

Massi broke down and let the tears of joy and relief run down his face.

In the following days, while the other cadets were put through their own Combis, Massi desperately wanted to catch up on the end of Sandy Attiyeh's trial. He could not even get to the TV in the break room, however, as the other cadets only wanted to watch highlight clips from the Combis. They had been filmed the entire time.

Massi's 'Harry, take my gun' moment was the most reviewed clip of all. The male cadets slapped Massi on the back as they watched and re-watched it.

At one point, Harry gestured to the screen and said, "This right here was the coolest moment of my life."

Massi relished being liked and admired, finally feeling as if he were part of a family. It was the feeling everyone said he would get in IC, but until now, Massi had never experienced it.

While viewing the footage of the other Combis, Massi noticed that every team had experienced a similar incident wherein one member got injured. Massi reluctantly acknowledged that it was the Academy that had hurt them. In his Combi, one of the wolves had probably dropped the caltrop, since whoever was watching them knew Jared had taken his shoes off. If it had not been a caltrop, it would have been something else. The Academy wanted to test their cadets' decision-making abilities and unit cohesion. Would the cadets leave a man behind or not? That is what they really wanted to know.

Massi had not seen Natalia since the team Combi. Perhaps, having inevitably passed her exams, she had gone home for the period between the Combis and graduation. He was grateful that he did not have to make any extra effort to avoid her. He was okay with not being around her, but he had not yet fully come to terms with the fact that she was out of his life for good.

Jared had returned to the Academy after two days in hospital. His foot was still bandaged, but there was no longer any chance of serious infection. His eyes welled with tears when he watched the footage of Massi carrying him, shielding him from the mace gas and protecting him from the bear. Liam and Zayn patted Jared on the back but could not look him in the eye. The memory of how they had wanted to abandon him had left them with feelings of guilt and shame.

Later in the canteen, Jared sat opposite Massi. He wanted to speak to him but could not find the words.

It was Massi who spoke first. "So how much of that do you remember?"

"Not a lot after it happened," he said soberly. "I should have listened to you."

"That doesn't matter now," said Massi.

The two boys sat in an appreciative silence.

"Thank you, man," said Jared, "for not leaving me behind."

"Don't mention it."

All that was left was to receive their scores. Massi still had no idea whether he had passed or failed. He was reading in the barracks when he heard the announcement that the scoreboard was up. He leapt out of bed and, along with the other cadets, raced to the front of the Academy.

His team had passed the Combis. Zayn Jackson, eighty-five per cent. Liam Greenshaw, eighty-five per cent. Jared Fletcher, seventy per cent. Henry Macey, ninety per cent. Matthew "Massi" Moretti, ninety-five per cent.

Massi would graduate from the Academy with high honours.

CHAPTER TWENTY-NINE

It was the last day of Sandy's trial. She rose from her chair in the dock to hear the jury's verdict. Without her usual supply of chemical aids, she had struggled to suppress the onslaught of traumatic images that had revisited her for the duration of the trial. A journalist had even remarked that she looked gaunt, withdrawn and preoccupied; the observation accompanied a not-so-subtle suggestion that these were signs of Sandy's guilt.

The clerk read the jury's statement: "We find the defendant not guilty of conspiracy to commit domestic terrorism and not guilty of treason. We commend the defendant for her wholehearted cooperation in this investigation."

Sandy heaved a sigh of relief, and felt like a cooling chill was rippling through her body.

"While we find the defendant's testimony to be credible," the clerk continued, "and we believe that she knew nothing about Maria D'Souza's murder and that she deliberately prevented Lyndon Hamilton from committing acts of domestic terrorism, we have to state for the record that we find the defendant's behaviour to be worthy of condemnation. The defendant has a position of seniority within the IC ranks, yet she helped build a model, which, by its very nature, violates multiple statutes, abuses the trust of the public that IC serves and dishonours its ranks."

Sandy nodded in agreement. She felt shame and a twinge of humiliation. Justice Braddock nodded in agreement too. Throughout the trial, Sandy had found his face expressionless and unrevealing. Now his eyes seemed hardened, and Sandy thought she saw a touch of disgust cross his face when he looked at her.

"Lieutenant Attiyeh," Braddock said, "though you have been found not guilty of treason and conspiracy to commit domestic terrorism, you have already pleaded guilty to serious data violation breaches. These breaches would normally carry a sentence of twenty years, but you made sure to secure a pardon before you cooperated with Intelligence Command, an entity in which you hold a senior rank. Having already been a recipient of one pardon, I'm sure you know that a pardon requires signatures from all five members of the Ruling Council. This whole situation calls into question your character and judgment. It also calls into question your loyalty to your command, and in light of this, your actions during the Long War will need to be re-examined. It is for this reason that one member of the Ruling Council has refused to ratify your pardon: High Ambassador McCawley."

Sandy's jaw dropped in alarm.

Justice Braddock continued. "As a result, I sentence you to twenty years in custody. You will serve this time in a maximum-security federal prison. You will be eligible for parole in ten years on the basis of good behaviour. Good behaviour that comes without any conditions. You will also be stripped of your rank and commission in Intelligence Command."

He swung his gavel and left the courtroom. Sandy felt the world swirl around her. She stayed still at its centre, frozen within the eye of the storm, numb and unable to think. Military police took her by the arms and led her to a van waiting outside the courtroom's rear exit. At least she was out of sight of the protestors. She had been betrayed. She had been lied to. She choked back tears as she was yanked into the vehicle.

Inside the van, Sandy regained her composure. She had been travelling in the windowless vehicle for fifty minutes. The two military police, officers she had never met before, frequently made eye contact with her but had not yet said a word.

"Do you know the interesting thing about these cuffs?" Sandy asked them, breaking the silence. "They have a subtle kink in their design."

She manoeuvred the wires and twisted the whole contraption until she heard a click, which signalled that they had come undone. "And like so, they can be removed," she said.

The military police officers stared at her intently but did not react, much to Sandy's surprise.

She stood. "I've done my time. My service in the war was a sentence. If you'll excuse me, I'm leaving now, and if you cooperate, I won't beat you to a pulp."

The male military police officer shook his head as a sly smile crept across his face. "Shut up, Sandy."

Sandy tilted her head to the side, equally annoyed and curious.

"We're Drummond's people," the second officer said calmly. "Muro doesn't know. Sit down, please."

Sandy hesitated for a moment, then obliged.

"Where to?" Sandy asked.

"You don't need to know," the first military police officer said.

It was another two hours before the van began to slow. When it finally came to a grinding halt, the doors of the van sprang open, and Christopher Drummond's dark face appeared. He stared calmly into Sandy's eyes.

As Sandy climbed out of the van, she turned to Drummond and said, "So what is this? My freedom, for not spilling the beans about Surabaya and Hazirat? I didn't think you were on my side."

"We are and always have been on the same side."

Sandy stared at him blankly.

"I need you alive and out in the field, Sandy. You'll be in hiding for a time, and we'll change your appearance, but you'll be working directly for me now."

She nodded, then said, "McCawley stitched me up."

"McCawley helped me set you free. You owe him. He arranged to have you sent down for data violations as a favour to the CAR in exchange for no inquiry."

"But you wanted me free," said Sandy.

"I need you free. And people can't go to jail for doing the things I ordered them to do. If people think they'll go to jail for following my orders, they won't follow my orders."

Sandy nodded and said, "You should have told me it was going to happen this way. I don't put myself in fights I don't know I'll win."

Drummond ignored her. "Things are never as secure as you think they are," he said.

"What will you say?"

"I'll tell the press you're a... you were always a loose cannon. Uncontrollable. An exception we made excuses for in wartime. But not an exception we make excuses for now. We're going to tell the CAR, and everyone, that you assaulted the guards and escaped. They won't know for sure that we set you free. If they call us liars, then we tell the world that the new regime running the CAR was willing to drop the inquiry into Hazirat altogether in exchange for putting you behind bars for something else. That's political suicide for them."

Sandy closed her eyes, trying to comprehend what had happened. She was a piece in a much larger game. She looked at Drummond. "Don't use the word <u>traitor</u>. Promise me you won't say I'm a traitor," Sandy pleaded. "Sir, please, I never did a single thing that wasn't for you. I followed every order you gave me."

Drummond stared at her blankly before finally saying, "You don't make the rules."

Sandy looked down again.

"Get into the plane," he said. "You need to leave now." He gesticulated at a waiting flight pod.

Sandy turned to leave, but her eyes were still locked on Drummond's. "It was worth it? Surabaya? Hazirat? It was all worth it, right?" she said.

"We won, didn't we?" he said, holding up his arms and not expecting a reply.

She climbed into the cockpit of the small plane and strapped herself in. When the plane began taking off automatically, Sandy realised she had no control of the vehicle. Its destination had been preset.

She did not know where she was going, but she was going away.

Word of Sandy Attiyeh's escape would not ruin Massi's graduation day. He had not even decided how he felt about it yet. Something about the whole thing violated his sense of justice. She had been pardoned, then seemingly unpardoned, and things she did in the war—things she had been pardoned for years ago—were brought up and used against her. The whole thing stank. Today, however, he was determined not to let it bother him.

Massi and his fellow cadets had been instructed to line up beside a raised platform in the Academy's front field. Their parents, beaming with pride, sat before the stage as Colonel Mathers delivered a speech saluting the cadets' achievements. He acknowledged the talent and skill necessary to have made it this far.

When it was finally Massi's turn to receive his diploma, he walked onto the stage and shook hands with his new commander, Claudette Muro, as she handed him a neatly folded white bundle: the uniform of Intelligence Command. There was a glint of recognition in her eyes. His moment on stage was over so quickly that he had no time to wonder if she remembered his name.

Before being allowed to join their parents, the cadets had one final task to complete. To be fully fledged officers of IC, they needed to have their juvenile civilian chips removed from their arms and replaced with military ones. Inside the Academy, they were hustled into changing rooms, where they would leave their grey uniforms behind. They were then shown to a queue for chipping.

That was when he saw her. He turned away, hoping she had not seen him, but then she spoke.

"Hey, Massi," said Natalia.

He turned to face her but did not respond.

"So, you graduated?" Her face was relaxed and pleasant.

He nodded.

"I saw your Combis." She paused. "You were very impressive. You deserve this."

Overwhelmed with emotion, he realised that it was all over. The Academy. The fun he had had there, the challenges he had aced. The doubts and frustrations the place had brought him. Whatever relationship he had enjoyed with Natalia was over too. Everything. Everything was over.

"I'm glad you think so," he said.

"Good," she said, smiling warmly. "You look great in a white uniform. I'm so proud of you. I hope you're happy with the regiment you find yourself in."

"Thank you," he said, "you, too."

He smiled at her, then turned to present his left wrist to the chipping technician, who held an instrument that looked like a cross between a syringe and a gun. The technician took a firm hold of his arm and deftly inserted a large square chip beneath his skin.

###

After the graduation ceremony, Muro had returned to ICHQ and was now seated in her office, perusing various files in their physical and electronic forms. Most of them concerned Sandy Attiyeh's escape. She carefully examined the profiles of the military police who had let Sandy slip through their fingers. All competent agents. She knew she should have formally reprimanded them or sent them for extra training. Maybe a disciplinary panel? Perhaps they had felt unable to hurt one of their own, even in retaliation. The truth was…she did not really care that Sandy had been allowed to escape through incompetence, and that was a reflection that made her feel guilty. Muro was surprised by her own lack of emotion about the whole fiasco.

Then again, this was exactly the result she had wanted. Sandy had moved on from her sad, little existence of begging Muro for work. Muro did not know where she had gone, but Sandy was not in her office, and Muro was quietly confident that she was not a threat to either IC or the country. It had been Sandy who had thwarted Hamilton, after all. Throughout the trial, Sandy had not seemed to enjoy the attention her own antics had brought down upon herself. Muro sensed she would lie low for now.

Muro decided not to look a gift horse in the mouth. If Sandy had dropped off the face of the Earth in any other circumstance, Muro would have been thrilled. She picked up Sandy's physical files and tucked them away. She also decided that devising consequences for the people who had let Sandy escape would not be a priority and, instead, carefully thumbed through her other orders of business.

It was at that moment that Gerald burst through her office door, startling Muro enough to make her reach for her panic button.

"Ma'am! You won't believe it. It's a miracle," said Gerald, struggling to catch his breath.

"A miracle?" Muro asked sceptically.

"The treatment. It worked. He can talk. He can talk." Gerald gesticulated frantically.

"What?" Muro stood, her face changing from a look of annoyance to one of stunned hope.

"You have to come to the hospital, Commander. He wants to see you. He's been asking for you all morning," Gerald said as he attempted to compose himself.

Muro dropped the papers she had been holding and dashed for the door.

She gritted her teeth as she travelled to the hospital. She had been through this before: hoping that he had finally recovered only to have those hopes so suddenly dashed. In this regard, she empathised with Sandy. Muro's breathing quickened as she made her way down the familiar corridor. She paused and took a deep breath before twisting the doorknob and letting herself inside the hospital room.

The man in the wheelchair looked at her. His body was still partly broken, his limbs were atrophied, and it took a while for him to properly focus his gaze on her.

Muro rushed towards him and threw her arms around him. "My darling…my darling," she sobbed, "they say you can talk?"

"Hello, Mother," said Martin Muro as he embraced her.

Muro, her arms folded, stood in Christopher Drummond's office. Martin Muro was seated in a wheelchair in front of Drummond's desk. He was already more alert and animated. In fact, apart from his inability to walk and his atrophied limbs, he was entirely back to his former self.

"Tell him how you were injured, Martin," said Claudette Muro.

Martin lifted his eyes to meet Drummond's curious stare.

"I was electrocuted in a savage attack and left for dead by Sandy Attiyeh. My own fellow soldier. Attempted murder. By a member of my own command," said Martin, his voice articulate and unwavering. "I was going about my own business, and she attacked me without provocation. She thought I wasn't the right person to lead the three regiments taking part in the Locket Vault operation. Look at the records. She had made complaints about me; she said I wasn't fit for leadership. Just look up the records. She didn't like that I got the lead on that mission, and Lucian Scott didn't. No one else agreed with her, so she decided to mutiny against my leadership by taking me out."

Drummond relaxed back into his chair, considering his next words very carefully.

It was Muro who spoke first. "I want her dead, Christopher. I want her dead."

Drummond nodded; he had a deep understanding of the desire for vengeance. "Claudette, I know you're angry, but I've been reading the disturbing reports from your people about a cyber terrorist calling himself 'Corio'. Don't you think that should be where your priorities lie?"

"Corio is small fry. I'll assign someone good to that case, and it'll be dealt with. But dealing with Sandy Attiyeh—that's about justice."

Drummond shrugged. "The trouble is that she has already been pardoned for her crimes, Claudette."

"She was pardoned for the crimes she committed against the enemy. Not the crimes she committed against her own side," Muro protested.

"I believe the pardon covers that, too," said Drummond while looking downwards to avoid her glare.

"She's dangerous, Christopher." Muro, her voice quivering with hurt and anger, stepped forward. "It's an absolute scandal that she escaped custody in the first place. She's a rogue agent."

"I agree." Drummond nodded.

"High Commander, we need to bring her to justice. For all her crimes," said Muro planting her palm forthrightly on his desk.

Drummond sensed that she was unyielding.

"All right," said Drummond, "I'll give you all the resources you need to track her down." He stood and approached the window to give himself time to think while avoiding Muro's forceful expression. "Preferably, I would like her taken alive. But dead would also be acceptable."